C.W.G.

(CAMPAIGNING WITH GRANT)

C.W.G. is Peter Minack's first novel. He was born and lives in Melbourne.

C.W.G.

(CAMPAIGNING WITH GRANT)

PETER MINACK

V
VINTAGE

A Vintage Book
Published by Random House Australia Pty Ltd
20 Alfred Street, Milsons Point, NSW 2061
http://www.randomhouse.com.au

Sydney   New York   Toronto
London   Auckland   Johannesburg

First published in Australia by Vintage 2000

Copyright © Peter Minack 2000

All rights reserved. No part of this publication may be reproduced,
stored in a retrieval system, or transmitted in any form or by any means,
electronic, mechanical, photocopying, recording or otherwise, without the
prior written permission of the publisher.

National Library of Australia
Cataloguing-in-Publication Entry

Minack, Peter.
C.W.G. (Campaigning with Grant)

ISBN 0 091 84186 0.

1. Grant, Ulysses S. (Ulysses Simpson), 1822–1885 – Fiction.
2. Historical fiction. 3. United States – History –
Civil War, 1861–1865 – Fiction. I. Title.

A823.4

Design by Gayna Murphy/Greendot Design
Typeset in 10/13pt Sabon by Midland Typesetters, Maryborough, Victoria
Printed and bound by Griffin Press, Netley, South Australia

Every reasonable endeavour has been made to contact relevant copyright
holders. Where this has not proved possible, the copyright holders are
invited to contact the publisher.

10 9 8 7 6 5 4 3 2 1

For my father

'When I feel that we two meet in a perception, that our two souls are tinged with the same hue, why should I measure degrees of latitude, why should I count ... years?'

from *History*,
Ralph Waldo Emerson

The American Civil War lasted from 1861 until 1865. In 1864, after three years of defeat at the hand of General Robert E. Lee's southern Confederate army, Abraham Lincoln finally found a commanding officer who seemed capable of leading the Union forces to victory. This general was Ulysses S. Grant. The first battle between Grant and Lee was the Battle of the Wilderness.

1864

ENTERING THE WILDERNESS – CROSSING
THE RAPIDAN – TWO DAYS IN THE LACY
MEADOW – THE BATTLE OF THE
WILDERNESS – THE FINAL CRISIS – THE
MOVE BY THE LEFT FLANK – END OF BATTLE

I shat myself in the Wilderness. I thought, 'It's back to Galena.' But I feel I performed in that battle, especially when it seemed everything we had won was at risk. As Horace would put it, the enemy was truly – literally – at the tent door. Horace was always talking like that: like some documentary voice-over from 1864, full of emotion-charged nobility. 'I looked in his tent,' Horace would later write about Grant, 'and found him sleeping as soundly and as peacefully as an infant.' Horace was a nice bloke, but a dickhead.

For most of the first two days of the Battle of the Wilderness, General Grant had done well. We were getting shitted on, but this was as everybody had expected, more or less. Everyone – troops, officers, public – had premonitions of defeat. It was the first time Grant had fought against Lee; and it was in the Wilderness, with its thickets still full of the skeletons of soldiers who had been killed in our last battle here.

'If it is true that the spirits of the dead walk beside us, we unknowing of their presence, then it is surely so that they walk here.' That's what Horace said to me as we were crossing the Rapidan river to enter the place. 'Everything is rank and shut in,' he said. He could truly be a mordant fuckwit.

Crossing over Germanna Ford, everything *was* rank and shut in. The Wilderness was a huge scrub full of mongrel timber, with slashes cut away by the battle this army had lost here last year. Grant and I were not in charge then. I rode to Grant's left; for this battle, he'd dressed in his best uniform. He looked ridiculous with riding gloves.

The night before, we had made camp near a deserted farmhouse, and had the fence rails made into a fire because of the gloom all around.

'I heard the men talking,' Horace had whispered to me. Grant and Meade were sitting in front of the fire. Meade was visiting us from his own encampment. Horace was acting like he was present at the signing of the Declaration of Independence. 'One infantryman put a skull on his bayonet, and said, "This is what you are all coming to, and some of you will start toward it tomorrow."'

Ooh, *spooky*, Horace, spooky, you Pennsylvanian prat. Tomorrow we're pretty likely to get the white whipped out of our asses by Massa Robert, meaning Grant – which also means me and you, Horie – joins a long list of generals who spend the rest of their lives pissing in the pockets of history, trying to convince everyone they didn't get beaten because they were pompous, blundering half-wits able only to look good in dress uniform and contract gonorrhea. That's what we might start towards tomorrow: back to Galena, back to that stinking law office, and years of petulant letters to *The Century Magazine* complaining about Burnside's late move up the fucking

Orange Plank Road, or the true import of the dispatch we sent Sedgwick that he didn't receive. What odds our skulls on bayonets tomorrow, Horace? Smaller than us getting our *arses* on bayonets, and getting them pointed towards history with Lee screaming, 'Kick this.'

I replied: 'Look, Horace. The General is offering Meade his silver tinder box; the wind makes it hard for him to light his cigar.' This was the small, human detail I knew Horace liked, because it made the whole event so portentous.

'Yes.' Pause. 'Do you feel that the French would call that tinder box of the *briquet* type?'

I knew he would like it. It's yours, Horace; use it.

∽∾

My name is John A. Rawlins, and I was General Grant's chief of staff. We had a strange relationship, and I want to tell you about it. It seems like a funny trick of perspective that the same events – the same life – when described, even by the same person, can produce such different stories, depending on when the story is being told. If I'd written about it all at the time these things happened, I wouldn't have written a book like this. Even if, like Horace and Grant, I'd waited twenty years after the war, it still wouldn't have been like theirs. But I waited till now, and that's changed everything. Now, I'm not even much interested in the American Civil War. You get those Civil War Dickheads who just lap it up, though; your real Star Trek Fan type, 'cept with the Civil War they think it *really* happened. What happened in the Civil War changes every year: I should know. I was there.

I've chosen a strange perspective, that's true. The more time passes, the more I think things from years ago change. It's far too hard for me to explain what happens when you're dead. It's not what I want to talk about. If you can't accept that –

if you want to know about that – give up now. You mightn't believe me, but I can tell you that I find it's knowing what happened during my life that's the really hard thing. I thought I knew back then – but right now I still don't know just exactly where all the lies in my book are. Horace and Grant both wrote books, too. Any Civil War Dickhead could tell you that. But what CWDs don't get is that their books have as many lies in them as this one, just in different places.

It's a fact that two days into the Battle of the Wilderness we had lost over seventeen thousand men killed, wounded or captured, and all that drew me towards Grant, all that I wanted from him, had shown itself.

We spent the two days near the old Wilderness tavern on a little knoll called the Lacy meadow. You couldn't see anything because the scrub was so thick. Our only knowledge of the battle was based on reports from adjutants who'd rush in from various corps commanders. We could hear the sounds of rifle fire drift from our left to right as the battle moved up and down the front. Being the commander-in-chief's General Staff, our job was basically not to pack ourselves to death. Many men were killed on the first day, and, especially in that dark underbrush, a lot were hysterical with repressed fear. Horace was in his element, riding messages to Hancock and the other corps commanders. Horace Porter was a lieutenant-colonel, one of Grant's aides-de-camp. Grant got him a brevet rank of major in the regular army for it. Don't worry about working out the difference between ranks and brevet ranks and lieutenant-colonels and brigadier-generals and obersturmwaffenautobahnvolkswagenführers: it's like DOS commands and Nintendo – only fourteen-year-olds care enough to understand. Wounded men would straggle back past our position, at first in ones and twos, then in great masses. Many were not wounded, but nothing could have made them return to fighting. Once or twice, shells and bullets flew overhead, showing us how badly we were losing. At about two o'clock on the first day, one of our generals came riding up and dismounted in front of Meade.

'I wish to report to you directly, sir, the loss of my guns and many of my brigade. I was unsupported on my left and similarly unsupported on my right. I wish that the devil himself would take command of what is happening in this battle, because he could not be any god-damn worse than the fool in charge at the moment.'

George Meade was commanding the Army of the Potomac – if you want to remember which army that is, remember it's the one losing this battle. Meade was only one of the commanders under Grant, who had just become overall commander of every army in the country. Meade let the complaining general get back on his horse and go back to the front. Grant wanted him arrested, but Meade told us, 'That's only his way' as we watched in disbelief. It was like we were at the fucking grouse hunt, and one of the old boys had been whining about the lack of game to the hunt master. We hadn't been here in the East long; we'd won our victories in the West. No fucking wonder they'd been shitted on for years.

That night there was fire in the brush, and the wounded men were burnt alive while trying to crawl away. 'The resin in the saplings makes the trees burn like torches,' Horace said when we woke the next morning, 'but by dint of extraordinary exertions, great numbers of the seriously wounded are being brought to where they can be cared for.' Yeah.

The next day, the second of the battle, it was the same thing: us in the Lacy meadow, while officer after officer came in, bringing news. The whole time, Grant – the hero of Donelson, Shiloh, Vicksburg, Chattanooga, recently promoted to Lieutenant General, only the second person since *Washington* to hold the rank – had been whittling while sitting on a tree stump: for two days, whittling, making nothing. I had been with him for every one of those victories, and I still didn't know what to think. In anyone else, it would be an affectation of studied, careless unconcern. But, even given what happened later that day in Grant's tent, I don't think so. It's stranger, I suppose, if it wasn't just a show, and he really was just whittling away. Horace, of course, was immensely impressed *because* he thought it was an affectation; and it shat Meade up the wall. I could see Meade trying not to look, talking with that prat adjutant of his, Adams, then looking back and thinking, 'He's *still* whittling.' Meade was relying on everything he had to keep it together: his sense of duty, his breeding, his Pennsylvanian ancestry, his rank – but Grant was just whittling. I grabbed Meade by his whiskers and pulled his ear down: '*He's* the commander-in-chief of all Union armies, George,' I whispered. These pompous Easterners, they'd all heard the rumours. I'd seen them as they looked slyly at each other after Grant had passed and take a mimed drink from the invisible bottle they held in the air. 'He's got the job you want,' I hissed. 'You're his glorified errand boy – *and all he does is whittle*.' I didn't really. I didn't suppose I could just say, 'Sorry, George, that's only my way.'

The final crisis came at the end of the second day. It was nearly dark. Colonel Hyde, of Sedgwick's staff, came galloping up to Meade. He was bleeding. If you get confused with all the names, and with working out who are the Union ones and who are the Confederate, and who wore blue and who wore grey, don't worry too much. It's not important anymore, for you and me both.

'General, we have been flanked and routed. We are trying to form another line, but the panic amongst the troops makes it impossible.'

'What has General Sedgwick to report? This is nonsense,' said Meade.

'I have no news from General Sedgwick. I come from Wright's division. Brigadier General Seymour has been captured, along with his whole division. Wright is attempting to reform a line.'

Meade cracked it: 'You will return to Sedgwick at once, Colonel, and get a report that is not this nonsense. Pay the commander my compliments.'

We could hear the small arms fire swelling over to our right. Night was falling, and the darkness came on quickly because of smoke from the burning forest. An adjutant from Wright's division ran up. He had lost both his mount and his self-possession. His face was distressed, as if something terrible was about to happen, some huge disaster was hitting, and all he could do was look on. There was no saluting or anything.

'Wright and Sedgwick have been captured. I have run from there. They are on the Germanna Ford Road.'

Out of the scrub came another one. He stumbled up: 'The Georgians are on the Rapidan. Gordon has captured Brigadier General Shaler. They are behind us.'

'Shaler?' said the first one. 'The North Carolinians have Sedgwick and Wright. If they are at the Rapidan, they have the ford and the road.'

Meade repeated, 'This is all nonsense. Adams, get me a map. Show me Wright's last position. He cannot be further back than here.' He jabbed at the map, and sort of half turned it to the two panicked men. It was too dark for them to see anything anyway; and they were so gone that if it had been a map of their own buttocks they couldn't have pointed out the arsehole.

'I will reinforce Sedgwick from Warren.' Meade spoke to Adams: 'Captain, tell Warren to send Wadsworth over to Sedgwick.' Meade was as lost as you are, trying to work out all these Civil War names. He turned back to the two panting adjutants. 'Will you report something that isn't nonsense? Tell me where Sedgwick is, so I can send Wadsworth there.'

In the circle of failing firelight in the Lacy meadow, I could read the letters already:

Oct 11, 1885
Mr Johnson and Mr Buel,

Though it occurred over twenty years ago, as editors of The Century Magazine *surely you are aware that on the second day of the Battle of the Wilderness the collapse of our right wing, which resulted in the subsequent rout of the whole of the Army of the Potomac, was not due to the fact I am a pompous blundering half-wit only able to look good in dress uniform and contract gonorrhea. It was the fault of all the other generals – except Lee, it wasn't his fault at all, I had a handle on him the whole time. I think it's time your magazine implied they are the pompous blundering half-wits. I don't care who you pick, but remember Grant is a pisspot. I must go now, it's time for my penis swab.*

Yours,
George Meade

Even at the time, I was thinking I should remember this, that I might need to know this: if you are standing in May 1864 on a dark knoll in the middle of horrifying wilds, and an army of over 118,000 people is collapsing (just like it has for the past three years), and you are on the General Staff of the commanding generals of the disintegrating army, and you're hearing the frenzied reports of bleeding adjutants as they bring you the knowledge of your coming defeat with repetitive, cumulative detail, what you do is your duty. I know, because I saw people do it.

You might think commanders and generals and chiefs of staff would no longer have to monitor themselves so they don't betray their panic to others. But I can affirm that these soldiers, too, must still try to check their tone of voice, and how they are holding themselves, to make sure of their effortless bravery. I know that is what you'll have to do, you poor turd, if you're ever there. Horace, I think, might have been preparing to die; he was all erect and immobile. I learned later that during that whole day he faithfully kept track of how many cigars Grant smoked: 'Deducting the number he had given away from the supply he started out with in the morning showed that he had smoked that day about twenty, all very strong and of a formidable size.' There was Horace: he was going to die for his chief, and if that meant adding 'It must be remembered that it was a particularly long day. He never afterward equalled that record in the use of tobacco', well, he was doing no more than his duty. Which was the same as the rest of them. 'Gentlemen,' I could have said, as an implacable darkness, suffocating as the brilliance of Lee himself, was about to collapse in on our fire and us, snuffing us all, leaving only the trees swaying and sighing rhetorically in the soft wind over this place, our bleak and overwrought crematorium – 'Gentlemen,' I could have said, 'Our duty is plain. We must each allow ourselves to be interviewed by Ken Burns for his groundbreaking documentary on the Civil War, and put before the small but influential percentage of people who watch public television the truth that none of us were at all responsible for the collapse of this army.' Well, I'm pretty sure – if it was their duty – and, godsblood, that's what they knew the commanders of the Grand Army of the Potomac had to do at such a time: their *duty* – I'm pretty sure old Meade and his main man Charles F. Adams Jr. (son of the ambassador) and Horace and the lot of them, and me too, would have sat down and done exclusive one-on-one interviews with Ken, minus even an appearance fee. Grant wouldn't have, though.

Meade kept commanding the two adjutants: 'Tell me where Sedgwick is. Captain Adams will lead Wadsworth there.'

Grant, at last, stopped whittling, and moved over to them.

He spoke to the first one, taking Meade's map and folding it as he did so. He said: 'It is easy to feel panic in this place.'

The two men waited. I'm not sure if they knew he was Grant, but his calm tone seemed to assure them that he was someone they should listen to. I find it very hard to describe Grant's voice, except with what seems like an understatement; but he sounded unconcerned. 'Did you yourself see your general captured?' he asked one of them.

'No, not myself.'

Grant kept folding the map, getting a little muddled as to the order of the edges he should fold next to make it sit right. He turned to Meade: 'This map confuses me.'

Both adjutants stared at the map, as if its unimportance had suddenly been made clear to them. Grant, still folding, spoke like he was remembering a boring lesson learnt in childhood. 'How many troops were captured?'

The adjutant answered, his voice less urgent, as if he knew he'd look ridiculous remaining hysterical in the face of such tedium.

'How many troops did you see running?' asked Grant. Everything he said to them was simple. Where was the reserve line? Was this line broken? How far was it from the front line? While the noble officers of the Republic prepared to die, Grant whittled his way to the facts, as if fear and bravery, cowardice and panic, dishonour and duty were sticks you pick up from the ground when you're bored and you don't wanna make anything in particular. He handed Meade back his map and moved back to his tree stump. He lit a cigar, but it wasn't like in the movies: there was no ostentation or swagger. When Grant lit up, it was as sexy and dangerous as drinking herbal tea. He sat on the tree stump and spoke, looking up at us. His face was small, like a child's turned suddenly old.

'The enemy have attacked us continually for two days. They have only had small and temporary success, followed by repulse. They must be exhausted and confused. There is a possibility of an advance if we can get information about their lines, and we organise quickly. I feel we will reform our line a short distance from our initial position.' Grant addressed the adjutants: 'Go in the direction of your last position and try to find your general – he should be in the rear of your last line. Inform him that we will try to advance.'

Grant wasn't worried; that was his schtick, and it had played well so far in the provinces. But did this mean that we were going to win them over, here in the big city? Horace thought so – certainly, years later, he was sounding confident: 'It was in just such sudden emergencies that General Grant was always at his best.' Meade looked as if he'd been in front of the urinal too long, and was holding the map in his hand like it was his reluctant old boy.

If we all seem like fools now, to be complacently mocked in some smarmy modern farce, we were no more so than you are, looking back and sniggering about our beards. The thing was, we were beaten. I'll tell you about it, about how the Ghost General came and warned us and everything. We were beaten, but only Grant, sitting still while the skeleton of the huge forest seemed to shift under us, wasn't pretending when he acted like we could still win. You'll be trapped, one day, too; and if there's a man who can lead you out by tilting his egg-shell head like a toddler towards the ground and saying, 'Inform him that we will try to advance,' you'd write a book about him as well.

Officers like the two we'd just sent away kept coming in, reporting disaster.

'I have come from miles away,' said one. I remember him because rather than being panicked, his voice sounded like he had just woken up. Only the lamps provided light now, and he had walked uncertainly up to the tents, not knowing to whom he should report.

Adams said, 'You can surely then advance some yards further.' He was glad to encore the old pompous outrage for what might well be one last time before Lee took his place in the band.

'I have come from miles away without stopping,' repeated the adjutant as if he'd fluffed his first line. 'The air is full of missiles. Along every mile I saw our men retreat. The rebels pause only where the wind blows the fire back at them.'

Meade did not look at the man. He said to Adams, like Adams was at fault, 'From whom does this soldier report?'

The adjutant swayed, his chin down, but said nothing. Adams was about to scream at him when the soldier suddenly looked up, remembering something: 'I reported to General Shaler the disintegration of our line.'

'Is General Shaler captured?' said Meade.

'I delivered my message to General Shaler,' said the adjutant wearily, still shuffling. 'He was sitting on his horse. He said to me, "Very good, sir".'

The man somehow thought he had finished and turned to go. I seemed to smell smoke on my own clothes, as if being too close to this man was like standing near young trees burning.

Adams said, 'General Meade has not dismissed you.'

'Is the General captured?' repeated Meade.

'From where I have come, had daylight lasted one half-hour longer,' said the adjutant, 'I too would not have avoided the rebels.' Even in the shaking lamp light I could see his eyes almost closed over; he held his head back to prevent it dropping down again, and looked up weakly at Adams. It's hard to blame him for what happened next. More men had died on this day than on most days in the history of America; but he shouldn't have yawned. His eyes opened in shock even as he did so. The outrage of what he had done woke him at last.

'General Shaler rode towards the gunfire,' the adjutant said, standing, finally, at attention, 'and was taken.'

Meade stood up. 'General Grant is watching you. Are you unaware of that?'

The adjutant was now as still as a corpse waiting to be cut down from the gibbets.

'Captain Adams, assist this man. He is to be bucked and gagged. This will train him to control his mouth.' Meade's phrase sounded stupid, like he was reprimanding the adjutant for swearing. Adams called for a guard. None came. For that completely shocking moment it was as if there was only the five of us left there; that beyond the light everyone else had fled into the miles of bone-filled scrub over which Confederates swarmed, black as ants. We were beaten. For hours they came to us, adjutants like this, every one of them bringing some new exhausting drama. Grant's unconcern might be proven correct – Lee might not have enough troops to push home his attack. But try telling us that, just after Adams had said, 'Guard, I want you to take this man for punishment,' and out of the darkness no-one at all stepped forward. 'We are alone!' I thought, even though I knew this was impossible. Another person's hand squeezed from my heart a more powerful beat. 'We are abandoned in the Wilderness!'

It was in just such sudden emergencies that General Grant was always at his best.

'I have ordered new entrenchments dug,' he said. 'I have detailed the guard for this task.' The back of his head seemed to stick out too much, just like the kid at school who always got picked on. 'With your permission, General Meade, I will send this man to join them.'

Meade was lost. New entrenchments meant Grant was preparing to stay here. Lee was coming at us. The only thing stopping him from being here now was that he kept tripping over our dead. This was the final battle. One member of

Grant's staff was quoted later as saying, 'The coming of officer after officer with additional details soon made it apparent that the general was confronted by the greatest crisis of his life.' That man's name was John A. Rawlins. (You wouldn't've heard of him.) The commander-in-chief of the Union forces didn't wait for Meade to answer; he knew the words needed for this emergency:

'Go,' said Grant to the adjutant. 'Find a shovel.'

When they heard that command, I couldn't work out if it was more or less fear that Meade and Adams felt. I will write more fully later, when I have more time, about this crisis. Soon after, Hancock returned from our left flank, exhausted. Meade, Adams and Horace crowded around him, as if at last a soldier had come to lead them. The whole polite fiction, the whole grand story of the Battle of the Wilderness, had lost its appeal, like when an author finally stops writing in mid-sentence and gives the whole thing up.

'There is plenty of fight left, General,' said Hancock, 'though the fighting has been desperate, and exhausting. The men exhibit signs of fatigue.' I could see Hancock's knuckles. There was a welt right across both hands, like he'd been fighting in a bar. 'I have seen my men fire through the flames, until it has become too hot to continue. The enemy is compelled to halt for the darkness, and their own crossfire. Ordered movement is still possible.' Around Hancock his three groupies nodded in sympathy. 'Much of our army can still be saved.'

Grant said, 'All proper measures have been taken.' It was like he was reading something into a court record, and spoke only so the words could be looked up later. Grant stood, and patted each of his pockets in turn. He seemed confused; but then his face cleared. He took out a cigar, and gave it to Hancock.

Meade, Adams, Hancock, Horace – all looked at him. Grant had led more than another 100,000 men into this place who, had they seen him right then, would also have looked at him and been similarly amazed. Hancock took the cigar, but I saw him drop it soon after, forgotten or unwanted.

Meade's camp was half a mile down the Germanna Plank Road. He and Adams rode away. Hancock left us.

At 8 p.m., Grant went to his tent.

Now here's where I got frightened.

I followed him into his tent. He collapsed on his cot, and began weeping. He was face down, sobbing. A little tingling ball of despair was forming between my shoulder blades. I became sensible of the top of my scalp. Behind my ears and near my temples a despairing, undeceiving hand was moving, its fingers probing lightly. This was what I always knew. Here, in the East, against Lee, it was all ending.

The canvas of the tent made the light inside a dull gold. I moved slowly, as if with enforced reverence, towards Grant. My hand reached out and touched his shoulder. He was the commander of all Union armies. I watched with wonder, more full of awe than horror. Under the palm of my hand Grant's uniform was moist with sweat. When you see your father crying, is it pity or contempt you feel?

Had I not promised to expose him if I found him inadequate? No-one could know more fully than I the depth of the failure revealed in that moment. To see him weeping – weeping after only two days against Lee; the Lieutenant General weeping as if in surrender – showed me how unfit I was for such a task. I was caught and humiliated in the glare of my own self-deception. I was in front of my father all over again, and he had reached out too suddenly to lay his cold hand rough on my head.

'General.'

He kept crying.

'I'll just try and sleep,' he said then, still weeping. 'I'll just have to try and sleep, and it'll be all right.'

And this, this was so brave! It was the bravest thing I heard from him. He was going to sleep, and when he woke, he was going to go on. Everything was lost, now, and, like a child, tender and small, he was going to go on, but first, 'I guess I'll try to sleep; I'll just try to sleep.' He pulled his blanket up around his face.

'General.' I was whispering. 'General.'

It seemed as if I'd heard this crying before, from a dying child I'd abandoned years ago.

Then, in walked Meade's staffer, Adams. I was propped on the side of Grant's cot, my hand on the blanket that covered his shaking back, leaning over him, and whispering, 'General, General'. Adams! It couldn't have been worse if it was Robert E. fucking Lee and the whole of the Army of North Virginia. Adams, to Meade; Meade, to the world: the collapse of the Lieutenant General, in full colour, with all the action. 'Drunk Again – This Time On His Own Tears' says *Time* magazine.

Adams took it in. The enemy was at the tent door, then turned and left. I caught him as he got to his horse. I said, 'The General is stirred to the very depths of his soul.'

Adams had his bridle in his hand, one foot in the stirrup, ready to mount. He stopped, and turned to me, his foot still in the stirrup. 'Sir, the General is unmanned, and unable to command himself.'

'That he has given way to the greatest emotion is true,' I said. 'The last two days have been ones of great crisis.'

Adams bounced on his heels, making that small preparatory movement you do to give yourself a little momentum to help pull your weight onto the saddle. I wanted to reach out and touch his arm, but that would have been near enough to grabbing it, showing him how desperate I was. The long campaign was near over; Grant's two days of hard calm had collapsed, revealing to Adams this pitiable man.

I knew how badly Adams wanted to expose Grant's failure

as Lieutenant General, and how quickly he could get Meade in that job if he did. This battle with Lee wasn't over yet, but it was the battle with our side that looked closest to defeat. Instead of grabbing Adams, I took the bridle of his horse in my hands: 'But General Grant has not displayed any doubt or discouragement about the progress of our arms, or the course we have followed and must continue to follow.'

Isn't it always later, when the moment has passed, that you think of the best replies? I could've broken down and pleaded with him: 'Adams, before you go to Meade, did you know that my pisspot dad used to line us up and beat the bejesus out of us when we were young just as if we were ordering meals at a fast food shop? "Number Twenty-three, please come to the counter, your left hook to the solar plexus is ready".'

Or threatened: 'Captain, you know how much Lincoln likes Grant. Lincoln doesn't care if he is an alcoholic. Jesus, if he wins the war, Lincoln wouldn't care if you told him you saw Grant after every battle in a full Spandex body suit with "Satan Lives" on it, drinking goat's blood and sacrificing virgins to the Dark One. So you wanna be the one to tell the President that his favourite general's a sissy?'

Or bribed: 'Let's talk about this, *Brigadier* . . .'

Or reasoned, sort of good-naturedly: 'Oh, come *on*, Charles. We march brainlessly straight into a sepulchral scrub called the Wilderness with 100,000-odd men, lose 17,000 of them in two days of morbid horror, not having won enough ground to even erect a decent monument to the dead, and then you find the commanding general weeping in his tent. So? Let's have a drink. Anyone can have a bad day.'

Adams bounced up on to his horse and said to me in parting: 'That the General is confident about the progress of arms is welcome news indeed, sir, as in that he truly stands alone. Let us hope that confidence is more inspiring for the troops and the nation than it seems to be for himself at present.' He jerked his bridle, turning his horse's head out of my path. 'You will hear from General Meade presently, I assume.'

Très witty, dickhead. 'Let us hope that confidence is more inspiring ...' Mincing turd. But I didn't have time to waste on abusing the smarmy prick. I had to pull out a good one. Here's what I came up with. It was one of my best ones, but if you don't know anything about the American Civil War, it won't be as good for you.

I told him this. 'Captain Adams, General Grant has ordered a forward movement by the left flank. The objective is Spotsylvania Courthouse.'

It worked for Adams, though. He suddenly reined in his horse, and faced me. 'General Grant orders a forward movement?'

Bash that one up your ginger, Benny Hill. We're going forward, pal. Lee has met us in the Wilderness and slaughtered our army as comprehensively as he did against your succession of losing Generals for the last four years, but we're not going back. There's more of this, Charles. This stricken army is going to march down the Brock Road about a dozen miles, and it's all going to happen again. Think about that one before you ride off to Meade and tell him Grant's lost it.

And he was thinking about it, too.

'When?' he said. He didn't believe me. It was perfect. He had already stopped planning the celebratory sherry soirée he and Meade were gonna have. Instead, the news he would take back was that whoever was left over from this bash got to have another go. The only problem was, the last time I saw Grant, he was weeping on an army bunk.

'General Grant has not asked me to draft final orders yet. I presume you will receive these sometime tonight.'

'This is absurd. General Grant would surely expect General Meade to be informed of such a movement immediately.'

My every experience told me that Grant was lost. My deepest fear was that he could no longer get us out of the Wilderness. A second ago all I wanted was for Adams to get off his horse and stay, and now all I wanted was for him to stay on it and go. Such is the unpredictability of battle.

Adams dismounted, and walked to Grant's tent.

And then, reader, I had a sort of epiphany of fear. The camera pans back and above the meadow where the headquarters had been for the last two days, revealing it to be only one circle of firelight in a darkness freckled by many such others. Stretching over miles of Virginia, towards the Rapidan and out to the Rappahannock, spilling out to the Ni, blazing even – it seemed to me – over the famous Potomac, there was a spreading river of light, made up of soldiers' camp fires, fires kindled by soldiers alive and dead; American soldiers camping across the Virginian theatre, from the Rapidan to the James, from wars fought before or now or later, all gathered here on this night, a strange soldiers' night of ghosts and the living, all camped in a great arc of land in the heart of this nation.

From way, way above the clouds – clouds that seem to me to be themselves seeded with bones, and ready to soon rain – the camera comes zooming in, back to the Lacy meadow in the Wilderness; and there is the jacketed back of Charles A. Adams, stiff with a mixture of disbelief, respect and disappointment, entering Grant's tent. I can remember that my awareness of my own body came back to me as he entered the tent, but that doesn't make sense, because here is where my fear and misery were at their peak. I was left outside, waiting for the inevitable revelation of defeat. Adams would confirm Grant's collapse. Grant was weeping on his camp bed while the generalship of the Army of the Potomac passed on. My fearful hallucination hung around me, the hysteria gone, but leaving me still with appalled elation. Adams came out of the tent.

'The General wishes Warren to have the lead in the march,' he said to me, 'marching to the rear of Hancock. Sedgwick will go East, by Chancellorsville, then South by Piney Branch Church. Burnside will follow Sedgwick. He asks you to go in and help him draft the final order for the movement so I can take it to General Meade.'

Grant had ordered a move by the left flank. It was as if I was hearing this for the first time. Adams was handing me a slip of paper. I took it from him with slow amazement, but his own bewilderment and confusion was even stronger than mine.

'Here is the General's rough draft of the order. He wishes you to read it, and give him your thoughts before the final draft.'

'The General has done a rough draft?' I asked Adams.

He looked slightly puzzled. 'The General was preparing it as I entered his tent.'

I stood there.

'You are to see the General,' he said. 'I must go to General Meade as soon as possible.'

I went into Grant's tent, and we wrote the order for the move by the left flank.

It was about two hours after this that Horace claims, 'I looked into his tent, and found him sleeping as soundly and as peacefully as an infant.'

This ended the Battle of the Wilderness.

1861

OUTBREAK OF THE REBELLION – SPEECH AT GALENA COURTHOUSE

On the night of April the 16th, 1861, I gave a speech to a meeting in the Galena Court House. If you want to know about the social and political background to the American Civil War – the *antebellum* years it's called now – that's another thing you're going to have to read about in the books Civil War Dickheads write. I'll tell you about the courtroom I gave the speech in.

It was on the second floor of the Galena Court House. Looking back, everything was small and tacky, but everyone before the speech that afternoon was acting like they were setting up for the Lincoln-Douglas debates. Flags and bunting were lying in a jumble on the mass of chairs at the back of the small room; near one end, a small speakers' platform was being put together under the long dusty windows. Workmen and court officials moved about, carrying posters and lists and tablecloths and jugs for flowers. All this has a cumulative effect, as if the Lincoln-Douglas debates were something people might remember.

I'd appeared for seven years in this shitheap of a courtroom, which was better at least than seven years on that shithole of a farm my shithead of a father never once worked on; in fact, apparently (and I'll quote from one of the General's CWD biographers) 'Rawlins snatched what schooling he could ... and read books by torchlight in the charcoal pits in the woods.' Then I 'embraced the law so fiercely that by October 1854 Rawlins had passed the bar ... and was established in a surging career'. If it's in books, then I suppose that's what happened.

Later that night, the courtroom was full. From the darkness outside, I could hear the rumble of the crowd, and sudden bursts of applause or stomping. The glow from the courtroom was lighting the whole street. When I walked in, it seemed three times as large as it did in the afternoon, and the enlarged space was crammed with heat and smoke. I felt suddenly breathless, and coughed for air.

The speaker before me was Elihu B. Washburne, congressman for the district. Good name, that; I think he played blues harp on Blind Willie Johnson's seminal early recordings of *Mother's Children Have A Hard Time*. Actually, that can't be right, 'cos Washburne was the sort of support act the main performer likes: not very good. I had his measure, I knew. His fat politician's lips moved slowly as he spoke.

'Citizens,' he said – to my nervous hearing it sounded like he was pausing after every syllable – 'The na–tion binds us all. How terr–i–ble it is to a–ban–don our fellow men.'

I could see the crowd grow restless during his speech. He seemed to have no sense of what they wanted. He was a softcock. He was deluded into thinking they were debating whether it was a good idea to go to war, but I knew they were debating whether they wanted to go to war. Looking back, I know I didn't have a fucking clue if it was a good idea: I mean, I was twenty-nine and had lived all my life in the backwoods of Illinois, and was a big shot in Galena, a town that would've been proud to be worth one horse's dick. But none of them knew either, except for Grant, and he wasn't saying much. I tell you, if there was one person there who I knew I could fool, it was Elihu B. Washburne.

'It is hard to go to war,' Washburne said, concluding at last. 'We need not condemn ourselves. We can at least be easy in the knowledge we are doing what we must.' From where I was sitting, behind Washburne on the speakers' platform, I could see Grant looking down, as if miserable and bored.

Then I got up, and they went quiet. They'd come to see me, after all. I said, 'Everything is changed.' I paused, melodramatic and false. Grant looked up.

'Everything is changed,' I repeated, 'and I am full of fear. When this war comes, will you find me out as a coward? Will you find me, skulking at the back of the battle, overwhelmed by the terrible voice of the cannon?' I paused again, for exactly the amount of time it would've taken for me to whisper, *sotto voce*, 'As fucking if.'

'I may seem confident now before you; and you have heard Mr Washburne, who speaks with the majesty of the Congress. But soon you may hear me weeping in terror and shame, lost and alone, as around me nobler men face what I cannot. After this war comes, maybe they would disdain to hear speech from one like me, wretched and dishonoured. For all is changed.

'And when I come back to Galena from this war, I may come back knowing this is all I am. I will take from the shelves again my law books; take up again my pen, and know this is all I can do. Deep in me I may find there is no other, greater man. All will be changed, once we are visited by the God of battle.' Listen to me – 'All is changed . . . all will be changed.' I sound like a train conductor.

'And yet, the God of peace also finds the truth about many a man. You know that under this God, I have not wavered. You know me; you knew my father . . .' This really shut them up. There was an embarrassed, intense stillness in the room. They had known my father. '. . . And you know that I have not allowed myself to suffer in his defeats. The God of peace also gives us to struggle. Without shame I appeal to you and say, "Have I not won?" Have I not won, when many a man would have cowered and cried "I am lost!" and been ranked amongst the defeated?

'Why then do I declare before you that I fear myself a coward? Why invite dishonour? Because all is changed. What do my past victories avail me, if the greater loss in war should be mine? Amongst us, let me tell you, there are two societies, two worlds. You see the ranking order of one before you today. You see me, the Congressman, the Mayor; why, we are in the courtroom where the powers of our Republic are enforced, where there,' – I pointed to the judge's chair – 'one man has been given power to judge the man there.' I pointed to the dock. 'But there is a second world. In this world, men are ranked by their hearts and their bravery; and this second society has its own Congress, made up not of the successful but the resolute; its own courtroom, where judgements are passed so deep in the soul guilt can never be denied. And with the coming of the God of battles, this second world is stirred to life, and in that great and terrible moment it shrugs off the skin we see in this room now, to reveal bone – to reveal the real order of things.'

Well, I was afraid my metaphysics was going to lose them. But their faces, even Grant's, were all still and looking.

'Where will you be counted in that new world?' I asked. 'Where will you be ranked?

'Do not be deceived by the trappings of rank you see before you. They are worthless, now the new God is here. I have from this night only the desire to prove myself anew, to prove myself to be a patriot in the new country this war has founded. All is changed. There is no John A. Rawlins, now. That man is gone, and the person that stands in his place has done nothing in the new world. There are no mayors and congressmen now; there are no lawyers and judges, drunks or dignitaries, prisoners or presidents; there is no Galena, as yesterday we knew it; there is no State; there is no Democrat, no Republican, no parties, no politics. There is left now only two countries: one of patriots, and one of traitors.

'We will stand by our country, and appeal to the God of battles!'

Well, ladies and gentlemen, *lay-dees and gen-tell-men*, the crowd rose as one; and then John A. Rawlins left the fucking courthouse. As my limo drove me away to my waiting hotel room, full of bitches and lines of cocaine, I could hear the MC yelling into the mike: 'Ladies and gentlemen, John A. Rawlins has left the courtroom.' That's exaggerating a bit, because in those days they didn't have mikes.

I went home to my wife Emily, who I knew wouldn't let me enjoy the bitches and cocaine. The nurse was asleep outside of Emily's bedroom door.

'You may go to bed,' I whispered to the nurse. Her mouth hung open, peculiar and ugly. 'I have returned from the meeting.' In her sleep, the nurse's lips came together as if she was chewing. By 1864 they had killed so many of our men that all the cemeteries were full. We dug up Robert E. Lee's front lawn, and started a new one there. Coming into the quiet of the house after the noise of the courtroom, I felt like I was carrying a gravedigger's shovel. Every time I moved, no matter how carefully, it swung around, clanging into another thing in the room. The nurse woke.

'I am home,' I said. 'Go to bed.'

'Your wife's coughing continues,' she began, 'which tires her more. She refused her food, but drank a little. I have continued to –'

'We can talk tomorrow,' I said. 'Leave.'

The candles had began to stink. Emily's door stood looking at me, impassive as a coffin lid.

It was time for another speech. I don't want you to be sad about Emily, she's not my heroine. This isn't a chick-flick; it's not *Steel Fucking Magnolias*, where the whole show all the strong women – *strong* women – stand around freshly dug graves and emote in a strongly empathetic fashion. Brave women! – bonded by their gender, together able to celebrate undaunted the fact that, no matter how little regarded by the world, no matter how incidental to the greater concerns of men, their efforts have in some unknowable but vital way helped make a movie of nearly unalloyed purulence.

It was time for another speech because my first one had worked so well. I was off to war; and I hadn't even thought once about the speech I'd have to give now to my wife. It's not Emily who you need be sad for.

'I am going to battle.' I composed the words in my mind, looking at Emily's blank bedroom door. I sat; the warmth left over from the nurse's body was still asleep in the chair. 'Tomorrow I will join the army, and soon I will fight in this war. My darling wife, my deepest pain would be if you did not believe you are made more dear to me now. What part of love was hidden by the happy customs of peace is now revealed by the rent war tears between us, and as the earth we stand on is large beyond our sight and can be revealed only by ascension, so too more love than I could have known has now been shown to me. Emily, you are more beautiful than all else in this world, more precious; and yet we must be apart when death itself threatens. What I face alone I do so with you always in my thoughts! Not battle, nor war, nor death will ever be so dread that it will separate you from my heart. There is no fear so great that it does not drive me to love you more. Battle will join me in love to you by a bond more fierce than that which peace has forged. How can I be lost? How can I be alone? I have you always, Emily, my darling wife.'

Don't I talk fine? As I rehearsed the speech in my thoughts I could hear from outside the last hooligans from the courthouse audience calling to each other as they went home. Twists of smoke sucked straight up from the dead candles, as if by a mysterious force; the flame on the last candle was dying. I sat in the chair feeling the colder darkness behind Emily's bedroom door.

'Emily, do not abandon me! In faint hearts strong love must die. Will you leave me so defenceless on the field of battle? I will have no ally if you do not believe that by leaving you now I love you more.'

The cold face of her door stared, unwooed. It looked at me as if I'd said, 'OK, Em, fuck ya. I'm off.' Hadn't this fucking piece of wood even seen *Steel Magnolias*? Didn't its little brass knob brain know that women are brave and strongly empathetic in response to tragic separation? How did it know – a fucking dead tree, mind you – how did it know more about me than I did? It had witnessed this scene, I guess:

Nearly one year ago I had been sitting, just as still, in the same chair.

'John,' said Emily, 'John.'

I did not move. My face was stuck, tilted to the floor. I had nowhere to move nor any way of holding myself that did not make me ashamed of my feelings.

Emily was standing near me. She coughed softly, and placed

her hand on a chair; then she let herself sit down. It's hard for me now to think of her outside that bedroom. It's like there are two of her: the one I remember, bedridden and shrunk, and another person who could stand there and look at me before sitting gently, like she was someone else's wife.

I didn't move to look at her. 'Was the mark of the blow still visible?' I asked.

'No, John. He was attended with all proper display.'

I had nothing to say.

Emily was distressed. She had not seen me like this. I gave her no clue as to how to help me. The door to our bedroom was open, showing the sunlight and paintings inside. Emily's face would change so quickly when she was grieved. Around her eyes the skin seemed to show the delicate bone below. Her cheeks formed deeper, older hollows. Some toll was being taken of her, beyond her command, deep within. When I first kissed her, I could feel my lips as if alone from the rest of me and they were touching on the face of another world, my self lost already in the richer, blood-dark lands beyond.

She came over and knelt next to me, and put her beautiful face close to mine. 'John, you will never see him again.'

I was distraught, and knew that if I moved I would collapse. Even in this distress I sensed her perfume, like the delightful detail framing a painting full of pain.

'It will be the last time you will see him,' she said, as if my father was still alive and waiting for me.

The embalmers in Galena had a sign:

Embalming The Dead
Free From Odor or Infection

I always liked that: 'Embalming The Dead.' Who else do you embalm?

As I stood up I shuddered, but did not start crying. 'I ask

you to leave me now, Emily.' She looked helpless and lost. 'I thank you for visiting him, but I do not wish to.'

She was still kneeling. Moving and speaking had shown me I could keep doing so without fear. 'Emily,' I said, one year ago, in front of that door, 'I do not wish to look at that face.'

That door didn't forget. By now the last candle had so little flame that the eye of light on the wall behind had shut. Only the red wick could be seen imprinted in the dark, like the sun on your closed eyelids. I was going to leave Emily; but don't feel sad for her. You want to know how I felt, sitting in the darkness like a blind man, after that courthouse speech? I felt like it had been a great gig. It was a great gig. I didn't know it right then, but Grant was never the same. 'I never went into our leather store after that meeting,' he wrote way later, 'to put up a package or do other business.' I knew it was great when I saw the amount of stuff they were sweeping up the next morning. The room was returning to its normal self. Some court attendants were clearing the papers and crushed handbills. Candle wax, fallen flowers, lost handkerchiefs and broken ribbons were being swept away, and chewed tobacco was being mopped up. It was a shithole again, but now it was the shithole I was leaving, because now there was a war.

I was exhausted by exhilaration, not sadness. John A. Rawlins had left the courtroom another man. I finally got up to leave. I could talk to her tomorrow. I left Emily's door closed. The pity I felt for her clung to my fingers as I let it go.

1846

ANCESTRY – BOYHOOD – THE MEXICAN WAR –
THE TRIP TO ST. LOUIS – ENLISTING

My father was a complete arsehole. He was one of those passive weak arsehole fathers – those arsehole fathers who go through a life crisis when the kids are just starting primary school, and leave the wife in a pissweak attempt to get another life. You've seen them, maybe. I heard of one guy who drove around for nine months before he left his wife. He didn't go to work – he'd got sick leave, but hadn't told his family – and he'd get up every morning and have breakfast and off he'd go, and just drive around. He'd park in shopping centre car parks and eat his lunch, and go down to the beach and sit there in his car. When it was 10.30 in the morning, which was morning-tea time at work, he'd find somewhere to park and read the paper. Nowhere special; he'd just pick some suburban street to turn down, and take a few corners until he found himself in a court or one of those small U-shaped avenues, and sit and read. Then he'd come home at night. He did that for nine months. Just like carting firewood around, pretending you're selling, but really you're begging or hoping to bump into an old army buddy. You take a drive down by the bay on a wet weekday about 1.30 in the afternoon. In every carpark it's peak hour: blokes sitting behind the driver's wheel having a look through the paper, then staring out through the rain on the windscreen at the bay. Why do they decide to drive away? They turn on the ignition and just let it idle for a while in indecision about where to go next before they move off. Then another one'll come a few minutes later and take the park. There's a constant supply of arseholes like that out there.

But my father wasn't just one of those. He was also an active arsehole. He'd go out of his way to be a cunt. He didn't want to just leave his family and fail. He wanted to use us as well. I don't know. It was always hard to tell just how much he was knowingly exploitative, and how much was so ingrained in his genes that it was as automatic with him as it is for a dog to spray its scent over what it thinks it owns.

Maybe if he'd had a car he would've just driven around like those other guys, and then made the big decision to leave his wife, and then gone out and got another wife exactly the same. But you didn't really have the option then. He'd take his gun and go out hunting round the woods he'd claimed back in '27 (*1827*, that is, son). He never did much else, except get drunk and piss off for months on end. Not like 'I'm leaving forever, but now I'm back' piss off; more like 'I'm so sure of myself that I just feel like fucking off for a while' piss off.

You've got a few problems when your father's an arsehole like that. There's all the obvious ones, but the big one I reckon is this: you're him. You're him. If you could get the major developmental stages of your soul shown on ultrasound, like they can do with foetuses these days, and then viewed the video later when you were older so you could see in that grainy sequence your whole inner self unfolding in frame-by-frame summary, what would happen is this:

'Oh, look, Mum, look at this one,' you'd say. 'Remember this? This is when I hadn't realised yet that Dad was a cockhead.'

'That's right, darling. Look! Isn't it sweet! Look at your childish innocence and confusion! Oh, John, you were such a *hurt* young baby!'

'And here, Mum. Here's when my consciousness was just beginning to grasp that him pissing off on us, and him drinking and going out shooting all day and leaving me and the others to cart the charcoal to the smelters, was plain simple selfishness.'

'It took a long time, I remember, dear. See here – that's when you kept trying to come to some other conclusion, isn't it? Hold it a bit closer, darling, I can't see this one ... Yes! That's the one! That's when you deep down knew he was a ...'

'Turd.' [Said together. Much laughter.]

'And I couldn't admit it!' you'd add.

'Oh, John, and here's when you finally gave up the attempt, and just said to yourself, "He's a prat. My dad is a prat."'

But by this stage, you've fallen silent, because you've seen the following frames, and your mother hasn't. Your eye has searched with increasing comprehension the grey blotched images on the screen, and what you see is what you always knew.

'Well, let's see the rest, darling. Come on.'

'Nah. It'll wreck the machine if we load too many images on, Mum.'

'Oh.' You know she's not convinced. 'Well, I wouldn't know. You'd know better, dear. I don't understand all this modern what-not. Switch off the light, dear, will you, if you're going to pack up. They cost a lot to run, those fluorescent ones.' And you've fooled at least one of the people there.

But not the other one. The thing is, when your Dad's a complete turd, so are you. Deep, laired in your most private cave is that knowledge. Even when you spend your whole life being what he isn't, you are still him. You can become a lawyer, a politician, a Chief of Staff; work obsessively; exhibit all the drive and courage and reliability he didn't; fanatically denounce the Demon Rum and never touch it – but it doesn't work. You're still him, deep down. Why, the fact you're trying so hard to prove you're not him, proves you are. He is the one great alternative of your life; he is what you'd be if you weren't trying not to be him the whole time. He is hardwired into you; and all you can do is run different software. In the final frame, you've seen what you always feared: his face.

The Mexican War broke out in 1846, when I was fourteen. I secretly and obsessively planned to enlist. It takes no great insight now to see it was a secret that helped me hide my real secrets. Hauling carts of wood to be burnt, I'd give speeches to the men before battle. When I heard adults talking of the war, I'd listen with a sort of self-righteous condescension; after all, what did they know, compared to me, who would soon be there? The Illinois volunteers were based at St. Louis, and that's where I was going to head. I knew that I'd be too young to be enlisted in Galena, but in the big cities they didn't care about your age. In the evening, standing on a ridge overlooking the long valley that ran through the woodland, I'd be a preacher, like I'd heard at my mother's meetings: 'The Lord calls forth from the breast of Man the courage to do His bidding and gives unto Man's hand the power to enforce His Will on those who do not follow in the paths of the Goodly. Go, yonder mighty Host, in the knowledge that with your banners and on your battle flags the Almighty Father's blessing follows.' It seemed like each of my words would lift into the air of the valley, at first only a little above where I stood; and then I could sense the distance from the earth to them growing greater, as they floated precariously further into the air; and sometimes I could seem to feel in my stomach the dropping ocean of distance that gaped between them and the tops of the trees as those words accelerated away.

I think my father must have overheard me, though, because one day he announced to my mother: 'Lovisa, after the paddocks are cleared, John and I are going to St. Louis to join the army for Mexico.'

Our surprise wasn't just his plan, but that he'd bothered to announce it at all. It was strange – of all the arsehole things he'd done, why tell her about this before he actually did it? Normally he just up and did anything he wanted. But I had another reason to be shocked. He was fulfilling the very wish I had been harbouring so closely.

'We're going to fight the Greasers, and come back,' – he looked at my brothers and sisters, pathetically and obviously currying favour – 'and tell you all how we did it.'

I was torn: here was my wish come true at the hands of my father, of all people. Yet he was the reason I had so wanted to go. I didn't want to go with him. I wanted to go to escape him. Also, I'd never thought of my mother – but now I had to.

'Don't take him,' she said to my father. 'You can go by yourself, and let us stay here.'

He hitched his hunting bag over and around his neck. This meant he was going out alone. I carried his rifle and ammunition bag when we went hunting together.

'I'm going into town to find out 'bout enlisting.' He turned to me: 'We'll go after the last two paddocks are done. Take a load up to the smelters today.'

'St. Louis is too far for him,' my mother said. 'You go to St. Louis yourself.' She spoke quickly to convince him before he left: 'He is too young. They will not accept him. See them yourself, and then come back if they'll take him. You'll not want him on the journey. We will clear the trees here when you're gone.'

'We're gonna fight the Greasers with General Scott,' he said to my brothers and sisters. He opened the door. 'I'm going to town. You start clearing, and take a load today.' He looked at my mother. 'You wanna go fight the Greasers, John?' he asked, still looking at her. 'You want to come to St. Louis and join with me?'

When I said yes he closed the door and left.

For the next three weeks he kept it up. I was incredibly frightened that we'd miss the war. It was a long way to St. Louis, and I wanted to leave then and there. But he'd insist on another paddock being cleared, and more charcoal taken to the lead smelters. 'I found out that uniforms are provided,' he told me one day after work, his voice full of excitement. He'd always make sure my mother was there.

'Look.' He held up an advertisement from the newspaper. 'Chetlain told me that it was in this paper.' Chetlain was a merchant in Galena; my father bought drink from him. 'Read it,' he said to my mother. He held out the paper to her. He couldn't read.

She looked at the paper.

'Go on.' He shook it at her. 'It says about the uniforms for me and John to wear.' He was making her his instrument, forcing her to help him take me away. 'The boy wants to hear. Chetlain has marked the place. Read it. He wants to hear about the Dago war.'

She took the paper, all the time thinking of some way out.

What good was it saying that a uniform wouldn't fit me, or that I was too young, or that the war would end too soon for us to get there, or that Chetlain had marked the wrong passage? She knew all of these could be easily countered, and that they weren't the point anyway. The point was his refined cruelty, his rat cunning way of making her and us hurt even more. Was it time for her to try and challenge him on that? It was easier to read the paper. She took it from him.

'"*A grand opportunity*",' she read, '"*is afforded for patriotic persons to enlist in the service of their country under the command of as able officers as the country has yet furnished. Pay and rations will begin on enlistment. Uniforms will be provided.*"'

We – my mother and I, and my brothers and sisters – could all sense there was some ulterior motive. His enthusiasm to take me must be either fake, or part of some plan. That's what I figured, but it didn't stop me playing along with him, hoping that by some fluke it was real, and we would go. By this time I had changed. Now, I secretly wanted to go with him, though I wouldn't admit it to myself; together – James and John Rawlins, father and son, stars of the saccharine sitcom *Meet the Rawlins*, where the final scene before the credits is invariably me hugging my Dad and saying, 'Thank you, Dad, for all you've done for me' – we would bond better than the blokes in a shaving cream commercial.

'We have cleared the woods up to the creek,' I told him hopefully, trying to save my mother having to read any more, and also wanting to convince him to take me soon. My brothers and I had been working on this clearing for three days.

'There is more, Lovisa,' he told my mother, ignoring me. 'Chetlain read it to me in the shop.' He turned to me. 'It says about the Dago war, and how we'll get to see everything there. There is more, Lovisa. The boy wants to hear.'

She looked at me. I did want to hear.

'"*This regiment*",' she kept reading, '"*is second to none in regard to discipline and efficiency, and is in the healthiest and most delightful country. Pay and rations begin on enlistment. Citizens of Illinois should feel pride in attaching themselv –*"'

He interrupted her, swinging around to look at me. He asked for more forest to be cleared: 'You go to the fence line,' he said, eagerly. He took the newspaper from my mother, and held it out to me. I looked up the creased and ragged arm of his jacket to his leering red brown face.

'You read,' he said. 'You are smart. It tells about how we're gonna go fight the Greasers.'

I began reading where my mother had left off: – '"*attaching themselves to regiments from their own State. Come one, come all! God and your country call!*"'

'We're coming, aren't we, Johnny? We're coming!' he jeered at me. I was silent.

'We're coming,' he continued. 'We're going with General Scott. Keep reading, John.'

He hit the paper. 'Keep reading. You're smart.'

'"*Bounty has been liberally voted for the brave volunteers. Persons joining the ranks of the army will share in this magnificent provision of the Commonwealth's riches*",' I stammered out.

'Riches, Johnny. That's what we're gonna have. Riches. It says so. Old Chetlain sure put me on to a good one here. I vote thanks to Chetlain.'

And so on, me reading, him parroting and mocking the great times we were going to have in Mexico.

Meet the Rawlins – might rate well, but I never said the show had class.

One day I returned home early; we had cleared the wood all the way to the fence line, and I wanted to see what to do next. I could hear him talking to my mother. I stayed outside.

'I'm going to take John tomorrow to Galena to watch the

volunteers leave,' said my father. It had gotten so that everything they said to each other was part of their battle; so this, innocuous as it could have been, was delivered as a taunting challenge. I doubt whether they could have thought of one sentence, no matter how trivial or mundane, that would not have contained within it somewhere the whole story of their marriage. I could hear all they said from where I stood, the shaft of the coal cart still over my shoulder.

'Leave him,' my mother replied. 'We are going to a meeting. A preacher has come from Chicago.' There was a pause, and then my mother started again. 'James, leave him. I need him with me now. You leave if you want, but do not take him with you. I need him now. He is too young.'

'You have Alton, Lovisa, and I want to take John to the war.' My father was referring to my older brother. Even this was cruel; Alton was always sick. He had tuberculosis, though we called it consumption then. He would be no help to my mother. 'I know John is young – everyone here knows he is too young. That's why I am taking him to St. Louis. They take boys in the big cities. No one knows us there; we can be who we want.'

Our house was slumped onto trodden earth in a clearing in the woods. It was as simple as a child's drawing of a house: roof, two windows – one each side of the door – and chimney stuck on top. Like a child's drawing, it did not have many straight lines: the planks were haphazard and rough, the stone chimney was piled leaning onto one side, the frames of the door and windows were scabby with dirt and wear. There were other details a child would not include, splotched over the poor kids' butcher paper like Dad's beer stains: the rags hanging on the beams, the tins and pans scattered around the front, the disabled ladder leaning uselessly onto the rotted roof, the steps punched in and moaning near the door, the refuse piled in the dark spaces where the bottom beams had fallen way to reveal the gaps in the floorboards. The clearing it was in was heaped with old piles of dirt full of mangled branches and stumps. The house stuck painfully in the middle of the broken ground, keeping it raw and wounded. That's enough. I'll just get my daycare teacher to write 'John R' in texta on the top, and you can stick that up with your fridge magnets to show the neighbours.

I could hear their voices, and I didn't even take the shaft of the cart from my shoulder because my father said, 'I'm gonna take John to the war, and we're gonna fight with General Scott. You can have the others, but I want to have John with me when I go to the war. He is smart. He can do things for himself. He ain't like me, Lovisa; he can work and stick to things. I want to go with him, and together we can be soldiers; and we'll come back when it's over.'

'Why take him?'

'Do you think I don't know who I am, when I am drunk under a tree? When I go off and I am wandering and shooting and drinking and no place to be and going down to Chetlain's shop for another jug? What do you think? That I don't know what they are saying in Galena? That I don't know when you go to your prayer meetings you pray for strength and to be rid of me? That you take John with you so he won't be like me?' He wailed and lamented, as pathetic as a drunk, though I was pretty sure he wasn't pissed. 'I don't want him like me. I want to take him to the war. We will be soldiers and shoot some Greasers. It won't be me who Chetlain laughs at with Stevens when I've bought my jug and I can hear them behind me after I've left the shop. I'll've shot some Greasers, and that is more than they will have shot, 'cos you don't find many Greasers to shoot sitting in the front parlour of Isaac P. Stevens office, Lawyer and Advocate.' He snarled the last phrase. 'And when they mutter "Shame 'bout the boy", well, the boy and me will have been to Mexico and fought with General Scott and that's more Mexico than you'll find in all of Chetlain's jugs. You won't find Mexico there, or General Scott none; all you find in his jugs is rum and whisky.'

Slowly, so they wouldn't hear, I picked the shaft off my shoulder, and began to tenderly lay it on the dirt.

If my mother said anything, I couldn't hear her. I was bending over the cart, frozen at the moment I had finally rested it on to the ground.

Inside the house, my father was shouting, 'I am going to take him. You can have a baby, and another too, before I won't take him. It's but once we'll get this war, and there'll be plenty of people dead before we get another one. Tomorrow, we'll see the volunteers march; then we'll leave to follow, and go to St. Louis.' I could tell he was concluding, but by the time he got to the door I was off belting through the woods. Was I happy or sad? The coal cart was left sitting there trying to work it out, staring at the house and my parents in innocent amazement.

Three days later, James Rawlins and his son John floated down the Pecatonica River on a wooden barge, the baby river pushing up against the surrounding valleys' careful protecting strength, then running off, then back again to make sure they're still there, and then off once more, the hills never resisting the wet hand of the river, and never letting it stray too far. When the Pecatonica turned into the Rock River, the land around began to press less closely, letting the river search further and further into the distance before returning, then wandering away again through confident plains of corn and hay. Walking between the Rock and Illinois Rivers the father and son could see those plains become enveloped in a huge contented horizon that encircled prairies of adolescent wheat learning how to move together up towards the giant patient sky.

Of course, I was fourteen, so at the time if you had asked me to describe the trip to St. Louis, I would have said me and my dad were going down a river, past some trees and over some farms. All I could have told you that I cared about was that we couldn't miss the war. But behind that was the happiness that my father and I shared this obsession. Of course, I couldn't have said this then, but it seemed he and I had both been seeing the Mexican War as the same opportunity: me to escape him, and him to escape him. It was a foolish, innocent and driven search to change our lives, and here we ... fuck me, *Meet the Rawlins* is getting worse.

So. Me and my dad sailed south down the Illinois River to St. Louis, but to get to the Illinois River we walked from where we'd got off the barge on the Rock River. It was on this walk through the still hilly and marshy fields that one evening, just on sunset, there started the sound of wolves calling. Wolves have the ability to make the call of only one or two animals sound like the combined signalling of a huge pack. The prairie grass was long, and we couldn't see far into the fields on either side. The animals were moaning with a weird misery, the location of the sound distant and changing. The grass parted and closed around us as we walked.

'Wolves 'bout,' said my father. 'Not out of this country yet.'

Wolves normally kept to the high Dubuque hills; they must have been hungry to be down here on the settled plains.

As the noise grew, the evening light abandoned the tops of the grass. The distance was already a predatory black. We seemed to be walking straight for the sound, but then it would swing around, and the calls would be behind us. We had been walking all day, but now for the first time I could hear our footsteps clearly, and they got louder as the light paled and ran away. We walked on. I was carrying his rifle and for the first time, this weight started to bother me. I didn't know how many wolves there had been before, but there were clearly more joining them. Their bizarre keening sirened over the plain.

'Four miles yet to Wyanet.' My father calculated the distance to the nearest town as if he was unaware he had done so out loud.

In the closing blackness around us the grass was moving in great undulations that were not violent, but spread through the vast crop like a scent in the night wind. I was on my way to war to fight and kill Greasers, but that was in Mexico, and we weren't even at St. Louis yet. And that was a dream: what was real was padding bestially alongside of me just behind the corn. As I walked behind my father, I began to sense the wolf as it stalked parallel to us. It was just beyond where the shafts of growth now screened it in the dark. I couldn't stop myself imagining the sharp, foreign hardness of the hair on its coat, and the heavy, repugnant power of its hide. I sensed them following us, a little behind and to our left, moving expertly through their feeding grounds.

'How many of them in that pack?' asked my father, his voice close in the dark.

At the sound of his voice, the misery of their grief changed pitch, like the sobbing around a grave when the coffin is lowered.

''Bout twenty,' I replied. I seemed to hear my own voice as you do with headphones on, as if it was someone else's.

My father gave a strange grunt. He sounded disgusted by my wild underestimation. I'm convinced now that he knew all the time how many there were; he'd wandered around enough woods to know that.

My panic tunnelled through me. The howling was now continuous and overwhelming. Each time I found new courage inside myself, like a circle of cleared calm in the forest, my fear would dig under it and burst out of the earth, plunging me back into the prairie grass with my father.

No matter what direction we went in now, we seemed to go further towards the wolves' singing throats. I was only aware of two things: their yell, full of carcasses and pushing snouts and greed around the kill; and my father. I can remember, as a distinct, separate moment in my fear, the realisation, 'This is happening and I am alone *except for my father.*'

Have I told you about my dad? So was it more or less fear I felt?

He said to me: 'I need my gun. Be quiet.'

I tried to grab the stock of his rifle from the sling over my shoulder, but it slid out of my hands.

'I need my gun. The wolves are here,' he whispered.

The stock slipped. I felt the sick frustration you feel in a dream when the action you most need to complete is repeated again and again, but for no good or understandable reason it remains never fully finished. I was grabbing over my shoulder, my elbow bent awkwardly to the sky. Later, the muscles in my upper arm and wrist would ache; but I felt nothing now.

He stepped towards me and pulled the rifle from its sling, wrenching me and grazing the side of my face with its butt. I staggered slightly away from him. Then he knelt down, pulled a cartridge of powder from his belt, ripped it open with his teeth and emptied it into the barrel. He looked up and around. I thought he was looking for the wolves, but when he saw me he stood, caught me with one hand to steady me and took the ramming rod from the sling with his other. He rammed the powder, and placed in his shot. My memory of this has a rarefied quality, as if my conscious self was not present, and it was only some primitive involuntary part of my brain recording these events.

Horribly, from just behind the next tufts of prairie grass I could hear a beast move. They were all howling, celebrating the final irresistible union of the pack into a whole army. When I think about it now, I'm sure my father knew exactly what was there.

He stepped through the bushes. In the darkness I could see two wolves – two, just two – pointing their snouts together and skyward. We were upon them before they knew of our presence. The sound of the gun didn't shock me. One of them fell suddenly, as if it were hurtling dead weight that had been dropped from way up. Before the shot wolf hit the ground, the other had sped terrified into the stalks of corn. There were no more wolves. The howling stopped.

Scared and astonished, I saw my father move to where the animal lay. He prodded it with the barrel of the gun. He was grinning.

'Hey, that'll learn ya, hey,' he said. He poked its carcass. 'That'll learn ya, get in the way of James Rawlins going to Mexico and kill Greasers. Can't kill Greasers if you're scared of a couple a wolves. Not worth going. Stay home with Chetlain. Sell jugs.'

Whatever reaction sets in after great fear had set in with me. I stood by the wolf and my father, shaking a little. I was weary in all my limbs, and my shoulder and wrist hurt. My father was still looking at the corpse, but said to me, 'Take this.' He handed me the gun. I struggled to lift it.

'Not worth the trip, let a couple of wolves howling scare you.' He was talking to the wolf now. I don't think he was scared then, or had been for the whole time. I think he knew the whole time what was happening.

'Think we're near Wyanet. Not half a mile,' he said, moving off. As we left he said, 'That'll learn ya'; maybe to me, maybe the wolf.

So we sailed south down the Illinois to where it joins the Mississippi just above St. Louis. You've got to remember that I was fourteen, the son of a cruel father and unfathomable mother. So if you'd've constructed some fancy metaphor about the junction of those two rivers, making the weaker Illinois represent my half-conscious obsession about the Mexican War, with its connection to my father and his fundamental hollowness; and made the Mississippi the deeper, subsuming current about which I was wholly unaware but which swallows the smaller stream because the more powerful river is who I really was: if you'd've constructed that metaphor, I'd've abandoned it as crap. Abandonment of crap was what this trip was all about.

I had never been to a city, and, looking back, that was important in what happened. Here was the place where I'd really change my life; here, I'd join the army with my father. What had seemed unreal back in Galena was about to happen. Approaching the landings and wharves, the chaotic Mississippi, Missouri and Illinois river traffic could be heard across the water, the sound all the more imposing because its rumbling was still neutered by the distance between the wharves and our boat. As our boat moved it seemed impossible to me for the captain to know where to go. How could he distinguish one wharf from the next? Dock hands swung screeching cranes shifting cargo; there were shouts for ramps to be raised; loads slammed onto waiting carts, while other hands, right next to them, were sitting at tables playing faro, their jobs (whatever they were) obviously done. St. Louis was the biggest town I'd been to, and those wharves, full of black men, made Galena's one wharf seem timid and silent; but it was the tables of faro players that created in me the most unfamiliar sensation. There they were, amazingly indifferent to the whole scene, more interested in a card game so simple that even kids played it back in Galena. The isolated mute tables of faro players showed how different St. Louis was: here, people were bored and unimpressed by St. Louis; no-one was bored by St. Louis in Galena. Our boat closed in on the wharf. As the confusingly gentle thud shivered up through the railing, I could sense that now I was part of a place that didn't know or care for me. For these faro players, I was less interesting or important than the next card to be turned.

My dad was nervous. The recruiting station was next to the St. Louis barracks. The barracks seemed to belong to a whole self-contained world. The stone buildings stood in straight uniform rows; even the curtains in the windows were tied back in the same way. There was an imposing separateness to it all: inside that place, things were different. They could've put a sign out the front: *You're in the fucking army now*. Looking at the place, I was less happy than I'd thought I'd be.

The recruiting station was not inside the barracks proper. It was a small temporary building, and advertisements were pinned in its windows promising 'chances for travel' and swift promotion. But these, and the meek bunting tacked onto its porch, were like the poor stalks of flowers in a lonely bachelor's home, serving only to make the sense of despair more emphatic.

We walked in.

The office was cool. It was still and calm, different to the crowded hot wharves, and there was that dark office smell that you get in public service buildings, the smell you sense in places where everyone's got to line up for hours to re-register their car.

A sergeant was behind a desk. He addressed my Dad. 'What do you want, sir?'

'We want to enlist.' My father said this, bashful and embarrassed. 'We want to go to the Mexican War with General Scott.'

You dickhead! You poor dumb dickhead! Couldn't you see?

I couldn't see, but I was only fourteen. What's the fucking sergeant gonna do? Call up the General on his mobile and say, 'Hey, Winfield, before you plan your greatest campaign, from Vera Cruz to the Halls of the Montezumas – what? You know, the Mexican campaign . . . Yeah. No, the *Mexican* campaign. Right. Well, before you set out on that, could you pop down to the St. Louis recruiting office and pick up James and John Rawlins? Yeah. James just came in and said he wanted to go with you. OK. Ta. The *St. Louis* office. Yeah, near Illinois. Righto. [pause, and then the recruiting sergeant sighs patiently] The Mexican campaign. M–E–X–I . . . look, I'll tell you when you get here. See you then.'

Is any pity stronger than the pity you feel for your father? As I stood behind him, I came to see him with the sergeant's pitiless eyes. This war – our Mexican War, I mean – didn't have anything to do with their Mexican War. Our Mexican War is all about you and me. It's our shared obsession and why we're obsessed that's important: and they don't care about that. General Scott probably don't want to even *know* about that. Ain't no Greasers involved.

I was entangled in different emotions – contempt, humiliation, fear, bewilderment – which were confused and unidentifiable. I'm able to disentangle these things *now*; that's the only important thing you need to know; that's what's got to be real, what you've got to accept. We all grow into awareness, don't we? Don't be distracted by how far it might be between now and then, because it's irrelevant.

The sergeant began to speak. 'The recruiting officer has taken the recruiting roll to headquarters.'

I could not listen to the recruiting sergeant's words. My father's nervousness and distraction seemed to increase as the officer spoke. The officer looked at both of us. I thought my father was worried that the sergeant would say I was underage. 'Go outside, son,' my father said to me, quietly, when the sergeant turned to call his superior officer.

The heat and light struck me. From the porch outside the office I could see down the St. Louis street. Along one side of the dirt road was a broken slithering gutter. The piles of soil that had been dug to make it had been left on the road. All the awnings and window sills and guttering and door lintels – every horizontal – seemed carelessly, shoddily out of alignment with each other. The advertisements in the shop windows sold

> 'MARVELLOUS CORDIALS, REFRESHING TO ENER-VATED LIMBS. REJUVENATES THE MUSCLES AND MIND. AN ELIXIR FOR THE GODS'.

They remind me now of the newspaper reports of the great victories of 1864: 'BRILLIANT STRATEGIC MOVEMENT OF THE UNION COMMANDER. MOVE SOUTH BY LEFT FLANK. "WE WILL FIGHT IT OUT ON THIS LINE IF IT TAKES ALL SUMMER.' THE REBELS FOOLED BY THE PLANS OF OUR GENERAL." But right then I was not thinking like that. There was nowhere for me to go. This was the St. Louis street, indifferent and real.

I stood in a perplexed despair. With every direction, with every move, it seemed my whole life came dragging along with me. Where to? There was nowhere. I could not run down that street, so crowded and foreign. I could not go back into the office, where I thought my father and I were to be shackled together in self-delusion. I felt sick. My back hurt, as if a great weight was on it; my stomach was ill with disgust. I was tired of this. There was no help for me. I was abandoned, alone. I wanted some miraculous chance occurrence to save me: to faint, for a carriage to overturn, for a trumpet to call the soldiers all away, for my father to piss off down into one of the drinking houses. I waited, but all around me went on, implacable as the faro players. I couldn't step off the porch. There is a beautiful pause between the convulsions of a patient struggling for breath, the brief rest of the lungs before the next inadequate breath is drawn. You gotta draw that breath. But back then, it was so hard.

I went back into the recruiting station, to my father.

He wasn't there anymore. I blinked in the gloom. There was the desk, but this front room was empty. I had the sudden, horrible conviction that my father had run off, that he had been lying all the time, that he never really wanted to go to the Mexican War, and so had turned back home. I was alone. I suppose the person who can best sense the hugeness of the ocean is the man drowning in it. I doubt anyone has ever thought St Louis a bigger town than I thought it was right then. I didn't know it at the time, but I was wrong about the whole thing.

I heard my father's voice coming from another room. I walked behind the recruiting desk, with its limp bunting, and down a short corridor towards the sound. My father, the recruiting sergeant and another man, a higher ranking officer, were talking in the officer's room, just beyond and out of sight of the front desk. All three in the room looked earnest and concerned; they did not notice me outside. I leant with my back to the wall of the corridor outside, my fingers gripping the frame of the door jam that opened into the office.

'My son is only fourteen,' said my father.

This new officer replied. He had a falsely patient tone that covered the irritation of having to repeat himself in an effort to be understood: 'You have told us about his age already. There is no need for the rest. That is your business.'

'Without the rest he will want to go somewhere else,' said my father. 'He knows that some recruiting stations are less strict that others. He will ask me to take him further south.'

'We will make it clear. It will be official. I can show him the regulation.'

'And he will still want me to go. I cannot go, with him so sick. He must be shown that we cannot go anywhere and be accepted.'

The officer was silent.

Standing there unseen looking into that room, I knew that suddenly, totally, I didn't want to go to Mexico. I felt as if I had never wanted to go.

Deception! Deception! Was I not raised on, suckled by, joined to, born of, deception? You are your father: you're him! Try and deceive yourself, and that very act makes you him: has he not colluded in the same deception? Aren't you both unable to solve the same problems, and this joins you further together? And at last – in some visceral way – are you not finally undeceived?

'We have come from up north,' said my father. 'Do not make him go further. I have told you he is sick. Our doctor in Galena says the disease will show soon. He needs to be home. I do not know of medicine. But I am his father, and do I not know him as well as a doctor can? This desire of his to go to the war is surely the effect of it on his mind. Let him be cured of at least this before his body is taken too.'

'Why do you not tell him? If he is sick, why have you brought him to us? You should have stayed and told him at home.'

My father paused. He started his sentence, but stopped. He started again. Although it was all lies, his voice whispered as if he was making a confession he could not force himself to hear:

'Captain, I have not been a good father. I am weak. I drink and leave. I have lied to him too much. He would not believe me. I had not the courage to tell him this; I am not good enough to. He would not believe me, and I could not do it anyway. There was no time. I have tried to tell – at every bend in the river, at every new wharf I thought: "Here. Tell him here." But I could never. I said, "Then there, at the next bend." Always the next bend.' My father stopped, as if gathering strength. I could sense the stillness in that inner office, even from where I stood unnoticed beyond the partition. 'Can you not have pity? I am a weak man. Help me.'

To my father the officer said, 'You are a weak man. I hope you find the strength that your son will need and that his years may not give him.' His voice softened, became unconsciously patronising, as if he did not know how to say some awkward, sensitive thing. 'I give my regards to your wife.'

Then the officer came to a decision. 'Go,' he said. I could tell he was speaking to the sergeant by his commanding tone. 'Get the regulations. Then bring the boy in.' He turned to my father. 'I will talk to your son when the sergeant returns.'

I hadn't had time to work it out fully, but I knew that I shouldn't have been listening to this. I could feel all my dreams of the Mexican War slide into a deep chasm inside of me and disappear. Here, this smell, this office, was the real thing, and I didn't want it, not a bit of it. I felt sick. And it was so swift! I was scared, I was fourteen, and now I didn't want to go. For so long I had been dreaming of this war; carried it with me in the coal cart to the smelter; preached about it to the valley behind our farm: but this long incubation meant nothing, now. I didn't want to go. I didn't want to go south and leave my home.

That a change so deep, about a belief I had held onto with such strength for so long, could be overthrown this quickly and completely! I was humiliated by my own cowardice. I wasn't a soldier, and that's for sure. Shelby Foote, the noted CWD, said Grant had 'four o'clock in-the-morning courage'. He wrote, 'You could wake him up at four o'clock in the morning and tell him they had just turned his right flank and he would be as cool as a cucumber.'

Before the officer finished, I was off, back outside. I figured they should find me out on the porch, where they thought I was. It took what seemed to me a very long time before the sergeant came out and told me to enter. My father was now in the original reception area. He said to me, 'An officer wishes to speak to you.' He was annoyed and nervous and impatient.

The officer came in. He had put his gloves and sword on. He spoke in an official tone, but as if he were acting his part, rehearsing for some future performance.

'Are you James Rawlins' son?' he said to me.

'Yes.'

'You wish to enlist in the army to fight in the Mexican conflict?'

I was silent; he could not know what that question was for me then. But he seemed to wish his performance over, so he helped me rush it on to its conclusion.

'You and your father have come to St. Louis from Galena for that purpose?'

'Yes.'

'And what age are you, John?'

He hadn't asked my name; I hadn't told him.

'I am fourteen.'

'You are too young for the Illinois regiments, then. I am holding a copy of the regulations concerning recruitment.' He held it out to me, as if I wouldn't believe him, and read the minimum age requirement. After that was over he said, 'You are too young for this regiment. You cannot go. You will not be able to enlist in any place in any of the United States. The United States army is not able to accept you. No state will allow you to go. You can only go home with your father. It is no use going any further south.'

I understood this, but he kept on, now lapsing from his official act into another equally forced character: 'It is best for you. You need to go home, and be with your family. You will need strength, and God and they may provide.'

He looked at my father and said, 'I can say no more.' Then as if he had just remembered his lines, he turned to me and added, 'You understand, no matter where in the country you go, you will not be accepted. The United States are unable to accept youths of your age into their army.

'You are very sick. You have a disease called consumption. You are going to be unwell, and you will need strength for this time.' He was not looking directly at me – he seemed to be looking at my forehead, or my face, but our eyes didn't meet. I was too ashamed and scared. Then he said, 'Sergeant, I wish to speak to you.' Now he did all his talking to the sergeant. 'Sergeant, this boy has consumption. He seems well now; but he will be sick very soon. If we take him, he will be in hospital within a week, and we shall have to send him home.'

'Well, we shall not take him,' said the sergeant, like the straight man in a comedy routine.

'I would also recommend that we not enlist his father. This boy needs to go home. His father should take him. His father is also a risk to the regiment,' said the Captain. 'I recommend both these volunteers be declined enlistment.' Without looking at us further, the Captain left the room.

'Yes, sir,' said the sergeant, his voice hollow and emotionless. He turned to me: 'You cannot go to Mexico. You have a very serious disease called consumption.' They kept saying that. 'Your father cannot go. He will take you home. Forget your desire to join the army. You need strength now for another conflict. Let your father join you in that battle.'

My father led me out of the recruiting station, joining me, I'm sure he didn't think, in another battle.

Ain't no more. My father and I spent three days in St. Louis. He got drunk and left me alone for most of the time. I'm still not sure why my father had lied to them about me having that disease. It wasn't true, at the time. Afterwards, he never once mentioned it to me, nor was the Mexican War spoken of again between us. We'd both had enough of it. I think he needed more than just my age to let him off the hook. Maybe he really thought I would make him find another recruiting station if this one rejected me because of my age; maybe he couldn't stand the thought of admitting to me he never wanted to go. I think he also wanted to shit on me a little bit more; but he never said, he just went off drinking for three days.

He sailed with me most of the way back to Galena, but took off when the boat docked at the town just before home. He didn't come back for six months. Then, in 1849, three years after I'd got off alone at the Galena wharf, and just after I turned seventeen, he pissed off to the gold fields in California for a few years.

1853 – 1856 – 1860

A WORD OF WARNING FOR THE SICK SOLDIER –
A MARRIAGE PROPOSAL IN NEW YORK –
TWO CEMETERIES

'I rub my arse on your tongue.'
With the branch I had in my hand I beat upon the dirt road a rhythm of imprecation at the beast:
'You fuck – *whack* – ing, fuck – *whack* – ing, fuck – *whack* – ing, fuck – *whack* – ing, fucking, great fucking – *whack* – fucking four-legged fuck.'
The branch broke. My shoulder hurt, and the dirt from the track fingered my face and throat. I held the stub of the branch out at the ox in front of me.
'I'll put this down your cock and pull it out sideways.' I pulled the placid head of the ox down with one hand so its nose was near the dirt, and I knelt on the dirt and I beat the dirt an inch from its snout. 'Fucking, fucking – *whack* – fucking, fucking – *whack* – fucking animal beast fucking shit down my throat *fuck*.' The last 'fuck' was a final, defeated

noun; and with it, I jerked the animal's head away from me. It didn't care at all. My arm was weak, and as I stood I felt in my whole body that strange ghostly resistance you feel when you straighten your fingers after they have been clamped hard around something too long. I uncurled the shredded stump from my fist.

Below me I could see the Dubuque hills. At the bottom of the valley the Galena river was shining orange. At the horizon's liquid edge the sky merged into the mountains, then rose up into a curved inverted ocean, suspended at some hugely distant point centred over my head.

It was the evening of a hot afternoon in late September, and my ox refused to move. You know the feeling. I had beaten the ground in front of it and nearly pulled the charcoal cart behind it clean up its arse and out through its dumb nose ring, but that fuck weren't moving nowhere.

Up and out of the twilight-infused air of the valleys in front of me, in the silences left between the breaths of my panting, I could hear animals calling in their nightly conspiracy to each other. With my back to the animal and the charcoal cart I took a vow: 'I will sleep here, in this coal cart, rather than return home. Those who are infirm of purpose cannot fulfill what God wills of them. The smelters will have this coal tomorrow. I will not abandon this.'

I turned back towards the ox. It had its head down, grazing at the side of the track. It was still in harness, and a little behind the cart the ground showed where the wheel had skidded into a rut and become stuck. We had not moved for most of the afternoon. Although I've changed some of the swearing in this chapter to make it more acceptable to a modern audience, none-the-less I can assure you some of my actual language was quite strong.

'I cum in your eyes,' I would've hissed, if I'd've thought of it.

Like I said, my father pissed off to the California gold fields in 1849. He came back late '52. By then, the farm was in my name; we changed the documents while he was away. Did it down the Stevens' law office, too. Of course, after the whole St. Louis/Mexican War thing, I threw myself into my mother's brand of obsession. I had attended one term at the Rock River Seminary at Mount Morris. I thought I wanted to be a preacher. I'd tell you about my 'John the Preacher' phase – quite like Picasso's Blue Period or Elvis Costello's country album – but that enlistment office in St. Louis had convinced me about the hollowness of my fanaticisms even if it hasn't persuaded you. I'd just be repeating myself. It was like Post-modernism: not worth worrying about. I was stuck on this hillside carting coal around again, just like I had when I was fourteen, because we couldn't afford the final term I needed at the seminary to graduate. So I had spent this summer in the middle of 1853 shifting shit. I was twenty-one.

That fucking seminary, though ... Let me tell you about my 'John the Preacher' phase. It's vital. You can imagine the farewell scene at home. It was winter, early in 1853: 'John,' said my mother, 'from those to whom a ministry is granted God expects even greater obedience.'

I said, 'Those given to the ministry find also an uncommon strength.' It made no difference what the words were, or how fluently they were spoken: we were talking as if in an unpractised language. Our unfamiliarity with the precise meaning of what we wished to say made us sound strange or ridiculous.

She held out her hand, and gave me a small folded pamphlet. I could feel its paper, thin as a flower, dry between my thumb and fingers. It was a religious tract: *A Word of Warning for the Sick Soldier*.

'I have heard the Seminary meals are sparse,' she said. She didn't touch me; she stood away, as if on stage and confused about what to do with her hands. Through the thin walls I could hear my father outside, laughing like a child. 'The Disciples are old fashioned in their devotions.'

'We all of us must face a trial. We can only pass with Another's help,' I said proudly. It was like the instruction manuals you used to get with old Japanese VCRs. I should have told my mother, 'First it in to plug, then when power – tape will on!'

She looked at me.

I could have slowed down every word: 'First – it – in – to – plug! Then, when power – tape will on!' Someone wasn't getting it. '*When power – tape will on!*' I might as well've said, my face expectant and happy, ready to see the first sign of comprehension in hers.

'When you have finished at Mount Morris,' she said, 'you can come back to me, John, if you like.'

Outside, as I walked to the trees at the edge of our clearing, my father was playing with my younger brothers. 'Here comes the red-eyed bear,' he was shouting, on all fours, his face down near the dirt. He slowly crunched his way towards the squealing children. I was sure this was a show, for my benefit. There was never much play in our house. I could see him without turning my head. Because of the cold, he wore a jacket and coat, the layers of clothing crumpled up his back, humping up near his shoulders as if he had grown the slouching neck of a beast.

'Here come the red-eyed bear,' he growled as they squealed in amazed delight. 'Here come the red-eyed bear, and he's angry.' Suddenly, he lunged at them; they ran as he collapsed into the dirt. I walked on, my head held still so that my steps took them finally beyond my line of vision. The trees stood glacially above me. The house seemed soon to be crushed. He didn't look at me at all as I left.

A Word of Warning For the Sick Soldier started like this:

In the hospital behind the field of battle the sick soldier lies. Around his ears arise the sounds of the great booming cannon. The sick soldier is surrounded by the crying of the wounded and can hear the calls of his comrades as they lay in their beds. But the sick soldier has a secret. The calls of his comrades, the sound of the cannon, the orders of his commander can not prevent the sound of that great secret from ringing in his own ears. The sick soldier knows he is not really sick. As henbane poisons the blood, so too did the sick soldier's cowardice poison his soul. Are you a sick soldier?

Fucking that'd get ya rockin', wouldn't it, if your mother gave you *that* and you read it with your mouth full of Galena frost as you toured your way through the townships of Forreston, Brookville, Eagle Point, Grand Detour, Leaf River, Pine Rock, White Rock and Scott to get to Ogle County and Mount Morris? 'Hel–lo Leaf River – we are the John A. Rawlins Experience, and here's the single from our new album, "The Sick Soldier".' Fucking yay.

'When you have finished at Mount Morris you can come back to me, John, if you like.' She didn't want me to go. You would've thought she'd've wanted me to go – after all, it was her religion, not mine. I'm almost glad I didn't work it out at the time.

I only lasted one semester anyway. I was expecting some grand basilica; but it was just another shithole of slanting huts. There was a small sandstone chapel. The Disciples would sing hymns with their breath condensing in the air in front of them. For the whole term I was there the footprints in the mud tracks didn't change from the ones iced solid since before my arrival. A line of mist could be seen rising up along the course of the Rock River, as if the stream's water had fallen in one tremendous snaking mass from above but had become frozen just as it rebounded off the iced river bed. Looking back, I'm aware now of the invisible condensation this place was accumulating unfelt in my blood, waiting, like the bends, for the time when I wanted to surface. The small porous details of the Seminary got under my skin. The sign outside the chapel would read 'A Sermon is to be made by L.D. Waldo, of Rockford, and D.R. Howe, of Lanark, on the subject of Swearing.' The Disciples would all gather before daylight, and listen like they were the only believers in the world. St John the Baptist proclaimed the Christ had come; L.D. and D.R. claimed that the profaner, 'like the silly fish, was biting at the devil's bare hook'. Before the evening meal G.W. Ross would stand and proclaim: 'This little church, the child of persecution, has a present membership of 93. The value of our property is $1,400. The enrolment in the Bible school is currently 120.' When the Rockford Rapper M.C. D.J. L.D. and Snoop Doggy D.R. warned about 'distilled damnation' and how 'blighting rum and sorrowful whisky will from the bottle their evils spread' nothing they said seemed to successfully slander my stinking pissfilled father. Careful lists were posted inside the chapel doors:

Founder: *J.H. Wright.*
Pastors: *G.W. Rose, J.H. Car, T.B. Stanley,*
                   J.B. Wright, C.T. Spitler, G.W. Pearl,
                   D.G. Wagner, D.F. Seyster
Those given to the ministry: J.H. Shellenberger; Z.O.
                   Doward, J.W. Baker.

Everyone had two fucking initials, like J. F. Christ. It wasn't that there was too much religion that made me dissatisfied – there wasn't enough. It was the two-initial religion. I wanted a fucking baptism; what I got was J.A. Rawlins. It was like the Rotarians – 'Chicken or beef, President-Elect Chubby?' 'I'll have the chook, Treasurer-In-Waiting Onan.'

Of course I wasn't aware of the reasons behind my dissatisfaction back then. Shivering in the sandstone, I prayed as hard as I had sweating amongst the charcoal. Old G.W. 'A-lecture-room-and-modern-improvements-are-to-be-contemplated' Ross met me one day and quietly told me that my 'induction into Christ would surely come soon after the next term's study' and that fees are paid in advance. I was secretly glad to go back to the charcoal furnace to earn the money.

In the six months I'd spent at the Seminary I'd read my mother's tract until its pages were thick with the oily dirt from my fingers. The image of the Sick Soldier lying with artificial awkwardness on his hospital cot resonated with me. I was lying on just such a bed in the narrow acolyte's cell I'd been given. I could stand up and touch the two opposite walls with the flat of my palms, not having to reach with fingertips, but pressing hard till the sandstone came off on my hands. Was I a sick soldier or not? Can the most polished officer in the Grand Army of the Potomac be certain about himself? You don't have to be lying in a camp hospital to be faking it. Read my pamphlet:

A WORD OF WARNING TO THE SICK SOLDIER
by J.A. Rawlins

The sick soldier sat in the brasserie, ordering bruschetta. Tomorrow he was to leave Washington to begin the campaign.

'Charles's haemorrhoids are playing up again, aren't they?' says his wife, leaning over to Charles in mock sympathy. 'You don't mind me sharing this, do you, darling?' Charles looks mock shocked, though he is embarrassed enough to make the other guests burst with laughter. 'I told him to get the cream, and that I love him so much I'd rub it on again.'

Guest next to Charles [holding up a fork full of whole wheat gnocchi in ricotta sauce]: 'I'm not hungry.'

Burst of laughter.

'No, really, I said to Charles, "Well, darling, four years ago at the start of the war I vowed to love, honour and cherish you till death and haemorrhoids do we part", and I meant it, darling, I really did.'

Burst of laughter. Surely no-one around that table was thinking of the battle to come.

'Of course, you seemed to be a young attractive adjutant back then – very high up with General Meade – and your bottom seemed very firm' – *another burst of laughter, each one reaffirming to the surrounding tables what crazy and crude and unworried people they happened to be sitting next to* – 'but I've found out since it's what's inside that counts.'

Burst of laughter.

Guest next to Charles: 'It's what's outside that should be in.'

B.O.L.

'Painfully true,' *says his wife.*

B.O.L.

Now Charles, in mock indignation: 'Really, I feel that this is entirely inappropriate, Sarah. Our guests are having a repast with us at our invitation, to celebrate the departure of our grand army, and they little care for your dissertation on my . . . delicate complaint.'

B.O.L.

'I don't want to get dogmatic, but I insist we change totally the tone of this conversation.' *Pause.* 'Anyway, Sarah's gynecologist says to me . . .'

Ending drowned in burst of laughter.

The sick soldier excuses himself, and heads quickly for the toilets.

I know enough about faking it to claim copyright, and I know it's not just up the back of an army that you find cowards. Here's my word of warning to the sick soldier: the fact you're malingering doesn't mean you're not sick. The fact you're willing to fight doesn't mean you've been cured. You can't tell from the front of a person what is going on out back:

'Go get Sarah,' says Charles F. Adams, son of the ambassador.

'I can't get Sarah, we're in the mens'.'

'You're a fucking girl, aren't you? You're in the fucking men's.'

Giggling.

'Go get her. Tell her there's not enough for Sammy.'

'Sammy's paid.'

'I know he's paid, but look, there's not enough. Tell her to come and have some, and then she can tell him.'

The Girl Getting Sarah hovers outside the cubicles. She's not really embarrassed about being in the mens' at all. She's doing drugs in the male toilet, and she knows everyone knows, and that makes it better.

Alcohol and drinking and buying jugs of rum from Chetlain's store will not help the sick soldier. The cocaine deal solemn as a Japanese tea ceremony in the brasserie toilet will not help the sick soldier.

'Get Sarah!' the sick soldier calls, desperate now, from inside the cubicle.

'I've really got a penis,' the Girl Getting Sarah laughs, calling back over the door, 'but I'm just a bit confused at the moment.'

'Get Sarah!' The sick soldier sounds ready to weep. The Girl Getting Sarah grimaces in distaste. 'What's wrong with him?*' she says under her breath as she leaves. Inside the cubicle, the sick soldier lets himself fall onto the tiles,*

palms flat on the suspicious wet floor, knees near the bowl.

'Get Sarah,' he cries quietly to himself, as if, when his wife comes, everything will be all right.

Sick soldiers are everywhere. You could be one.

So I slept the night next to my ox and cart; so? I looked out over that dark valley and felt the cold's wolvish approach. Brave vow, that: 'I will sleep here, in this coal cart, rather than return home.' I'd been exposed, you see: Mexico had shown my hidden weakness, and I didn't want to be exposed again about the strength of my devotion to this religion, despite its monkey-butler pastors and butt-doctor G.W. Ross. When I said, 'Those who are infirm of purpose cannot fulfil what God wills of them,' what I meant to say was, 'Rawlins – YOU'RE PINGED, SON.'

Looking back now, when the evening fell on the dirt track that was the road from our farm to Galena, the whole thing in front of me made sense. From high up, I mean. From high up, from the air, the curve in the Galena river that on the ground takes the ox and cart an hour-and-a-half to round, so that you're cursing the perversity of whoever put it there, is a logical step in the argument the river makes down through the valley and on to the Mississippi. And the folds of the hills, the way the oak line starts and stops, and the flat plain and where it begins to rise – looking back now, over the very last of the twilight when the river and the sky are glowing orange from within and everything else is dark, it all made sense.

But back then, all I knew was that it was getting cold. I decided to sleep on the seat of the dray. The ox was still harnessed to it – I wasn't going to take the fucker off – and when the animal slouched slightly to get at more grass, the cart trembled under me. I could smell the animal's fleshy manure-like odour in the black air. It shuffled again. On the hard wooden seat of the dray, it was impossible to get my shoulder blades and hips and knees all rested at the same time, so, on my back, I stared above. In the dark, I seemed able to sense the cold valley below. I lay on the ox cart, waiting for hours and hours before the sun would warm the black air to daylight. If I slept, then I was dreaming I was awake on the ox cart.

When I woke up the next morning into a new world of green, cold, damp light, what I did was jiggle the reins and say 'Hurrup' to the beast and the damn fucker moved straight away, easy as that. How come I couldn't work that out, either?

If I had, maybe I wouldn't have caught the cough in my chest that never went away. If you were hiding in the hills watching, amongst the far, foetal sounds rising across the valley of early morning light, you would have heard the tinkering, rolling movement of John A. Rawlins' ox and cart hoofing and wheeling its way over the hills, and just as it disappeared behind the next grassy crest you would've heard the comic splutter as the driver coughed for a first time, and then again.

That buttfucking ox stalled on the very next hill. It was too much. I walked to a nearby railroad construction camp and sold the lot – ox, cart, charcoal – for $250; good price, too, because the workers at the camp were from down near Springfield and didn't know exactly what the smelters were paying. I got to Galena by eleven o'clock, and by noon I'd seen Isaac P. Stevens in his office. He sort of seemed sorry for me – probably he'd been talking to Chetlain again. So I joined the firm, and was from that day a driven lawyer-politician for the Douglas Democrats. No more seminary. Told you it wasn't worth worrying about.

The facts in the previous paragraph aren't made up at all. Or at least, 'that' (as William S. McFeely, author of *Grant: A Biography* puts it) is what 'the story is'.

∽ ∾

I haven't told you properly about Emily yet. I've been trying to avoid the whole subject, just like I was avoiding it back then. I've been writing about the American Civil War, and how I was going to join up and change my life, and blardy blardy rah rah rah. You don't need to know about my law career – God knows, I've inflicted enough grief on you without you hearing about my great win in *The People v Shitforbrains* and how I told Your Honour to get off her. The law was a perfect profession for me – all those high ideals, and all the time what you're really doing is working in a factory.

By 1855 Stevens had left the firm. Thinking back to his tired, grey head as he looked up with almost no surprise when I entered his office just after eleven o'clock in 1853, I think he'd worked out by then what a shithole the law is. He sat and looked at me standing in front of him. I was too scared to sit down because of the charcoal dust still on my pants. I asked him for a job. I remember his office smelt cleanly, antiseptically impressive – the ink wells, paper, books, carpets, even the wall paper. Most rooms I'd ever been in had been full of planking, like I'd been brought up in the bottom decks of ships all my life. Isaac Stevens sat there in a room covered in leather and wool and paper; the ceiling was a perfect white plaster, like the skin of a beautiful dead girl. I could sense that I had the stink of the ox still hanging around me – I'd only sold the fucker a few hours ago – and felt as if I'd dragged in dung beetles that would breed in the walls. When I told him I could read, he got up and moved to pick a book off the shelves behind him. He moved slowly, seriously. He opened it and carefully found the place he wanted; then, holding a finger at where he wished me to begin, he turned the book towards me and held it out.

'Read this, John,' he told me.

It was from the Massachusetts Legislature's resolutions on the war with Mexico.

'Resolved,' I began. '*Resolved*, That such a war of conquest, so hateful in its objects, so wanton, unjust, and unconstitutional in its origin and character, must be regarded as a war against freedom, against humanity, against justice, against the Union, against the Constitution, and against the Free States.' How must I have looked, there in his office with my hair standing on end because of the dirt left in it from the boards of the ox cart, holding his huge book with my knobbly wrists poking out from my filthy grey shirt, reading these words? I was wholly unconscious of myself; the rhythm of the words rose like they were my own speech: '. . . and that a regard for the true interests and the highest honour of the country, not less than the impulses of Christian duty, should arouse all good citizens to join in efforts to arrest this gigantic crime . . .'

When I stopped there was a pause left in the room, like it was taking breath for a surprised second before it could applaud. How much did Stevens know then? He stood up again, and took the book from me, folding it shut.

'Clerk,' he called past me. A boy, younger than me, came in. 'This is John Rawlins,' Stevens told the boy. The clerk looked at me incredulously as Isaac Stevens said that from now on I'd be working with him.

I have observed in foolish awe
The dateless mid-days of the law
And seen indifferent justice done
By everyone on everyone.

But I've been wanting to tell you about Emily, and her illness, though. Back in 1861, it seemed very important; and, unlike most of the other stuff, it seems important still.

I knew Emily for five years. It was not enough. She died of consumption at the beginning of the war. I met her in Galena when her father, Alexander Smith, a New York Democrat lawyer and Senator, came through Illinois campaigning for Buchanan in '56. After they came through Galena, I wrote to her; and seven months later I went to New York to propose.

You know how long Emily and her father were in Galena campaigning for Buchanan in the election of '56? At the time the Republicans had got up torchlight parades, and chanted 'Free Soil, Free Speech, Free Men, Frémont', but we Democrats were trying to paint them as extreme abolitionists who believed in racial equality. Alexander Smith gave his standard speech with Emily sitting behind him on the platform. He kept referring to Negro husbands and Negro marriage; and there was his beautiful daughter right behind him, her wrists folded and delicate. 'The one aim of the party that supports Frémont,' he'd declare, 'is to elevate the African race in this country to complete equality of political and economic condition with the white man.' There'd be Emily, pushing her hair back over the perfect shell of her ear with one poised finger. And he'd say: 'No, there is more than this. These black Republicans wish also for the complete social equality of the black man. These black Republicans say that all the fruits that a white American man can pluck from the great sturdy branches of our nation, black fingers can grab for also.' Emily would look up at him with a daughter's innocent love, as if she was wholly unaware of the subtext. 'What is ours now will be the African's soon; what we possess – our pride, our country, our homes, our families, our daughters and sons – the black Republicans would let him have.' But every white male who could hear thin, pale Alexander Smith's anger, and see his child just behind him, knew the subtext: Emily's throat seemed already bruised with the abuse of some African devil. 'Save me from a nigger husband' may as well have been painted on her forehead. I saw him give that speech at least six times, and every time Emily sat poised and adorable behind him. When he campaigned around Galena for the '56 election, he repeated that speech word for word (every angry gesture and outraged tone the same) at least twice a day; and he was there for three days. That's how long I'd known Emily before I met her seven months later in the garden outside her father's house in New York – three days.

I proposed to her in that garden. That scene presents itself in memory unchanged from how it seemed to be then. Cold sunlight shone on the path and through the trees; and I could sense in the garden's air that moment's place in my life. Do you know – you must – how memory can transform the ordinary details of your past, so they now fill you with tender pathos? I can remember my brother Alton staring excited and ill in the light of the charcoal smelters, one side of his profile red with firelight and the other merged black into the forest behind him. I can see that now, in my mind's eye, and, oh, it is so pitiful, so powerful. Then, like as not, I was cursing him because he could not help with the shovelling. Somehow, it is the actual physical facts of the scene that evoke such elusive feelings. The actual tilt of his head, and the distance between him and me, and the smothering smell of the fire are now charged with an inexplicable significance. With such awareness, you seem to see that past time, and it is transformed:

> *I thought, How could I be so dull,*
> *Twenty thousand days ago,*
> *Not to see they were beautiful?*

Sometimes, these two great senses – the sense of the present, and the sense of a higher, though more distant, perspective, gained by the passing of time – coincide. You seem to feel in the present the full significance of the moment; it does not take long decades to burn away what is superfluous and leave only that gentle forgiving sense of pity. That momentous, calm sense seemed to be with me then, looking up at Emily's place from the garden. In that distance I could seem to feel something greater.

As I was staring, she came up the path behind me. She stood beside me, and said: 'You have come a long way, Mr Rawlins.'

Contrary to all the rehearsals of this moment I had enacted in my imagination, it was me who was surprised: 'Emily, you are here . . .' – beside me, I meant.

She looked directly into my face, smiling. 'The election is a success. You and my father must have succeeded in winning Illinois for Mr Buchanan.'

Who cares? Who cares? My sense of calm perspective left, not to return till I could see this all from a point of view that would have seemed impossible back then – who cares about James fucking Buchanan? 'The visit of Senator Smith, and his daughter, was for me of the greatest moment.'

'I am sure my father helped the cause you share with him, Mr Rawlins.'

She knew why I was here; why I was standing outside her house; why I had come all the way from Galena, Illinois, where they thought Alexander Smith a pale, small Yankee.

'Though that cause is dear to me' – yup – 'dearer still are matters that concern not the nation, but the –' I stopped, waiting for some sign from her beautiful face, some hint that if I said 'the heart' she wouldn't use her cream-soft brown eyes to laugh. Nothin', though. '– the self,' I concluded.

She looked away, pleased with the small lame silence after that. 'My father and I visited poor Mr Sumner. He could not talk at all.' She knew less about the caning of Republican Charles Sumner than you do. 'His son was very attentive to us, though. He offered to take us to the theatre. My father could not go, so, of course, I did not.'

Her dress was garlanded and ruffled, and her crinoline was worn larger than any woman in Galena would yet think suitable. I had so much to say – me, who was normally so full of talking, so bound up in driven expression – but in front of her, I could manage nothing. There was no use for small talk about bleeding Kansas and what the *New York Evening Post* said about Congressman Preston Brooks 'chastising us as they chastise their slaves', when she was there, like that.

'I am afraid my father is in Washington. You have travelled to New York for some other purpose, I hope. Such a long journey would be a sad waste without one.' She reached out, and very briefly touched her hand flat on my chest, and then self consciously drew back, saying, with a little laugh, 'New York is not such a big place that we may not possibly meet again, then, Mr Rawlins. Such a surprise would not be greater than the one of finding you here.'

As she was walking away I said, 'Emily, I have come to see if you will marry me', and she said: 'I don't know', and left.

I wrote her this:

12 DECEMBER, 1856

Darling Emily,

It is seven months since I met you, and in that time I seem to feel only more and more love for you. You know now that I want to marry you. I have come to New York to see if you will marry me. Will you?

In front of us I sense a future with no misgivings. There is no beauty or love possible if it is not possible and real between a husband and a wife who love each other. If this can not be, then I can see no joy anywhere. To what end, my state, or fighting for the Presidency, or Jo Davies's County, if true marriage is not true, and domestic love lost? There is no purpose to all America, if two people cannot share love.

Will you share my life? I can see the Galena river curving orange in the evening fields, and we two in that special light. Every evening, there is that light; it is no less beautiful for occurring every single day. We can have beauty, every day.

At times, when I think of us together in the future it is as if I am looking back on the past. What if every moment of the life spent together by two people in love were saved somewhere else; that, like a beach made of small gems, every present second of being together was not just lost into the past, but accumulated on the edge of an ocean in some other world, and there both could walk together when dead? How beautiful our life together would be; how beautiful all the moments we could have; how wonderful a heaven, to have them again.

Emily, I know that this may seem so foolish to you. If you do not love me as I love you, I will only be able to cover, not heal, the wound that is left. I know that my feelings will change: through grief, if you do not share them; or through joy, as our love becomes more and more true, and passion is strengthened by all that is new to be found out about ourselves. I know that in long years from now, no matter how you reply to me, you and I will be as different from the people we are now as age is different to youth, and young love to old. But whoever I am in the future, and whoever you are, I know that I could not change in

My love for you,

John

And this is the note I got back:

Dear Mr Rawlins,

It was indeed a great surprise to see you in the park here in New York, and receiving your letter left me no less unprepared. About these things you should talk to my father. He is in Washington. You have my consent to go to him.

I know I think of you as 'John', but forgive me if I find it too soon to write to you under such terms.

Yours,
Emily Smith.

It was my first time in Washington. It was the dump everyone said it was; before the war, people were fighting to give it away, not keep it. I met Senator Alexander Smith in the lounge in Willard's Hotel. He was another complete arsehole. I was no great match for his family – a six-toed spam-sucking Illinois shit-shoveller asking for the daughter of a senator – but he gave more thought to his choice of port than his choice of son-in-law. He kept looking around the room trying to hide his unease; every time a new table of guests arrived his eyes would quickly scan them. I had travelled over three weeks to be here and I was with him for no more than twenty minutes. He told me that Emily's happiness was of the greatest import to him, agreed we should marry soon, and left. He didn't want to be seen with an Illinois lawyer. No one worth his time had ever been an Illinois lawyer and, in 1856, it looked like no Illinois lawyer ever would.

There are two cemeteries in Galena. The closest is on the road just before you reach the town. Trees and shrubbery curtain the graves, even though from the road the headstones are visible through and above the leaves. The graves nearest the entrance are the oldest and some have footstones as well as headstones, as if the cot-beds that held the smaller people of the past have been buried there, with only the mattresses under the earth. As you walk towards the back, the bone-brown headstones become cleaner; and there, right at the back, the white gravestones and freshly dug earth wait impatiently like a new subdivision of housing for the builders to leave.

The other cemetery is six miles out of town. All the graves are new. It slopes up, alone and undisguised, in the hills high over the river. Every large tree or bush around it has been cut down. It faces the wind unsheltered; at night-time there is no warning of the snow that strikes before the land can flinch in protection, and in the daylight the cemetery can see the weather forming into tremendous grey-black shapes miles away. This sky comes over sides of valleys that drop down to the river so suddenly and so far that the animals who fall spin for long seconds before they hit the water. The storms balance precariously above the hills like huge slate slabs about to topple, and the earth waits unmoving for the slow spates of ice to rain cold into the eyes of the graves.

I put my father in one and my wife in the other. Cue violins. There's a little smartarse behind me pretending to be Paga-fuckingnini right through the next bit. My father was involved in a fight in January 1860 and, boom, he died in May. He didn't go back home to die, he went back home to get pity, to wake up and call for a bowl of water and for someone to wipe the muck from the wound on his face. If he knew he was going home to die, I doubt he'd've done it. Apparently, right to the end, he kept talking about his days campaigning in Mexico.

He didn't die because of the fight; at least, there was no way the doctor could connect the blows he received then with his death. He was fucked – years of drink had seen to that – and it was like the old person's hip injury job: one slip in the shower in the Beth Israel Rest Homes, and it's do not go gentile into that good night. Emily was writing a letter. There was a knock at our front door. I was preparing a speech for the coming elections; I paused to look at my wife just as she left her writing. I love to think of her now. She placed her hand on her chest, as if she were about to cough; but then she turned and left. I could see the paper and her empty chair framed by the open door of my study. I was making a particularly clever point about Stephen Douglas's view on the Nebraska Bill in 1854 and its relevance to the concept of popular sovereignty in territories under the Constitution having not yet fully attainedstatehoodregardingtheirabilityto excludeslaverypriortotheformationofastateconstitu –

I heard her crying, and when I went to her she was sitting in the entrance hall, looking straight ahead, weeping. Her face was red, as if she'd been crying for hours.

'Your father has died,' she said. She didn't stand. She looked up at me. 'A message just came from your mother. He has died.'

When her letter was finished, I thought later, how strange that it was begun when my father was still alive.

'Your mother wishes you to go there now,' she said.

'My father is dead?'

She nodded, crying.

'When did he die?'

She shook her head, confused. 'The boy did not say.' She meant the messenger. 'I think he came from the doctor's. He only told me your father has died, and your mother wishes you to go.'

I had no words for what I felt.

'Was it today?'

She shook her head, wiping her tears with the back of her hand.

'When, then?'

'I do not know,' she said.

'Then how do you know it was not today that he died?'

She shook her head, exactly like before, and gulped like a swimmer.

'I meant I do not know,' she said, whispering now. Because of her tears she could not seem to get enough air to speak. 'Your mother sent the message.'

'Well, who gave you this message?' I asked, as if something simple would be easier for this idiot I was talking to.

'I think a boy who works with the doctor.'

'He came from the doctor?'

My wife started crying with more force. In her distress, she began to cough.

I had to try not to yell at her: 'Is that right? He was from the doctor?'

Maybe, if I hadn't come upon her when she was sitting down; maybe, if she had come to me in my study, and she had told me with her hands held in front of her in compassion; maybe then I wouldn't have attacked her like this.

'He was from the doctor?' I insisted.

'I do not know for sure.' One of her hands was across her chest, gripping her other arm; this arm hung straight down. She clung to the limp arm up near the shoulder, like she was holding it there where it fell off, waiting in stupid hope that someone would come and assure her things would be all right and they were able to fix it back on.

I turned and left her, as if disgusted. I got my overcoat and hat, and went out without saying anything else to her. I came home very late that night and she was waiting for me but I said to her that both of us should immediately go to bed.

I would not visit my father's body when it was placed for

viewing at my mother's house. 'I thank you for visiting him, but I do not wish to,' I told Emily. 'I do not wish to look at that face.'

I put him in the graveyard away from town, cold and high up, overlooking the river. Once – sometime before the speech I gave to the courthouse in April of the next year – Emily wanted me to come with her to visit the grave. I would not go, I told her. She came up to me and linked her arm around mine. I looked at her in surprise, almost in shock.

'John,' she said. 'I do not want to be alone.'

Even as I told her that she did not have to go, that there was no duty incumbent on her to visit the grave, and that I felt my duties as a son to my father had been fulfilled – even as I told her that, I knew that wasn't what she meant. She let go of my arm. Things don't have to be dead before you bury them: *My poor, poor Tess.* You can place beauty, still alive, in a grave while you sleep.

Dead! dead! dead!

And love, long dead, can come back and visit you, entire and undiminished. She picked up the flowers she was going to take to the grave. I think of that now, and all I felt for Emily comes back to me. It can all come back, too sudden for you to deny what you feel, making you thankful for the pain.

༺ ༻

Here's something I bet you don't know about my father.

After he died, I was for a while childishly troubled at nights. I was afraid of meeting his ghost. I dreamed of him most nights. Ever after, this dream would occasionally come back to me. It came to me the night after I went to the front with Sherman's troops below Missionary Ridge.

In the dream I was six or seven. One hot summer's day we went out through the woods near our home. I had his rifle and ammunition bag slung over my shoulder. In the heat the grit of the powder seemed to find its way up my nose more quickly than usual, and into the pores of my skin. We were looking for honey.

On the way he told me a story: 'I went with my father to hunt bears once. He said to me, "Jim, if you ever get in trouble with bears, if they've got you cornered, you gotta talk to the most red-eyed one. You got to say to the red-eyed one, 'My name is James Rawlins and I am a peaceable man, but I'll not be hectored by a person of your size.'" So one day I was down by the Pecatonica and I had my hand right in a big honey pot when three bears came up behind me and even before I turned around I knew right away it was their honey pot and there weren't no debating they were prepared to do on the subject. Now I could hear them behind me, but I didn't turn 'round right away, I said to myself out loud: "There just don't seem to be no fairness around these days any more. Once when us humans went out after bears we did it fair and square and went out after 'em with sticks and arrows and the like just as the red Indian did and sometimes we got the bear and sometimes the bear got us and it seemed like in some ways we were dealin' fair with each other, in a rough sort of way, and no-one would complain 'cept perhaps the bears and the humans who were killed, but I'll admit if I was them I wouldn't take too kind a view of the deal either." I could hear them bears panting behind me, John, just waiting to let rip, and I think the only part left of me would have been the hand I had in that honey pot, so I felt I better get right on with my story and try and keep 'em diverted. "But then," I said, "but then we got traps and we hid behind bushes or some place where we knew the bears couldn't smell us, or we'd just go home and have our dinner and come back later, and there would be a bear in the trap howling like a baby and trying to chew its leg right off just to get out of that trap and find the damn villain – excuse my language but I do believe that it's allowed when there ain't no-one around to be offended anyhow – that done this to him." And I could hear those three bears gruntin' and breathin' behind me and I got a bit afraid that I had turned them even more against me than they were already but I could also tell that they sort of agreed with me too and wanted to wait till the end before they bit my head off so I said: "And that never seemed as fair to me, 'cos the odds on a one-legged bear getting back at the farmer who set the trap don't seem very good, even if the bear could find him before another trap got him, and that's if the bear did manage to get out of the first trap in the first place, which to me doesn't seem to happen more than once in a while anyway." I had my hand right down that honey pot, and I kept looking at the Pecatonica straight ahead of me 'cos I knew somehow that if I turned around at that point and looked for the red-eyed bear and said, "My name is James Rawlins and I'm a peaceable man, but I'll not be hectored by one of your size", it wouldn't have been good strategy, so I went on and said instead: "But then we humans got guns" – and I knew I'd hit the spot here, 'cos those three bears behind me gave this big grumble in agreement and I could hear one of them settle down on his haunches to get more comfortable and listen – "and that was just about the end of it, because you could shoot a bear from as far away as here to the other side of the river there and that bear doesn't even get a chance to know what hit him, much less who done it, he just grunts and falls over and you don't even have to cross the river if you don't want to, you can just keep on walking and load up again and wait for another bear. It don't seem right, even though I like honey and everything, that we can get bears like that and keep a whole river between us and them." I knew I was on the right track now; I heard the other two bears settle into the branches behind me, and they'd just about given up their low awful angry growling altogether, and I could hear them breathing and blowing out their nostrils, but not mad like. But still, I did want the honey pot, and I didn't want to get molested unfairly about it by those three, and all up I still wanted them to leave, even though I was changing my opinion of them just about as fast as they seemed to be taking a bit of a second think about me, so then I said: "But there ain't nothing worse than this new one, I don't think. When bears find out about this new one, they are going to be even more mad than they were before. I sure hope I don't have to be the one to tell them about this new one we humans have thought up, 'cos who ever gets that job – well, I wouldn't be surprised if the bears don't up right straight away and do something to him I don't even like to think on a lot." And I could just tell that if you'd paid those three bears behind me ten thousand dollars to rip in to me, they wouldn't have done it right then, nor if you had offered gold either. So I took my hand right out of that honey pot and took a big long lick of my fingers and then did it again just like I was making sure that I was really getting all that honey right down my throat, and before they got too restless but leaving long enough for them to imagine what that honey might taste like too, I said, "Yep. It's been done again. This here is another one of those poisoned honey pots, and I don't think it's fair either, and how those humans got it to be so that something that tastes so good to bears makes them scream so loud that it sounds worse than a baby in a bear trap I don't want to know. Why, if we humans went round and poisoned every single honey pot, we could just sit at home after that and read in the newspapers about how all the bears are gone and there'd be nothing to do but wait till the birds had picked all the bodies away and the smell stopped. It's not right; and I'm taking this pot with me, and I know a lot of humans won't be too happy 'bout me doin' it, and maybe bears neither, but the bears don't know it's for their own good and the humans don't need to ever find out." And, John, then I turned around and faced them three bears and pretended to look real shocked and scared, which wasn't too hard 'cos I was easier in my mind than ten minutes ago, but I wouldn't say I was all comfortable, and I looked straight at the most red-eyed one and said to him just like it was only then I knew he was there: "My name is James Rawlins and I am a peaceable man, but I'll not be hectored by a person of your size" and it was just like my daddy had said. Those three just sat there and looked at me, and they seemed more sad than angry, though that might just be me putting a little made up poetry into it all, I'll admit, and then they got up and walked away back into the trees and I let out the first really easy breath I'd had for a while and thanked my father, though he wasn't there so I did it to myself, for telling me what to say.'

The dream continued. My father and I climbed for a while up the side of the valley, and below us the Galena river was grey–blue in the yellow summer fields. I hitched the pouch up on my shoulder when it slung too low, and arched my back when we stopped in a cool shadowed place in the woods for my father to drink a bit. Sometimes, on a very narrow trail, there was a subliminal change in my sense of hearing, as if the woods were cupping a hand around my ear. Even in the dream the acoustics of our footsteps and my father's voice and the close calling of camouflaged birds seemed altered in my perceptions, and I could hear sounds, not more distinctly, but other, different sounds, which were always there, but normally beyond conscious awareness. Walking into a more open space, my ear was uncupped and the strange echo lost in the heat.

We found a honey pot ourselves eventually. He sat down by a large beech and I crept up to him, and he fed me honey with one hand while he took a drink with the other. One hand, then the other.

'John,' he said, 'you know, there ain't no such thing as a poisoned honey pot.'

It was the father he could have been; it was the person he could have been, if he hadn't always decided to be him. That afternoon, with the corrosive smell of his ammunition in my nostrils and honey lugubriously rolling in my mouth, he let me lie on his arm. I could at least dream of how he might have been.

1861

LIFE AT GALENA – THE BATTLE OF MONTEREY – A MEETING IN GALENA

On April 10th 1861, a few days before my speech at the Galena courthouse which I have told you about already – surely you remember 'We will stand by our country, and appeal to the God of battles'? Yeah, OK well; that one, anyway – I sat with Ulysses S. Grant at the back of his dad's harness and leather goods shop while he told me about what he did in the Mexican War. People called him Sam back then.

'At Monterey' – he was proud of this, maybe even a little boastful – 'the regimental fund had run down. I was quartermaster. The regimental bands were partially paid from the fund, and libraries and ten pin alleys and magazine subscriptions and other comforts for the men could be purchased from the fund.' He was speaking like an accountant, or a shop keeper, proud of his small business success. 'But when we were at Monterey, some of the musicians had been without extra pay for months. We couldn't get a good band leader because band leaders could get the pay of non-commissioned officers if they were with a wealthy regiment. I remember, our band lost its coronet player. He went to the 2nd Infantry. You couldn't get a good player if you couldn't pay them.'

In the storeroom where we were talking, the walls were lined with the goods stocked by Grant and Perkins, Leather and Hides Merchants. Everything was ordered in a meticulous hierarchy of demand. Harnesses, trace chains, bridle bits, whips, saddles, stirrups, awls, show pegs, axes, wedges, saws, augers: all were layered and, if practicable, tightly packaged. The goods that sold the most were on the most convenient shelves; the others disappeared up into the little used darkness of the topmost shelves.

Grant was thirty-eight; I was twenty-nine. I headed Isaac Steven's old law firm, and was a trial attorney. Grant was back with his dad's firm because he had failed at doing anything else after he came back from Mexico. That's why he was so proud of this deal:

'The thing I did was to issue the soldiers with bread instead of flour. I remember talking to Hays about it. He was impressed. You could give them either eighteen ounces of bread or eighteen ounces of flour. I gave them bread, because 100 pounds of flour will make 140 pounds of bread. See? By doing this I gain flour for the fund. In Tacubaya in the winter of 1847 going into 1848, I hired Mexican bakers and rented a bakery in the city and got a contract from the chief of the commissary of the army for baking bread. So with the saving of the flour I made more in two months for the fund than my pay amounted to for the whole of the war.'

When I had asked him if he was in the Battle of Monterey, I wasn't after his triumphs as a quartermaster saving the regimental fund from dishonour and death. That wasn't the sort of stuff Mexican War Dickheads (MWDs) like me were after. But there was always entangled in the shambles, in a way I could never fully unravel, another story. He did more than bake bread at Monterey; but for him, he was proud of that as much as anything.

He was perched on the storeroom ladder in indecision. His father Jesse had called from the front of the shop for a stirrup iron. Grant had no idea where they were kept.

'Lower and to your left,' I told him.

'Stirrups,' called Jesse.

'And you fought under Worth?' I prompted. I knew all about the Battle of Monterey, one of the major battles of the Mexican War. I knew General Worth attacked the west end of the city while Twiggs' division fought their way through the eastern streets towards the central citadel where the Mexican commander Ampudia was located. I knew this because ever since I was fifteen I had been a fuckwit obsessed with the details of the Mexican War.

'Stirrups,' called Jesse.

Grant made a feeble attempt to look for the stirrups: without thinking, his hand came to rest on one of the storage shelves, and then absurdly moved one of the packages there to one side and then back.

'No,' he told me. 'Worth's troops didn't advance through the open streets, where there was a lot of artillery fire. Instead, he cut his passageway through the walls of the houses, knocking down any structure in his path, going from one to another. He lost far fewer men. By the end of the day, he was in such a good position that Ampudia sent a messenger through the lines, and they surrendered by morning.'

Grant moved further up the ladder, towards the ossified upper reaches of the storage room. Stirrups, up there. Christ.

Jesse Grant burst through the door. 'Stirrups,' he said, this time more to himself than his son. He went straight to the second lowest shelf and picked up a stirrup iron. Grant was still up the ladder. Jesse turned and saw me.

'John,' he said. 'The stirrups here are for Washburne – he's coming later in the week for the meeting. Promised him a new pair last time. You like to come over?'

'I'll try, Jesse.'

'You been talking to the Captain 'bout Mexico?' he asked me. People knew of what they called my expertise in the Mexican War, and that Grant was a veteran from that war. Jesse liked this. He thought it would further his importance.

And I had been talking to Ulysses S. Grant about the Battle of Monterey in the Mexican War. Later, in his *Memoirs* (published in 1885 – mostly, we were all dead by then), Grant described his role in the Battle of Monterey. Here's the story I wanted from Grant at the time, but would only see later in his book:

> *My ride back was an exposed one. Before starting I adjusted myself on the side of my horse furthest from the enemy, and with only one foot holding to the cantle of the saddle, and an arm over the neck of the horse exposed, I started at full run. It was only at street crossings that my horse was under fire, but these I crossed at such a flying rate that generally I was past and under cover of the next block before the enemy fired. I got out safely without a scratch.*
>
> *At one place on my ride, I saw a sentry walking in front of a house, and stopped to inquire what he was doing there. Finding that the house was full of wounded American officers and soldiers, I dismounted and went in. I found there Captain Williams, of the Engineer Corps, wounded in the head, probably fatally, and Lieutenant Territt, also badly wounded, his bowels protruding from his wound. There were quite a number of soldiers also.*

> *Promising them to report their situation, I left, readjusted myself to my horse, recommenced the run, and was soon with the troops at the east end. Before ammunition could be collected, the two regiments I had been with were seen returning, running the same gauntlet in getting out that they had passed in going in, but with comparatively little loss. The movement was countermanded and the troops withdrawn. The poor wounded officers and men I had found fell into the hands of the enemy during the night, and died.*

'Yes,' I told Jesse Grant. 'He told me about the money he made with the flour rations. It was a clever business.'

Jesse snorted in disbelief. Grant was still foolishly up the ladder. Jesse held the stirrups up and at him, as if Grant were an infant and had never seen them before.

'Stirrups,' Grant's father said, showing him.

༄

Do you know that Johnny Cash song that goes

> *I shot a man in Reno*
> *Just to watch him die?*

When I think of this next bit, it keeps coming into my head. Anyway.

The evening after the courthouse speech I went to Jesse Grant's store again. I knew Elihu Washburne was going to be there. Washburne was a Republican, and so was Orvil Grant, Jesse's younger son, and so were the rest of them sitting around eating the oysters and drinking the alcohol that Jesse had laid on for the occasion. CWDs will know that the Republicans had won the election last November against Stephen A.

Douglas, whose policy of state self-determination proposed that in relationship to the issue of slavery . . . look, let's forget it. Two days ago South Carolina had shot at and captured the Federal government fort at Sumter. It was the start of the war. For the northern Republicans to fight, they needed the northern Douglas Democrats on side. That's what I had delivered to them, for Galena at least, last night in the courthouse; and so I'd come here to get my reward.

They were sitting by the stove in the front of the store. I tell you, the whole of Galena was like an unfinished building site. The pavements were made of smeared planks, hobbled together above rutted dirt streets. Looking at the raw wood of the railings and steps, you imagined splinters entering the meaty flesh of your palms. The buildings poked up beside empty lots, leaving around them a detritus of broken stone and abandoned dogs. The windows of the Grant store were too narrow to allow in anything but the rattle of smelly horses. The only unspoiled plane was that of the surface of the river, way below the town, and it was pressed cleanly from above by a healed palm of rare night air. But up here in front of 173 Main Street, Galena, I couldn't breathe that air; I didn't even want to. I hacked out a cough as I walked through the front door of Grant and Perkins into a saddle of smoke and sweating men.

I was welcomed by Augustus Chetlain. He took pride in being one of Washburne's Republican side kicks: 'A patriot! We need all such here, with us.' Deadshit.

'I bring myself tonight' – I stopped coughing – 'and soon many more with me, I hope, if I know the stuff of the people of Jo Daviess' County right.'

'Have an oyster, John,' said Orvil Grant, Ulysses' younger brother, holding out a pulp of flesh nearly as slippery as he was. 'Not cheap – up from New Orleans.'

'Going to get more expensive, anything from down South,'

calculated Jesse. 'We're not trading in specie now.'

I declined Orvil's oyster. The only person who hadn't stood up when I came in was Washburne. He sat closest to the fire.

'Let John have this seat,' he said quietly to Chetlain, indicating a place that I assumed had been Chetlain's. I sat.

'It was a fine speech, John,' he told me. 'The people seem to be rising as one. I have never before seen such a stern and deep mood. I remember anxiousness during the Mexican War, but also party division. We knew Polk and Marcy could not support Scott, fearing he was a Whig. Today, wisely or unwisely, we think only of the flag, and how to restore its honour. "There can be but two parties now – one of patriots and one of traitors": you have expressed exactly the thing.'

'The assault upon Fort Sumter has started us to our feet, as one man,' I told him. 'We shall shortly be an armed nation.'

'You know the President has called for 75,000 troops. I have been told Governor Yates has stated that the Illinois quota will be six regiments.'

'There is some sad and heavy work to do for those men,' toned Chetlain. 'War is dreadful.'

I could hear, in the back storeroom, someone shuffling around, as if lost and wanting to escape. '*Six* regiments,' I thought. I hoped getting information from Washburne was always going to be that easy. I said 'There is a lot of work to be done. A whole new nation needs to be built, a nation,' I looked at Washburne as I spoke, 'all people, no matter their party, can share in.'

And what mattered now was getting invited to the party. You didn't have to be a soldier to be in this army. At the start of the war, there were less than 15,000 men in the regular US army; by January 1862 – less than twelve months later – there were over half a million in the new volunteer service. CWD time:

The method of raising companies was left pretty much to the states and localities. The initiative was usually taken by local leaders who undertook to recruit companies – and get themselves elected to captaincies or lieutenancies. When an appropriate number of volunteers had been pledged (many deserted to other companies), the governor of the state would enroll the company in the state militia and assume appropriate expenses. Such matters as providing uniforms, arms, equipment, even provisions, were handled haphazardly; sometimes these things were provided by the rich men who raised the companies, sometimes by community effort, but usually by the states.

Every company needed captains, every regiment needed colonels, and there were brigadier and major-generals and generals above that. All over the country, the same questions were being asked: Who got to be a general? Who got a regiment? Where would the regiments come from? Who got the contracts? Posts in the Administration? The war was only going to last a short time, and granting places in the new army was a way of making sure the coalition in the north held. Military appointments in the volunteer army were made by politicians, and state governors and senators wrote to Lincoln telling him who was to be rewarded and why. Most of the volunteers didn't know what they were doing, anyway. I knew Washburne was set: he was a Republican Congressman, and had enough pull to even get a couple of letters from Lincoln. Here's one he got way back in 1860:

Springfield, Ill., December 13, 1860
Hon. E.B. Washburne.

My Dear Sir: – Yours of the 10th received. Prevent, as far as possible, any of our friends from demoralising themselves and our cause by entertaining propositions for compromise of any sort on 'slavery extension'. There is no possible compromise upon it but which puts us under again, and leaves all our work to do over again. Whether it be a Missouri line or Eli Thayer's popular sovereignty, it is all the same. Let either be done, and immediately filibustering and extending slavery recommences. On that point hold firm, as with a chain of steel.

*Yours as ever,
A. Lincoln.*

You CWDs gotta love that. I put all that stuff in for you, free. You could've told old Alexander Smith to watch out for Abraham Lincoln, the Illinois lawyer, back in 1856, couldn't ya? You guys never miss a trick – it's almost like everything's been written down in front of you and you're just reading it all from books.

I was calculating how much I could ask for. I wanted to know the deal.

'I believe we are thoroughly sympathised in our views and hopes,' said Washburne.

'Surely so.' Make an offer.

'I have heard also from Governor Yates that he will accept a company from this county.'

'A great honour.' Someone had to be captain – that would be the first prize up for grabs.

Here Chetlain got in the way again: 'War is dreadful, especially war with the excitement off and the chill on.'

Didn't he know there was a deal going on in front of him? All this was playing to my strengths: obsession and deception were skills I'd honed for years. Orvil said, 'There are so many worse things than gunshot wounds.' I could smell the oyster on his breath.

From the back storeroom, there was a comic crash and grunt.

I turned back to Washburne. 'Elihu, there is much to be done by' – I hesitated over choosing 'our' or 'your government' – 'by the government. We must maintain the integrity of the American flag –'

'Surely so,' murmured Washburne, with the others nodding on cue.

'– uphold the honour of the Constitution –'

'Surely.'

'– and show the peoples of our one country that the choice before them is not anything less than whether we shall have anarchy or no.'

'John, we strive together.'

He left a slight pause, and said, 'We will recommend the formation of a company in this city, to be offered to the governor.'

Now, I'll be buggered if Chetlain didn't say again, 'When the sound of the drum is heard, there will be heavy work, heavier than imagined now. I would pause before marching to such a beat.'

Then Ulysses S. Grant came out of the back storeroom of his father's shop. I can't describe how pathetic it was. We had our differences, us around the fire, but we were all united by the feeling that our conversation was important, that we were part of history. Orvil drank ostentatiously, leaning his head back until he had the empty glass poised above his throat; Chetlain crouched in secret concentration, as if in conspiracy; Jesse couldn't stop offering things to the celebrities in his shop – oysters, drink, tobacco, plates of small corn bread cakes. Only Washburne sat at ease in his chair alongside of me, his large belly and still hands contrasting with my driven movements. No-one cares, now, though; PhDs in History, maybe, with their *The Union Unified? Towards an*

Understanding of Illinois Political Activity in 1861 (Civil W. Dickhead, University of Chicago, unpublished thesis paper) – PhDs and us; they're the only two groups who've ever thought this was important. We sat around Jesse's stove like professors in the common room, the log fire burning, laughing complacently over a red wine about the unread thesis they've just graded. But Grant's entrance changed all that. Everything his face tried to do failed: ease, obsequiousness, eagerness, nervousness, diffidence – all seemed equally forced, as if he wanted to believe he felt those things, but couldn't really. It was plain; if his face carried any permanent expression, it was a sense of some sort of childish pained disappointment from long ago, forgotten now but commemorated in the small miserable eyes and the defensive, hidden mouth. Even Horace says that 'His face was not perfectly symmetrical, the left eye being a little lower than the right. His brow was high, broad and rather square, and was creased with several horizontal wrinkles, which helped to emphasise the serious and somewhat careworn look which was never absent from his countenance.' And Horace only knew him at his best: from the Battle of Chattanooga on, one triumph after another. There is a photo of Grant leaning famously against a tree at City Point, as indifferent in victory as in defeat, except in that photograph he was more handsome, more essentially himself. Then, in 1864, he was in the middle of doing what he was best at; it was the *only* thing he was really good at. No wonder he looked OK; but here, now, in 1861, he was still the embarrassing eldest son of Jesse Grant.

He came out of the storeroom he had been blundering around in, carrying a package across the front of the shop towards Washburne. We all looked at him in dumb surprise as he held it out.

'Stirrups,' he told us.

'Here's the man we can leave war to,' said Chetlain

condescendingly, breaking the awkward pause as Washburne accepted the package in surprise.

'My son, Captain Sam Grant,' introduced Jesse. 'He was all through the Mexican War. I got the stirrups wrapped for you last week, Elihu. Rubbed 'em down myself.'

'You can leave war to this man,' continued Chetlain. 'Of all of us, he has heard the drum loudest.' It was all bullshit, in Chetlain's mind, every word. He turned to Washburne. 'Ulysses was at Palo Alto, Jalapa, the storming of Chapulpetec.'

(It's Chapul*te*pec, dickhead. Dunno if that matters, though.)

'You have fought under Scott?' said Washburne.

'And marched with him in victory to the Halls of the Montezumas,' chimed Chetlain. 'May he be granted victory once more.'

Everything seemed less exciting around the fire when Grant was around it too. He said, 'General Scott's successes are an answer to all criticism.'

Washburne looked surprised: 'You could criticise the General?'

Horace has written, in his book: 'Grant never carried his body erect ... In conversing he usually employed only two gestures; one was the stroking of his chin beard with his left hand; the other was the raising and lowering of his right hand, and resting at intervals upon his knee or a table ...' I saw him do the last of these then, in the yellow humid light of the front parlour of his father's shop that to me now seems to be made so nauseous with imagination and obsessions; but I can confirm the reality of Horace's observation, at least.

Then Grant said, 'All events are plainer after they have occurred, Congressman Washburne. You would know that the most confident critics are generally those who know least about a matter. But it seems to me that the northern route to the city of Mexico might have been the better one to have taken. Puebla could have been passed and its evacuation insured without the danger of encountering the enemy. I know just enough about the Mexican War to differ with General Scott, and applaud his success.'

Here was Ulysses Grant, failed business man, failed farmer, failed real estate agent, failed debt collector, failed peace-time army officer, shithouse shopkeeper and, let's face it, probably a pisspot to boot, correcting the tactics of the man who was still, fifteen years later, commander-in-chief. Jesse and Orvil flopped around like those deep sea fish whose innards spring out due to the lack of water pressure when they are brought up to the surface.

'The Captain is proving invaluable in the store, now that my second eldest Simpson is taken so ill,' said Jesse, holding out a plate of corn cakes: 'Mr Washburne?'

'Let's leave Sam alone,' said Orvil.

'We talk of wars, and rumours of wars. Such things cannot be quantified.' This was from Chetlain. I've read it back to myself since, and it still doesn't make sense.

'John knows of the Mexican War.' Jesse directed Washburne's attention to me, away from his son: 'He talks with Ulysses out the back.'

Washburne was still staring at Grant in surprise. I said, 'There is no better soldier than the American soldier of the Mexican War. He is the great hero of the war – not the generals, not Scott, not Taylor, fine though they may be, but it is the professional officer and the disciplined soldier who won that war. The American soldier needs no martinet to command him. He has an intelligence that springs from the freedom that is his birthright, and it leavens his courage and provides his character. He is not like the driven Prussian or the hypnotised Frenchman or the slavish Russian or the arrogant Englishman: he has, unlike them all, something no other nation's soldiers can match – he has a spirit that tells him he is the equal of any man. He has the knowledge that the country he fights for is his; that the army he fights in is his; that the ideals he dies for are his ideals, freely chosen and his by right. They are not given to him; they are his to bestow. What match a Greaser, for such men? Such men need command and discipline, but they need no-one to provide them with bravery and nobility. They would scorn such a General. They know that these are theirs already.'

In the long narrow windows of the Grant store the night reflected the ugly scene back at us. My passion caused them to fall silent. In the window, I could not make out Washburne's face; he looked at me strangely, with some emotion I did not understand. The air seemed muggy with oyster juices. I hacked out a cough.

'Your spirit shines through you.' Washburne's voice seemed quiet after my speech and spluttering. It had in it a note I could not quite pick. 'We will need, John, such a spirit now. We must recruit the men to fight this new battle. We need leaders for those men. I tremble for our country, but am solaced when I know such as you march to defend it. The Galena company will need a captain. Think on it.'

'Elihu,' pleaded Chetlain, 'such a noble heavy burden must be chosen by the men.'

'I ask John to think only. A captain is needed. You know our nomination would carry much weight. Someone must have the honour of taking the company to Governor Yates at Springfield, to show Galena's unified commitment to the flag. It is an honour perhaps best given to those who are new to our ranks.'

Chetlain looked pained, but remained silent. He wanted the job.

I don't know where Grant went. He left. I thought Washburne wouldn't think of him again.

At the time, I thought I'd got Washburne to give me what

I wanted, stopped Chetlain, and saved Grant from embarrassment. It was win-win for John-John. As I walked out of the narrow door of Jesse's dingy shop I breathed in the satisfied air, cooled by the water below. My eyes adjusted to the dark. The river lay as if a thread of the moon had gently floated to earth, revealing itself to all who would look.

I worked out later – much later – now, if you must know, looking at this from here – what it was on Washburne's face when he offered me the job of captain in the Volunteer army. I just worked out what that note was in his voice after I had stopped raving on about the Mexican War, the very rave that I thought made him finally offer me the job: fuck me if it wasn't sadness. Fuck me if sitting there, looking at me, that great fat politician fuck, while wheeling and dealing in the arcane manoeuvrings of early American Civil War politics, wasn't sad for me. He heard my speech and saw me coughing and he was sorry.

When I hear that whistle blowin',
I hang my head and cry.

1861 - 1860

GRANT IS FOUND A COMMAND – MY FIRST MEETING WITH GRANT

In 1861, on April 18th, the day after we had all met in Jesse's shop to discuss the captaincy of the Galena regiment, Washburne came to my house alone. Outside, flags and bunting covered every building, like the town was holding a bellicose festival. Men – all men, not just Grant – walked quicker, and gathered in street corners like schoolboys who knew a fight was brewing.

Washburne and I had to speak quietly because my wife Emily was lying ill in her room. He asked to be introduced, but she was too sick. It was like there was already a dead person in our house.

'Augustus has signed up,' Washburne told me.

That fucking prick. Chetlain had told my dad about the Mexican War. He started all that farce; and ended it, too, in a way. And now he was trying to take my place in this war, the real war, the one CWDs would obsess over later. There are no MWDs anymore, unless you count me.

'It is impossible to enlist too quickly,' I said. I had not enlisted yet.

Washburne sat in my study and looked at me. The nurse walked past the study door, her mien that of someone at work, briskly carrying out her duties. It was so sad, that, someone at work in your own home, tending to your dying wife. Our voices were quiet because of Emily, and things seemed more intense because of this need to keep to a whisper. I wondered why he was here.

'We must elect officers.' I said. 'I will go to Hanover, a town south of here, to get recruits. I will do all that is possible to boost our numbers. Have no doubt about my commitment to the cause.'

Washburne sat calm and unmoved. 'John,' he said, 'I have no doubt of that.'

When we weren't talking, the house was very still. Nothing could be heard from Emily's room. There was a sense that if anyone had done anything to cause noise, the nurse would've come rushing in to admonish them. Before I could reply, Washburne quietly held up his hand: 'John, I know that Augustus wishes to nominate for the position of captain. It is an election, after all – the men have a right to choose.'

I had delivered what Washburne wanted in my courthouse speech, and he'd promised me my reward last night at Jesse Grant's. He sat there, plump and calm, as if he weren't double-crossing me. Chetlain was to be captain. I could join as a private, another farm boy in the ranks, more likely to die of dysentery and loose bowels than desperation and loose bullets, or I could stay stuck here with my dying wife. Isn't it horrible, war? I heard nothing from Emily's room. It was like she wasn't there.

'What nation is it that we are fighting for, Senator? Is it one built on deception and broken trust? If the allegiances we hold to party are greater than those we have for our flag, then the motivations with which we fight are forever suspect. Nothing is more contemptible – not even cowardice in facing battle – than entering battle with dishonourable cause.' I rose. 'Senator, at this time the demands imposed on me by my family are no less critical than the demands of the nation.' I walked to the door.

Washburne didn't move from the chair, like this was his house, and it was me who was to be thrown onto the street. The nurse passed outside again, stiff backed in disapproval. I wondered if I could lift him out of the chair by force. His fucking fat ox-arsed face looked up at me.

'John, I have not made myself clear. We are united in this fight. Alone and apart we will be lost and defeated. I have come to ask for your help.'

I was still standing as if, at any second, I was going to suddenly leave and let him have it all: chair, books, nurse, wife.

Washburne continued. 'Ulysses Grant talked to me after our meeting at his father's. He said that he will be joining the army again. He told me he feels that as he has been educated at the government's expense he is duty bound to offer his services.' That was typical of Grant. Of all the crappy reasons, secret and public, there were to join this war, of all the reasons he needed to change his life, he would pick that one: he's got a debt to pay off, like some taxes on money he should've declared. 'Grant told me that he feels, given his experience and former rank in the regular army, he doesn't know if he could accept a place in our volunteer regiment as a captain only. He wants to write to the Governor of Ohio to see if a commission as colonel could be given to him.'

Colonel! Colonel U.S. Grant! I knew, immediately, sitting there with my wife not twenty feet away, what I wanted.

Mexico – ping! Seminary – ping! Lawyer – ping! And Emily? *P*-fucking-*ing*. It was going to war with Grant I wanted now.

'There are so few men with military experience. In these matters most of us are blind, John. But I have heard rumours that are not flattering. He resigned from the army some years ago. He is quiet and shy. People are prepared to say he is still a drunkard. But you cannot think him so. Your speech showed enough of your repugnance for that evil to make me think no man who shares this sin could find in you a companion.'

I wondered how much Washburne knew about my father. Did he just deduce this from my speech, or had people been talking to him? Had fucking Chetlain talked? Of all the people who knew about my pisspot father, the guy who sold him the piss knew most.

'Ulysses is a man who is used to failure,' I said carefully. 'But I find in him a man who has qualities unlike many other people – unlike most, in this town.'

Washburne looked at me. 'I talked to Chetlain this morning,' he said. 'He told me that Grant was not fit for the post. He talked of intemperance. He claimed Grant was forced to resign from the army because of drink.'

Long before Washburne said this I had sat down again.

'Would you recommend him as colonel?' asked Washburne.

Somewhere, sometime in the past, I had felt things move this swiftly in a new direction. Washburne repeated the question. 'If I were to write to Yates and recommend him as a colonel would I have your support? I am asking for your help in this.'

I raised my head, as if listening for Emily's call, and looked unseeing at her door. I was thinking of Grant. 'Grant is needed for our effort, not for Ohio's,' I said. 'I would follow him were he given such a high command.'

'You have such regard for Jesse Grant's son?' he asked. 'He is a man of courage?'

'Courage,' I said, 'is about the commonest thing you can find in a man. Many more successful men have had their courage tested less often than he.'

I thought the nurse was about to move across the passageway again, but this time she came into the room.

'Sir,' she said, 'your wife has woken. She asks for you.'

Immediately, Washburne rose to leave.

'Tell her I will be with her soon. I will finish my discussion with the Senator.' Washburne made to protest. 'Senator,' I said, 'this war may not last as long as people are predicting. Surely neither side will fight for the full term of the three-month volunteers. I myself doubt if the South will fight at all; certainly, one great battle must dissuade them of their purpose. It is time now to decide this.'

He looked at the nurse, trying to judge how serious the cause of this interruption was. She did not look at Washburne; she heard what I had to say, and left before I had finished.

He asked, 'Do you think Grant can be trusted with such a command?'

'Who trusts totally his own strength? Men need to be tested before they are truly known. Some cowards are found out when exposed by battle, some heroes remain hidden because they are never brought to battle at all. I think in Grant there are such hidden qualities.'

'John, if I were to recommend Grant for this post, I would want to be assured of his character. You would be prepared to serve with Grant? You know, John, a colonel has the right to his own adjutants and staff officers. Would you join a staff under his command?'

'Senator, I would follow Grant.'

Then he asked: 'John, does he drink?'

'If I was to serve on Grant's staff, I would not allow it.' I thought of my father, lying on Chetlain's floor. 'Senator, you have described already my repugnance for this evil. It is impossible for me to express the abhorrence with which I regard this sin. Be assured of the fulsomeness of my recommendations about this man. But no matter what loyalty I feel to Grant now, I promise you that any weakness in Grant would be exposed. That the foolishness of my own judgements would also be made clear could not prevent me from describing Grant's true character; I would submit to be humbled by such revelation.'

Washburne was quiet. I could hear the drilled intensity of my voice only after I stopped speaking.

'I could not doubt your honesty, John.'

From outside men could be heard yelling nonsense to each other. Somewhere, a whistle was blown, and another seemed to answer it.

'John,' he said, 'I wish to ask more favours of you. I hesitate, because I am aware of my great impertinence in this matter.' I can remember feeling that I knew what was coming – that, as he spoke, I could have read ahead, if I wanted too, from his script. 'In these times, somehow, we are brought more violently to know ourselves. Swift action rather than slow reflection leads us on. We risk more, so we may win more. We come closer to those with whom we share dangers.' Everything he said, all this careful preparation – it was as if I had written it for him, but forgotten the text. He paused, then said, 'John, I want you to know that there is no shame if you feel the duty you bear to your wife is greater than the duty to your country.'

How could he outmanoeuvre me with this? Where did he find this order I'd been drafting to myself but lost? 'Congressman,' I said, 'those two sacred obligations are not in conflict.' I stood up. 'I will not be one of those who shouts, "Go, boys". I'll be one who says, "*Come, boys!*".'

'I have no doubt of that, John,' he said.

'My brother died of this disease, sir. I know that to be left alone is horrible. You can teach me nothing of that.'

He wanted me not to enlist. 'You must stay with your wife –'

'Do not tell me what I must do.' All this was still in a whisper. The nurse could be heard softly scraping something out in another room. 'Do not presume to intrude upon private affairs of which you can have no knowledge. I will enlist.' The whispering made it all sound ludicrously powerless, like a child stomping his foot in a tantrum. Hadn't I tried to enlist once before, and failed? Wasn't I bound to reverse that failure?

'My impertinence, John, I can only excuse because I wish to offer you my help. I wanted only to tell you that you must stay with your wife if that is where you feel your greater duty lies. I will use my position to guarantee you a place with Grant in the future. I will make sure you need not accept a rank of less importance than were you to enlist now. No matter how long the greater personal obligation here may call upon you, I will work to place you high in our common cause.'

I wonder, have you had a dying wife? You remember her with pain; and one day, years later, the day you recall her and feel at ease, you wonder perplexed why it is you now wish for your pain back. Eventually, everything is made precious.

'My wife, sir, is dying.' That was a sentence I had never said to anyone before. 'Nothing could prevent me from joining the cause but knowing that she must not be left to bear this alone.' I bowed my head because I could feel my lips, without my consent, begin to draw themselves down in grief. I drew in a long breath. I must tell you, I wanted nothing more than to go to this war. I wanted to leave Emily. 'We are all tested, John,' he said, 'but the field of battle is sometimes not of our own choosing. I will ensure no-one takes your position in the nation's fight when this other battle is finished.'

'I do not want pity,' I said. 'I ask for strength.'

For a moment he looked as if I had not understood him.

'You are needed for our cause, John,' said Washburne, 'together with Grant. Yet sometimes to those whom we love we feel such a sacred bond that none should break. No man can be condemned for that.'

I nodded. Some fresh scent, its source unplaceable, had somehow found its way to this house. Without meaning to, I reached for my forehead, and was shocked at the sweat I could feel.

'At least for now, while I find this place for Grant, you stay with your wife. I must go to Springfield to see Yates. I will not forget you, John. I will not leave you.'

I closed the door behind him as he left. Behind me the nurse stood, waiting for something. I looked at her, puzzled.

'Your wife calls you, sir,' she said. Her voice was pert.

I looked in surprise at Emily's door, and then I went in. Outside, women were laughing and children shouted in sudden delight, as if some rule had been lifted from their behaviour, just for the time of this carnival. Some of the townsfolk had tied bells to the harnesses of their horses. Crooked, dirty, small and miserable things had no place in this new world; everything now had been ennobled anew. Somehow, I can remember that I heard and sensed all this as I walked into her room.

You can see, the campaign with Grant began years ago, years before I met him. Did slavery cause the American Civil War? Complex question. Grant got to Galena in January 1860, having spent the years since his resignation from the army failing at every job he tried. I needn't tell you: it's all the same. He failed with the same inevitable pattern that a drunk begins drinking again. One week or so after he'd arrived in Galena, Augustus Chetlain sent a little boy to my law offices, who told me I should come to Chetlain's shop.

'Who sent you?' I asked the child again, surprised. He was no more than ten years old.

'Mr Chetlain,' he repeated. He looked up at me, over my desk.

'I am to come to his shop?'

The child nodded. He was staring at me, as if I was the messenger to him. He was waiting for something.

'Why?'

The child did not change his expression, he just repeated what he'd been told. 'Mr Chetlain said your father is drunk.' He placed one hand on my desk, and let his chin rest on it. He was just tall enough. He looked at my books and papers, but saw nothing interesting. He pursed his lips, and forced a bubble of bored air out between them, as if he'd been working at this job for years.

Back then, if I had only one photograph of my father, only one way I could remember his face, a last image to prevent him disappearing with the ordered inevitability with which we all disappear from the memory of the living – first our voices, the exact tone of our voice, and then the way we move, our mien and motion, and then our features, our limbs and profile – I'd've burnt it. I'd seen his face too often; can see it now, laying bashed to the floor, so distorted that it is impossible to understand, or forget.

In my anger, I nearly forgot about the child. When I was shutting my office door I saw him there near my desk, still staring at me, waiting for something. I closed the door, and he trotted past me, head low. If you want the simple answer, he was the fellow who started my campaign with Grant. That day, down in Chetlain's shop, was the first time I ever met Grant. The child ran off, disappointed.

Chetlain's wasn't a proper tavern; he was a liquor and wine merchant, and his place was a storehouse full of jugs, bottles and large oak barrels. He had a small corner down the back, near a stove, where he'd sell booze in tin cups. It was cheaper liquor than the tavern. The huge barrels sat in the cool dark. The rest of his shop was clean enough, but the back stove's fire was fed on stale, sticky air, and around it the floor gave off a stench of slopped rum and whisky.

I heard my father singing as I walked down the long passageway between the casks. The white daylight from the windows ran in narrowing ripples over the barrels until it was thinned to nothing. Down the back, against the dark, the stove lit a circle of men in rummy orange.

'Lawyers nearest the fire!' said my father when he saw me. 'Lawyers nearest the fire!' He was sitting on a bench. There were two or three others, all facing the stove. There were benches right around the fire, the far one out of sight behind the furnace.

Chetlain grabbed me by the arm. 'John,' he whispered, 'he is not able to control himself.' Chetlain said it like he was being my friend, helping to protect me. I still hate him for that: the very cunt who sold the drink.

'Mr John A. Rawlins,' said my father, solemn, 'has been called to settle our dispute.'

'He cannot pay,' said Chetlain, still whispering. 'You must tell him he will not be served. Then he will leave.'

> *'I travelled to the farthest parts,'* sang my father,
> *'Saw the good man and the liar;*
> *In all the towns that I went through –*
> *Lawyers closest to the fire.'*

'You are called for a reason, John,' he said to me. 'There is a fight brewing. These two' – he awkwardly sloshed his cup at two men sitting on a bench – 'say I did not fight in the Dago war. My son here will tell you. My son knows. There is a fight brewing here. I was in Palo Alto. I was with General Scott. We shot the Dago army until they ran. My son here saw me enlist – he can tell you – down at St. Louis, and then I marched to Palo Alto with the General.'

I looked at the two men. They were obviously ex-army. Both wore faded blue army greatcoats and old slouch hats. They were looking at my father, angry and mocking. Both were drinking from Chetlain's tin mugs. One looked at me, sizing me up in case they had to fight me, but after one glance at my lawyer's dress collar, he looked again at my father, sneering like you might at a child.

'In that battle I shot and killed two Greasers. My son can tell you. I shot and killed two Greasers, and if I could find any Greasers here' – my father looked at Chetlain – 'why, I would shoot them again, just to show you how it's done.'

I didn't think he was drunk at all.

'I think I remember you, old man,' said one of the men. 'You shot two Greasers, and chopped off their legs to show us when you got back.'

My father was silent, waiting.

'Yes,' said the other, after a pause as if to recollect. 'I remember too. He chopped off their legs. That I could never figure. Why did you chop off their legs? Why did you not bring us back the two Dago heads to admire?'

The first veteran looked at his companion with incredulity. 'Are you stupid, you shameless drunk? Why, how could this hero do that? Someone had *already* done that.'

No-one laughed. The two just grinned, like they'd stabbed something small and they were watching it, still shaking.

'John,' my father said, pleading. 'Did I not join the regiment at St. Louis? Did we not sail down so you could see me join General Scott?'

This lie was not new. Returning from the St. Louis trip, my father had left me just outside Galena, and had disappeared for more than half a year. When he returned, he boasted to Chetlain and Isaac Stevens and the rest that he was back from the Dago war. I had been refused enlistment, but he had fought. It was true that he'd come back with a tan over his sodden skin, but they had not believed him. I was bound to go along with his story. His shame was also my shame; his failure, I shared in. I had never denied it, and not even Chetlain had the gall to ask me outright if my own father was a liar and a coward.

He stood up, and pointed to a scar on his left forearm.

'See where the cold steel of one dirty Dago has left proof?' I'd seen how he'd done that. One day he'd come back from the woods with a large and quite deep cut running down his arm. He carried his axe in his right hand, and his jug in his left, and when he put the jug down it left a ring of blood in the wooden floor of our shack.

'You been bucked and gagged?' asked one of the veterans. 'Last time I talked as much as you, I got four hours of it from my Lieutenant.'

Bucking was a punishment for insubordination. You were sat down, your wrists were tied together then forced over your knees, and a musket barrel was placed through the space over your arms and under your knees. A gag, like a piece of wood or a bayonet, was put between your lips and tied there.

'Cold day,' observed the other, thoughtfully. 'Rope hurts more.'

Have you ever been in a bar and seen two tinnitus-raddled lead guitarists shouting the lyrics of an Iggy Pop tune? *'Here comes Johnny Yam again,'* they begin happily, slapping the dusty denim on their thighs with both hands for the beat: boom-boom-boom, boom-boom-a-boom-boom; boom-boom-boom, boom-boom-a-boom-boom. *'Here comes Johnny Yam again,'* they sing together, thrusting their heads forward at each other in rhythm, eyes squinting like they're angry:

> *'With liquor and drugs –*
> *He's a sex machine.'*

But then there's trouble.

'He's gonna do another strip-tease' continues Tinnitus Raddled Lead Guitarist One.

TRLG2 stops the rhythm. 'You got that wrong, man.'

TRLG1 keeps drumming.

'Hey, you got that wrong. You got the wrong lyric.'

'Fucken no.'

'Fucken yes. It goes,

> *Here comes Johnny Yam again,*
> *With liquor and drugs –*
> *He's a sex machine;*
> *He's gonna win a million in prizes.*

'Then it sort of goes, "*Yo Yo*".'

TRLG1 looks at his balding, straggly-haired companion to see if he's joking. 'It goes, "*Yo Yo*"?'

'Yeah. "*Yo Y –*"'

'Are you fucking deaf? "*Yo Yo*"? Where'd'you get that? "*Yo Yo*"? What's "*Yo Yo*"? It goes' – TRLG1 starts the beat on his jeans –

> '*Here comes Johnny Yam again,*
> *With liquor and drugs –*
> *He's a sex machine.*
> *He's gonna do another strip tease.*

TRLG1 goes on with the bass line: 'boom-boom-boom, boom-boom-a-boom-boom.'

To prove his point, TRLG2 begins to sing over it:

*'Here comes Johnny Yam again,
With liquor and drugs –
He's a sex machine.
He's gonna win a million in prizes, Yo Yo'*

By now, a circle of grinning drinkers are looking at the pair. 'What the fuck song you singin', man?' says TRLG1. '"He's gonna win a million in prizes" – what the fuck's gonna happen? He'll win Tatts? What song is *that*?! "Lust for Lies" by Iggy Slop? "Last Four Eyes" by Jiggy Hop?'

'Shut up, man.'

'"Bust My Pies" by Tiggy Top?'

'Shut it, man.'

'"Burst My Pipes" by Reggie Mop? How's that go?

*Burst my pipes!
Burst my pipes!*

'And here's the good bit, man:

YO YO.'

TRLG2 lets his beer fall to the bar, and at the same time turns quickly and slams his chest into the other man. He holds himself still. 'Shut ya fuckin' mouth,' he says, like a child just managing to keep some self-control.

Suddenly, no-one can choose to look anywhere else. TRLG1 is knocked back in surprise. With both hands he feels the wet beer on his t-shirt, then looks up.

'Ya fuckin' cunt,' continues TRLG2. People have forgotten what they were doing five seconds ago, before this. Anyone clear-headed enough calculates that if the two are to fight, then it will happen very quickly now.

'Rope hurts more on a cold day, old man,' said the first veteran, standing up. These two men were from out of town, and didn't know they had to make allowances for the stupid boasting of the town drunk. Behind me, the rows of barrelled drink were silent in the dark, as if all had suddenly paused to look. The veteran who stood up turned so as to face my father more fully. Both vets seemed to know exactly what was about to happen. The other, still seated, put his tin cup down to the floor.

'John,' said my father. He sounded like he was crying. 'John.' He sat down, as if cringing, on the bench.

'Colonel,' I said – yeah, *right*, Colonel; if this guy had been a colonel, then my father had been President – 'does not the misfortune my father has so patently suffered not help you pity him? He wants only to share in the glory your army brought to these states. If he errs, his error is to want too much to be honoured as you are, soldiers of the Republic both. Forgive him this.'

Forgive him? Pity him? Me, telling them to forgive my father? It was never going to work. Part of me wanted to see him on the ground, convulsively trying to stop the boots connecting.

Both of them knew it was bullshit – I hadn't expected anything else – but I was counting on them at least appreciating the effort. I should've just stepped aside and jerked my thumb at him: 'Here he is. Boot party. Rip into the old bastard.'

'Augustus,' I said instead to Chetlain, 'these men may wish to drink some more. A bottle can be placed on my acc –'

But from behind me, I heard my father, pathetic and stubborn. 'John, tell them I went with General Scott. I marched with the volunteers, and fought at Palo Alto.'

He was determined to stick to this demented lie. Now, both men were expecting to have to fight me. The one standing up was still holding his cup; he reached out and rested it on my chest. I could feel it through my clothes, steel-cold and wet on my skin. As he talked, he tapped each syllable on my heart. 'You coward,' he said.

I could not speak. I stared at him, dumb. I was aware of how perfectly still I was. Every word seemed as if it would carve itself in the air, stay written as testament in front of my eyes.

From the far bench in the gloom, someone else stood up; another veteran. This third man tripped slightly on the rough wooden block that formed the leg of the bench, either because he was drunk or through clumsiness, and took four or five steps around the stove towards us. I remember it now, but at the time I was aware only of the astounded panic I was feeling. The first veteran and I remained still, as though connected at the core of things, held by centrifugal forces ripping at us from all sides.

The vet took his cup from my chest. My shirt stuck to my flesh.

'Mister, don't you want a fight?' he said to me. Then he turned to the third man and said, 'This your General, old soak? Hey, is the whole regiment coming? Look, it's General Scott.'

It took me a second to understand that this third man didn't know the other two, but Ulysses Grant was a veteran, we could all see that. His face was small, miserable, shrunk and pickled by failure. Grant looked up at the first man. He was not proud and challenging; he looked at the vet like you might at a flat tyre, or a stained shirt, or a splintered thumb.

'I am a man of peace,' said Grant, 'but I'll not be hectored by a person of your size.'

The second vet immediately stood up.

'You are not welcome here any longer,' said Grant. 'You must leave.'

'Looks as though you don't know when to keep out of things,' said the second vet.

'You ever fought a real soldier?' said the first.

Thinking back, it was what was lacking from Grant's voice that made it so convincing. He was neither mocking, nor aggressive, nor brave, nor scared. 'I served under Taylor and Scott. The war was an unfair one. It brought shame to our Republic. Its actions were more like those of an imperial empire. I fear,' he said, 'nations, like individuals, are punished for their transgressions.'

There was no doubting him: he had fought in that war. No man could speak so matter-of-factly, could choose to lie with such indifference, if there was any question as to the truth of what he was saying. His small miserable hand was held awkwardly across his stomach.

'I want another drink,' said the second vet, turning to Chetlain and pointing at the cup he'd left on the ground. Chetlain began to hurry for a bottle.

'Sir,' said Grant, 'wouldn't you prefer these men to leave?'

Chetlain stopped, and I could see his shocked face. Any time else, it would have been funny. Grant waited, then said, in explanation: 'If we must fight, it were best it's over quickly.'

In his *Memoirs*, Grant writes of his tedious school days: '... winters were spent in going over the same old arithmetic which I knew every word of before, and repeating: "A noun is the name of a thing" . . . until I came to believe it.' 'If we must fight, it were best it's over quickly' was spoken in the same spirit; a dull fact, worth learning, but not worth getting excited over.

'Who is going to make us?' the first vet said, outraged. He meant, who's going to make us leave?

'There are four other men here, and I think they will fight if led to it,' Grant said.

It was four against two – I hadn't figured that.

'Two drunks, a lawyer and him?' said the vet, pointing at

Chetlain, contemptuous. 'None of you have the courage.'

'Courage,' said Grant, 'is the commonest thing you could find in a man.'

A noun is the name of a thing. There was no doubting it. Right at that moment, I did not doubt. Grant's tired, delicately miserable voice convinced me.

'You are strangers here,' I said, 'and can expect no help. You should leave.'

The first veteran was looking directly at Grant; the eyes of the other, behind him, moved side to side, judging all four of us.

'I think these men may fight,' said Grant, to us. 'Prepare yourself.'

These are horrible moments. No matter how comic the dispute, men who are preparing to fight must feel a horror of it – I cannot imagine who could not. Battle may bring some relief from awareness; pain or anger may blind one as to what has happened or what may happen. Possibly, ignorance or stupidity might make us unable to appreciate what is to come. But to the extent one can clearly contemplate conflict before it occurs, who is able to do so without some horror? When the veteran had placed his cold tin cup on my chest, I had been transfixed by horrible imaginings – blurry red images of pain and panic – about what the fight may bring.

The second veteran shrugged theatrically. 'You're not worth it,' he said. 'They're not worth it,' he repeated, this time to his mate.

The first gave a little grunt, disgusted. He could sense what his friend was about to do. Turning his head, he looked back at his companion. He kept his body towards us, and held his arms out in surprise.

'Take your bottle. Let's go,' said the second vet. He didn't want to fight. He was backing down.

Quickly, the first man stepped away from Grant and me,

bent down behind a bench and picked up a bottle. He shook his head a little, as if he was just waking up. Four versus one was too much.

'Let's go,' said the second vet, pushing his friend very gently towards a gap in the benches.

The first vet knocked the other's hand, as if touched by fire. 'Don't you touch me,' he said.

'Let's go,' said the second vet, conciliatory. 'Who wants the drink here?' He again touched the other man on the arm, friendly but pathetic.

'Don't touch me!' shouted the first vet, outraged by this betrayal.

They moved quickly down the long line of barrels. Near the door of Chetlain's shop, there was a thump and crash. One of them, in final protest, kicked a small barrel, sending it back down towards us; then it was quiet.

'*Prepare yourself.*' Grant's words gave me my first idea of just how much he was prepared to lose. I looked at him, but could sense none of the jittery victory and relief I was feeling. He was staring down at his shoes, as if slightly annoyed by the realisation they needed a polish. Yet, I realised, Grant had been prepared to have the living bejesus beaten out of us all, would have fought until someone's head had been so horribly injured we would've all stopped and stared in shock, before he'd given in. 'Prepare yourself' – I was sure those words, absent of all inspiration, had caused the second veteran to give up.

Chetlain moved towards where the barrel stopped, but then turned towards my father, enraged at the trouble he had caused. 'You get out,' Chetlain said.

'"Let us pause in life's pleasures",' sang my father, still sitting on the bench, ignoring Chetlain, '"and count its many tears . . .".' His voice trembled, as if shaken by what had just occurred, and the song was the only expression he could find for his emotion.

'Get out.'

'"... While we all sup sorrow with the poor".' Then my father, still ignoring Chetlain, grinned at us:

> *'There's a song that will linger*
> *Forever in our ears:*
> *Oh Chetlain, he won't go off to war.*
>
> *'Tis the song, the sigh of the weary:*
> *Chetlain, Chetlain,*
> *He won't go off to war.*
>
> *Many days has he lingered*
> *Here in his liquor store,*
> *Oh Chetlain, he won't go off to war.'*

Chetlain walked quickly up behind my father, gaining some momentum, and with a stiff arm swung his whole body round, hitting my father on the side of the face. It was an awkward, amateur blow. My father fell off the bench. He stayed down, gasping, like he had been crying so hard no more tears could come. When he took his hands away from his face, I could see it covered in snot and blood.

Chetlain held his hand out in front of himself, looking at it like he'd caught it in a door.

'John!' said my father. He turned and sat, feet straight out, like a child, and looked up at me. There was a lot of blood coming from his nose. When he spoke, little films of it formed and broke on his lips. He held his hand below his chin, cupping it to collect the drops. 'John,' he said, whimpering.

'There were no volunteers at Palo Alto,' I said to him. 'The volunteer troops hadn't arrived until the army was at Matamoras.'

He did not seem to understand; his hand was still, collecting the blood.

'Sir,' said my father, appealing to Grant, 'did not we fight with General Scott together?'

'Taylor commanded at Palo Alto,' I said. 'You are not wanted here.'

'Tell them the truth about me,' said my father. He took his hand away, letting the blood drop freely on to his chest. 'You must tell them the truth about me.' He sat himself shakily back up on the bench.

'It is you yourself that have exposed these lies. Why should I join you in further deceptions?' I said. 'You are not wanted.'

Behind me, I heard Grant begin to exclaim something, but before he could finish, Chetlain had already hit my father again, on the same side of the face, with one of the tin mugs. This was a very horrible blow. My father fell completely over on his side. Behind him, Chetlain stood back, horrified. My father had dropped as if dead, offering no resistance to the fall, but I could see him, barely conscious, moving his wet eyelids as if trying to wake up from a deep sleep. He could not cry out, nor move. He remained exactly as he'd fallen.

I looked at Chetlain. My involuntary curiosity, or my shock, or delight, at seeing a man so viciously bashed overwhelmed me for some seconds. Grant was already with Chetlain, keeping between him and my father, holding him lightly by the wrist. Chetlain still had the tin in his hand; but he offered no resistance to Grant. Grant looked down at my father, and then away, disgusted.

My father's face was already swelling. The eye closest to the blow was covered, lost under blueish, distorted flesh.

'Get him out,' said Chetlain weakly, like he was offering an excuse for his cowardice.

I don't want to remember that face.

Later, at work again, I kept wondering what that little boy had wanted from me. What was he asking? I never could work it out.

1861

FIRST TIME IN BATTLE

Washburne kept his word. In these early weeks of war things that had waited for years to happen, things that would seem grandly inevitable years after, were experienced as trifles and whims. We counted our lives by days, even hours; and one week could do or undo more than whole decades of the past. The political lobbying for Grant was just another recondite squabble in the selfish scramble for position. Governor Yates said of Grant, 'He was plain, very plain', but Washburne convinced him to make Grant a colonel. After Grant got his Colonelcy, he took command of the 21st Illinois Volunteer Infantry. Marching with the troops to their new post in Missouri, Grant had been assigned to stop Confederate guerilla leader Tom Harris. He succeeded: the guerillas ran away. Illinois became entitled to four brigadier positions, and

Washburne was on the congressional delegation that parcelled them out. When he got Grant one, Grant's new post was Cairo, Missouri. After he was made a Brigadier-General Grant wrote to me: 'I am entitled to a captain and acting adj-gen: I guess you had better come on and take it.' Fucking Chetlain, of course, wanted the job, now Grant had risen so far so fast; and Emily was still alive. It was just under six months since my speech. Grant wrote to Washburne about my delay in accepting a position on his staff: 'I never had any idea of withdrawing it ... so long as he felt disposed to accept, no matter how long his absence.'

I replied to Grant: 'Fully appreciating your kindness and friendship for me, and believing from your long experience in and knowledge of military service and its duties, you would not have offered me the position were you not satisfied it was one I could fill, gladly and with pleasure I accept it.'

I was in Cairo ten days after my letter of acceptance. Emily died on September 3rd. Washburne had come to visit and because of that I waited those six months before joining Grant. I would not have stayed with Emily if not for him. In Cairo, I would wake up at nights in my bunk, hearing her voice. I did not want to think about her death. Years later, in the Wilderness, I was still dreaming of her, trying to remember her, and mourning each detail I could not reclaim upon waking.

I didn't go to her funeral, you know. I picked the cemetery, though: the one near the road, closest to town. I bought a grave before she died. Some of the townspeople thought it strange, but others knew how I had to rush to go to war. The nurse didn't stay, either. She went back East. She hardly said goodbye to me. I had offended her. I'd done something wrong to her, I could sense, but I didn't know what it was.

My first battle while serving in the Union army was on October 29th 1861, in the Cairo officers' mess. Cairo in 1861 is far more interesting on historical markers about the American Civil War than it was in Cairo in 1861. A trail of mud led into the officers' mess near the entrance, concentrated itself like the bud of a filthy flower, then spread in a rosette of dirt on the floor. You get the same sense of shamed shoddiness in bad shopping centre cafeterias and run-down pubs. And, after all, these things are not so difficult to imagine. It's not the fact all this happened in a mess in Illinois that makes this hard. Men are still men; what happens at your family dinner table is likely to be just as unusual and strange and unfathomable as the officers' mess at the command post of the Union Army's District of Southeast Missouri.

I'd only been there about five weeks, but it was time for action. I was Grant's adjutant-general. I had seen what Grant was up to, and I knew that I hadn't left Emily a minute too early. Grant was sitting in the mess drinking with two other officers when I walked in.

'... so my men have ordered me to propose this toast, General.' One of the colonels drinking with Grant raised his glass. 'To General Grant, who let us kill the Rebel weeds.' Grant looked pleased. They all laughed and drank the toast. They all had fucking stupid beards; everyone back then tried to make their facial hair as prominently idiotic as possible. I suppose it's because they didn't have hands-free mobiles yet. 'Captain Rawlins, join us to celebrate the great victory,' said the Colonel. 'My regiment have finally routed the Reb weeds. Mowed them down. Then gave 'em the cold steel.'

They all drank again.

'The men wish to fight, Captain,' said the Colonel. 'I have been taking my regiment across the Mississippi for the last three weeks, training them in the manual of arms. We've been taking aim and firing blanks at the same clump of weeds near the river bed since September. But, oh, those saucy and defiant rebel weeds stood . . .'

'. . . flouting the flag!' added the other Absurdly Bearded Deadshit.

'. . . flouting our proud flag,' agreed Colonel Turd, 'and insulting the honour of our arms.'

Absurdly Bearded Deadshit: '. . . of our arms, Captain! Of our volunteers new to the uniform!' They were all pissed, pretty much, and everything was funny.

'But the men wish to fight. So today I rode to General Grant, and said, "General, you must give us ball cartridges for my men's guns. Blanks will no longer do. These weeds must be routed. One final effort, and victory is ours."'

ABD raised his glass. 'Come on, men,' he said, 'Up and at 'em. Give 'em the cold steel. Remember today you are from Illinois. No quarter for rebel weeds, by god.'

Grant had the stupidest beard of the lot. His moustache was too big, bulging out from his top lip. His beard was normally trimmed short along the line of his chin; but right now he had a bib of hair, square and frizzy, below his face. The thing is, bullshit Civil War beards suited those other officers. They were normal blokes; they could get pissed and grow beards and tell funny officer tales – but Grant couldn't. He just looked daft if he tried. He was looking daft now.

'And the General said to issue the live ammunition. So today I marched my men to that very same clump of weeds, and we enacted such bloody slaughter that Jesus himself wept and part of me even pitied those weeds. But my men insisted I propose a toast to General Grant, who let them kill the rebel weeds.'

'To the General,' said ABD.

They all drank. Grant was pleased to be one of these boys. He was a General, now. Six months ago, he was working back of Jesse Grant's shop. He'd gone from bottom to top, and that'd be hard for anyone. When I saw him posing like that, I felt peculiarly ill. Imagine seeing Lincoln, sitting at his desk, say 'Fuck it', push aside his speech for Gettysburg, and start playing his Gameboy.

The Colonel turned to Grant: 'Now you can turn us loose on the southern Confederacy as quick as you please. We are again in the highest of spirits.'

I said, 'The General here seems pleased with your exploits, Colonel. You are a jolly fellow, and good for the spirit. When the time is right for such men as you, then you tell your tales. But for now I wish to talk to the General.'

ABD looked up at me in anger, but the Colonel wanted to be my pal.

'Captain,' he said, pouring another tumbler of whisky, 'sit with us and celebrate this victory.'

'Colonel, I could not give a pinch of dung for your jolly tale.'

Now there was silence. Grant looked at me, expressionless.

Colonel Turd said to me: 'You have no call for this.' ABD was about to speak, when Colonel Turd turned to Grant: 'There is no call for this.'

I turned to Grant. 'We must prepare for battle. I have just received a message that the enemy is being reinforced for an attack. We must demonstrate against Columbus. It is not for me to judge when or how we should carry out this order.'

Grant said, 'The men need to fight now.' He put down his glass.

'I have been told that Congressman Washburne has faith in you,' I said. 'It cannot be that he has more than I. You know I will write to him. How are we to face this battle? Our troops are untested.'

I promised Washburne by letter:

Have no fears: General Grant by bad habits or conduct will never disgrace himself or you ... But I say to you frankly, and I pledge you my word for it, that should General Grant at any time become an intemperate man or a habitual drunkard, I will notify you immediately and will ask to be removed from any duty on his staff (kind as he has been to me) ... For while there are times when I would gladly throw the mantle of charity over the faults of friends, at this time and from a man of his position I would rather tear the mantle off and expose the deformity.

Let's get this over with. Everyone thinks Grant's great secret was his drinking; and that I was the one who kept him from it. It fitted, after all – me, the son of a drunk, hater of liquor, keeping the old guy sober for the nation. CWDs have read the letters. Listen to me – 'I would rather tear the mantle off . . .' – Jesus fuck. First, dickwad, having me as your guardian against deception is like putting your lead singer in charge of the coke stash. Second, Grant's secret, the one I thought he kept hidden so well that even I couldn't be fully sure about it, wasn't drink. That wasn't what was going to prevent him dying a hero of the American Civil War. He was never going to die like a hero of the American Civil War.

Colonel Turd and ABD were both shocked. Fun was over.

'We do not lack for courageous men,' Grant said, though the faces around him might not have proved it.

I picked up the bottle from the table and turned to Colonel Turd. 'Colonel, my hands have recently held for the last time she who was so pure that I will never hold her with earthly hands again. Do not make me soil them so soon by making me touch this.' I dropped the bottle. It wobbled on the table, but did not fall. 'I want to talk to General Grant.'

Grant said to them, 'Captain Rawlins has stopped the mirth. It is best you leave us to talk.'

It was the first time I heard him command his officers, and it worked, too. As they were leaving, I said, 'Colonel, may you lead your brave regiment to even greater victories. I look forward to again drinking with the General to your successes.'

Grant took his glass, and, stretching out his arm, placed it further down the table, as if protecting it from me. 'Your anger intimidates those men,' he said. 'They are wanting to do their duty. The men wish –' Grant pushed the whisky bottle away, looking as he did so, at how much had been drunk – 'The men wish –' he said again, but paused once more in thought.

Look, I don't want to turn this into 'Why Grant Was My Hero' by J.A. Rawlins (age 12).

WHY GRANT WAS MY HERO
by J.A. Rawlins (age 12)

I'd seen Grant move awkwardly to the side of the fire as the peace-time heroes of Galena discussed their successes; I'd seen his leathered red face express nothing at all staring into the flame. Grant wasn't a man for peace-time heroics. That was a job for other men. You can't write your own history. Let other people do that, later. Your job is to live it. I didn't want Grant to die like those sort of men; I wanted him to kill those sort of men. I hoped that Grant's great secret wasn't his weakness; it was his strength.

Then he asked me: 'How are the enemy getting men and supplies for this attack?'

'By boat down the Mississippi and up the White River. We

are directed to prevent this movement if possible. We are to have the men ready to march at an hour's notice.'

Grant stood up. 'We cannot take Columbus. It is too strongly fortified now. I will write my orders. I will call you, Captain, when copies need to be made. Be prepared.' He walked out of the filthy mess, to his tent.

When he called me later, he dictated the plan for what would be the Battle of Belmont, his first major battle. He won, though it cost him 120 men killed and 400 wounded. He didn't need me for this sort of planning. He always knew what it took to win, and wasn't prepared to avoid anything in those calculations. After the battle, he issued this order congratulating the men:

> *The general commanding this military district returns his thanks to the troops under his command at the Battle of Belmont, yesterday.*
>
> *It has been his fortune to have been in all the battles fought in Mexico by Generals Scott and Taylor save Buena Vista, and he never saw one more hotly contested or where troops behaved with more gallantry.*
>
> *Such courage will insure victory wherever our flag may be borne and protected by such a class of men.*
>
> *To the many brave men who fell the sympathy of the country is due, and will be manifested in a manner unmistakable.*

I wrote it. 'There was never a battle more hotly contested' – I wasn't there to see the battle up front, of course. I was a member of Grant's staff. Man, I was *adjutant general*: my job was to go nowhere fucking near the 'hotly contested' stuff. But you've got to appeal to your market, and I mainly believed those lies at the time. 'Such courage will insure victory wherever our flag may be borne.' I was in the army at last.[1]

∽∾

That's how Grant and I fought our first battle together. It was time, it was time, it really was time at last. And after the next little bit, I will describe for you the Battle of Chattanooga.

Grant had asked for permission to fight before I got to Cairo, but had been refused. Grant was under the command of John Frémont. If you're a plaque-reading deadshit the strategic position of the opposing Confederate and Union armies in the Western theatre at this early time in the war is intensely interesting, so if you want to know about it, grab me some time, because there's some great historical markers I could tell you about. Frémont was called 'the Pathfinder' because of his great voyages of exploration in the West during the '40s, and he was the same Frémont who had been Republican candidate for president in '56. He dressed his aides-de-camp so they looked like Michael Jackson during the Thriller tour. He believed his own publicity. He was sacked by Lincoln in November '61 because war found him out to be an incompetent poser. Frémont continually refused Grant permission to

---

[1] Look, it's a technical point, but I'm a CWD after all: in Grant's *Memoirs* there's a footnote, written by E.B. Long, about the message that the Confederate leader Price was being reinforced from Colombus:

> *Exactly who sent this message and what instructions it included are not clear as it is not in the Official Records. Later, Adjutant General McKeever told Frémont that no orders were given Grant to attack Belmont or Columbus . . . Furthermore, there is little evidence that the Confederates planned to reinforce Price in Missouri from Columbus.*

So Grant's attack on Belmont was done on the basis of a false message. I wrote that lie too.

fight. Washburne could get Grant the job, but he had no influence over military manoeuvres. The only real task Frémont had given Grant, whom he knew was a drunk, was to march against the small Confederate band of guerillas led by Tom Harris in July 1861. This was before Belmont. It was Grant's first experience of command in battle.

Here's a favorite CWD passage – Grant's description of what he was thinking about during this action:

> *We halted at night on the road and proceeded the next morning at an early hour. Harris had been encamped in a creek bottom for the sake of being near water. The hills on either side of the creek extended to a considerable height, possibly more than a hundred feet. As we approached the brow of the hill from which it was expected we could see Harris' camp, and possibly find his men ready formed to meet us, my heart kept getting higher and higher until it felt to me as though it was in my throat. I would have given anything then to have been back in Illinois, but I had not the moral courage to halt and consider what to do; I kept right on. When we reached a point from which the valley below us was in full view I halted. The place where Harris had been encamped a few days before was still there and the marks of the recent encampment were plainly visible, but the troops were gone. My heart resumed its place. It occurred to me at once that Harris had been as much afraid of me as I had been of him. This was a view of the question I had never taken before; but it was one I never forgot afterwards ... I never forgot he had as much reason to fear my forces as I had his. The lesson proved valuable.*

Fuck me if my father didn't drop that wolf with one shot.

1863 - 1852 - 1854 - 1863

PREPARATIONS FOR THE BATTLE OF CHATTANOOGA –
HORACE IS OFFERED A JOB WITH GRANT – THE
FIRST LINE OF THE ENEMY IS CARRIED – GRANT AT
FORT VANCOUVER – PISSED AT FORT HUMBOLT –
MOVING WITH SHERMAN AGAINST MISSIONARY
RIDGE – A GALLANT CHARGE – COMPLETE ROUT

Grant, after Belmont, won the battles of Forts Henry and Donelson, fought at Shiloh, and captured Vicksburg. Doesn't sound much, now, I know, and I want to skip those others and tell you about Chattanooga, because for me it was a unique sort of battle in the American Civil War. This is because I'd fought many battles before, but Chattanooga was the first one where I'd faced bullets.

I know that may surprise you. But, as I say, I was a staff officer, and my job was to stay with headquarters rather than go near the line of battle. There was some danger, of course, but I had never had to charge the enemy, or fight hand to hand; I hadn't had to stand the gaff, see the elephant, dance the Minié waltz, close with the enemy, attend the opening of the ball, write my name, pluck the turkey, beat to quarters, smell the powder, go together by ears or feed the cannon. And at Chattanooga, I did.

If I remember correctly, at about 1 p.m. on the day before the battle back there in '63 I was at my desk, on the first floor of the unimportant, rutted house that was headquarters. This was near the river, on the far side of the town if you were looking down at Chattanooga from the height of the Confederate lines, on top of Missionary Ridge. I was writing a letter to Washburne.

I say it was the day before the Battle of Chattanooga, but there was still to be fighting today. This was only a preliminary skirmish before the next two main days of battle. This initial fighting was to take place over two miles away, behind the desk where I sat. Grant wrote the order for the attack in the room downstairs at eleven. I had a copy on my desk with me: 'Drive in the enemy's pickets.' The window in front of me had a splintered sill, and the panes of glass were imperfect, distorting the images from outside like a fishbowl lens. All day, I could see distended lines of troops moving from left to right, passing from one grubby pane to the next. The fighting was for positions on the plain in front of Missionary Ridge, around Fort Wood and Orchard Knob. The attack was due in an hour.

I can report to you that in the town of Chattanooga there was no grass left at all. In front of me, in the half mile or so between the headquarters and the river, every building seemed as if it had just been put up or was just about to be torn down. Some huge, ugly excavation had worked through the town, leaving piles of dug earth or flattened mud. Before Grant had got there, the place had been under siege and starving for two months. The troops had knocked down houses for firewood, and used planks still covered with wallpaper for their own shelters. Little lean-tos and sheds plastered over with cheap patterns were plonked in the dirt. On their sides whole strips of paper were missing, leaving neat blanks of bare planking, and often sections from two or more destroyed houses were butted up together, each section with different patterns of wallpaper, so they looked like children's cubby houses made from off-cuts left over from the family home. Everything was soiled.

It was still drizzling at ten o'clock. The constant rain meant nothing could dry, and you could smell the moulding canvas when you walked down a line of tents. Now Grant had broken the siege, a whole line of temporary sheds had been built by entrepreneurs selling goods to the troops. I could see the Dunlap & Bowdre Supply Center, its roof an amateurish foot lower than next door's M. C. Graham Boots Shoes Hats and Caps sign. Directly below me were rows of tents. They seemed especially neat, but I suppose that's because the Colonel knew his troops were encamped directly in front of the Commanding General's HQ. Tents filled the town, like some overwhelming circus.

None of the soldiers I could see from my first floor desk were to have any part in the fighting this day; those troops were already mustered on the plain, two miles away. The troops I could see over the river, marching across Strengel's Ridge, towards the mouth of Chickamauga Creek three or so miles upstream, were being prepared for tomorrow's battle. Because I was one storey up, I could see the Tennessee River from where I sat. It looked orphaned and cold, circuiting through the valleys and plains like a freezer coil, and from it came the mists and drizzle that rose up the sides of the mountainous ridges that surrounded the battlefield those two miles behind me and my desk.

The soldiers near the rows of tents in front of me were cooking. They had been issued with battle rations, which was three or four days' rations at once, and they tended to cook and eat them straight away. Three other soldiers were trying to get a horse to walk backwards. One sat on it, and the two others stood laughing and giving advice. Those three looked to me to be particularly brutal and stupid. The men cooking looked on, deciding if they were impressed. One yawned. I could see legs poking out from some tents, where some men slept. Stacked muskets were everywhere. Right through the streets, I could see hundreds, thousands of guns. Another man yawned. I didn't know if this was a sign of tension or tiredness.

Across the river, the wagons and men of the army moving to my right kept on. They were from Sherman's Army of the Tennessee. There seemed to be a lot of supply trains. Some of these came across the pontoon bridge into the town. Right across my line of sight came wagon after wagon. It was uncanny when you saw it at first, because they were all identical, and this created the impression that whatever huge workshop made these had somewhere, somehow, produced millions, and they were never going to stop passing.

Behind me, I knew 25,000 men were beginning to be moved towards battle. The soldiers around the horse got it to take two panicked stumbles backwards, and they punched each other in delight. The rest of the men, even those who had been ignoring these three, smiled at this victory. Grant and other officers had left at about 11.45 for Fort Wood, where they were to watch the troops. It was an impressive array. All were on horse, each commander with his staff, and most in dress uniform. As they rode off, the soldiers in front of me had kept on with what they were doing, but suddenly their clowning seemed artificial. After looking at the commanding officers, their heads turned back to stare intently at their frying, blackened rations.

Every once in a while, a supply carriage would continue to break off from the uniform line of carriages over the river, jumble across the bridge and into Chattanooga. I could see their awnings moving through the lanes hacked between tents and shacks. They seemed to be depositing a stockpile of material quite near this camp. My back and shoulders ached with tired stiffness. If I stood up to stretch, I'd stay facing north towards the window and the river. The Army of the Tennessee kept marching its supply trains and field artillery and ammunition and ambulances towards the right for their fight tomorrow. I could seem to sense the huge presence of the battle about to be fought behind me, and I didn't want to turn around to face it, thinking this would only be admitting that I was afraid.

About three-quarters of an hour after Grant and the other commanders left, one man came running into the group of soldiers in front of me. His face was ugly with anger. The others all jumped up and followed him, running, out of my line of sight.

I was sitting there alone writing the letter to Washburne because my job with Grant had been done. Grant's staff had been up since one in the morning. We'd heard a deserter had claimed Bragg, the Confederate commander, was planning to detach troops from Missionary Ridge to help Longstreet take Burnside in Knoxville, 100 miles upstream. No names you need to remember there.

The advance was to be sounded soon, but now all immediately in front of me was deserted. I was too far away to hear anything but cannon and musketry. I listened, but it seemed even more silent with the noise of the men out front gone. I had a growing sense of the 25,000 soldiers being drawn up in line of battle behind my back. It was uncanny, as silly and superstitious as the solitary frozen anticipation of a child whose arm has popped out of the safe community under the blankets, to be exposed and alone, suspended while some unimaginable thing waiting in the black night of the nursery rises to touch it. Then, right there behind me:

'I heard your nasty coughing, Lieutenant Colonel. Are you

not going to watch the armies in the field? None that I can remember is so well fitted for a display of soldierly courage.' It was Horace. Fucking Horace, bursting in like some idea from the melodrama.

'The amphitheatre of Chattanooga, bounded by the heights of Lookout Mountain and Missionary Ridge, will be on view from the parapet of Fort Wood. I have heard from Old Pap's adjutants that Wood's division is parading now on the plain! The Rebel pickets have come out of their pits to watch! The defeat of Chickamauga will be revenged.' He was smiling and proud. 'They suppose we hold a grand review!'

I don't remember coughing much.

'I am going now,' he told me. He pointed towards the ever-continuing march of Sherman's army, the army that had supposedly come to save the besieged and hapless garrison of Chattanooga. His regimental loyalties were moved: 'And so the Army of the Cumberland is to make the first offensive movement after all.' General Thomas's Army of the Cumberland had been ignominiously defeated eight weeks earlier at the Battle of Chickamauga.

We met Horace here in Chattanooga. He was George 'Pap' Thomas's Chief of Ordnance. He was being transferred to Washington, leaving very soon, even though Grant had applied to keep him here. As soon as I met him, I wanted him around. Exactly eight days ago, Grant had got pissed. I didn't keep him from drinking, I told you that. But, fuck me. He got *that* pissed, the very night before the fucking Secretary of War's inspector came to report on Grant's command. There he was, General David Hunter, just arrived from Washington, as big a ponce as the Army of the Potomac could produce, sitting with Grant in the room down below, and the hero of Vicksburg was as hung over as a fifteen-year-old. I was horrified when I looked at the white stiffness of David Hunter's formal paper-collar. The only thing whiter in the whole of the no-longer starving Chattanooga was Grant's face.

Hunter had taken one walk around the town. He placed his note pad on the table, and took his pince-nez from where they were dangling on a cord round his neck and put them on his nose. *Pince-nez.* I tell you, I was once Lieutenant-Colonel John A. Rawlins, Chief of Staff of the Commander in Chief of the Western Theatre, and I know that every person who wears a pair of pince-nez is an arsehole. 'General Grant' – he looked at his notes, then his voice filled with pert disapproval – 'it seems to me that there is a great deal of card-playing amongst the men in the army here.'

Card playing! And he'd said it with exactly the same intonation as if the words were 'anal fucking'. There was a moment of poised embarrassment at this rebuke. I am sure I mouthed the words 'anal fucking' in silent amazement to myself. Actually, I didn't. Grant had looked with his dehydrated, noxious features at Hunter and said, 'Well, General, I am sure that is about as innocent an amusement as the men could have.' And victory, yet again, went to the brave. But, fuck me, I didn't want too many Hunters around. I wanted Horaces around. Horace was intoxicated too – but with Grant, not Kentucky wine.

'Captain,' I said to Horace, 'here is a letter for Congressman Washburne. I wish you to deliver it to him privately when you are in Washington.'

'It is with the greatest regret that I leave General Grant,' he replied, 'but that regret is ameliorated in some small way by the pleasure I have in assisting his Chief of Staff.'

Can you believe that sentence? Horace's entrance seemed to bring the battle nearer. He was nervous, excited, pre-occupied. Horace had an over-large goatee beard and moustache, a real ABD job, and – to his credit – it seemed stuck on his face like an ineffective piece of stage make-up, not disguising who he really was.

'And here is a letter from General Grant himself.' I handed it to him. 'It is for General Halleck, to be delivered by you to him in Washington, asking for a recall of the order taking you to Washington, and assigning you to duty on General Grant's staff.' There was a pause of surprised delight before he reached out for the letter, just as you might imagine.

Talking to Horace, I felt the battle differently. Instead of that vague awareness of its enormity at my back, here he was, right in front of me, and soon he was to be with the troops. The conversation seemed to take so much effort. There was a huge job to be done, a huge task to be faced, and here we were, play-acting.

'If that would be agreeable to you,' I added.

'Nothing could possibly be more agreeable,' said Horace. I was so tired. Both of us had been up since one that morning. But it wasn't just that. It was like talking through a thicker atmosphere, viscous and dense, and breathing out the words needed special effort.

'I should feel most highly honoured by such an assignment,' he went on. 'My preparations to start East have all been made. I have stayed only for today's action, to see the Army of the Cumberland show its worth in the field; and now I leave knowing a desire I have harboured with scarcely less devotion may be fulfilled.' I was concentrating on his beard. It seemed to me that as he was talking his goatee went up and down of its own accord, synchronised as if by a machine to his words. It worked right through a sentence like that last one without a miss.

'And you, Lieutenant Colonel – are you not coming to see this initial movement?'

'I have more letters to write and work to do here,' I told him. 'I fear that it is tomorrow that the more bloody work will come for our armies. Such preparations that are to be made are best made now.'

You know how old Captain Horace Porter was then? Twenty-six. Was he taking notes then, somehow, with some part of his brain, so that thirty-four years later, the same year he completed Grant's tomb, he could publish *Campaigning With Grant*? Maybe that's how he handled it all. He was writing his memoirs in his head as he lived them, as safe and honourable as his book, distanced already from these events by time and his devotion to his subject. His beard looked fake, though. My guts hurt. I was nervous, like a kid, like I wanted a shit.

'Horace, in the General's letter he recommends your promotion to Brigadier-General. It is no more than a just testament to his regard for you as an officer. Need I say I share in that regard?'

'I can hardly express enough my gratification.'

'Your spirit shines through you. It will carry you through all the work you are yet to do for General Grant.'

After he left, I listened again for sounds of battle, like I had for most of my life. It was raining, and the drizzle spotted the window. I had the feeling that if there was some honourable way we could choose to stop this, some childish impossible *deus ex machina* to get us out of here, like an earthquake, or a telegraph announcing Lincoln starting peace-talks, or the Tennessee flooding, or Bragg suddenly following Longstreet up to Knoxville, we all would have chosen it with glee. But there was no way out. Somehow, we had all colluded in creating this situation, and now we were going to fight the Battle of Chattanooga even though, secretly, nearly every one of us would've chosen not to if we could've. Oh, but looking back now, I was too young for all that. 'Son,' I think now, 'why did you want to fight so soon?' There's no way out. Your pain leads you out. I was thirty-two.

Instead of battle, I heard the soldiers in front of me return. They were yelling and pointing to the north, over the river, though because they were not as high up as me I don't think they could see the march of Sherman's forces continuing. They were all united now, standing agitated and angry around their dead camp fire. Whereas I suspected their bored somnolence before was born from tension, now I suspected their anger was some similar form of release. One of them was holding a large cloth sheet, originally white but now, like everything in this town, blotched and dirty, and smeared with brown.

The constant rain meant there was no dust rising from Sherman's column. I could see his troops marching. I could not see the faces of individual men, but the form of the body of troops was somehow formidable. The Army of the Tennessee had already won a large reputation. They moved in the rain, blurred such that I could discern neither tight regimented march nor the bobbed rhythm of any individual step. The supply wagons that had been intermittently diverting into the town had stopped. Now all were intent on marching up river, conveyed by some invisible, inexorable motion, merged because of distance into one solemn omen.

I always hated writing to Washburne. I always got the feeling he was picking my prose apart – though not critically. It was as if he was *forgiving* me for it.

> *Senator Washburne,*
>
> *I am writing as the Battle of Chattanooga begins. I have written to you now for two years, and before other battles, all of which have called for subsequent letters announcing victories; let this letter, too, be followed by such a happy missive.*
>
> *General Grant is working in cooperation with Generals Thomas and Sherman. I do not doubt that the propriety of General Grant's removal of General Rosecrans will be confirmed by his achievements as overall commander of the Armies of the Cumberland and the Tennessee. When*

I carried to Washington the dispatches from Vicksburg telling of the country's great victory there, I talked with the President and his Cabinet of the greater victories to be won. It is with your help that General Grant can now further that cherished course.

Should this battle be ours, you and I know that, in some quarters, the General would gain enemies as well as friends; enemies that, no matter how heroic he proves on the field, the General has little weapons with which to fight. The enemies are Envy and Rumor, and you and I have faced them before on the General's behalf. Let us not fail him. Let us remember that our enemies have as much to fear from us as we have from them – nay, they have far more to fear, as the evil have always more to fear from Truth than the good.

But let us do more: let us take the offensive against them, and join them in battle on a ground of our own choosing. A man, like a nation, is forced by war to reveal what is within. The trauma of battle is the trauma of finding out who we are. Until this time, the nation was young. This war makes us children no more amongst the separate and equal powers of the earth. As it was at our birth as a nation, so it is upon attaining adulthood – we need a leader to show us that we can only act how we see best, and then trust to God to judge the correctness of our actions. Greatness lifts up in themselves those whom it favors; and through those blessed by greatness, we can all be so elevated. This army needs a new Washington, a Lieutenant General under whose unambiguous command all serve, upon whose shoulders the burden of action rests, by whose hand power is exercised, and from whose whole person we all draw moral strength. The risk of wrongly choosing such a commander is outweighed by the certainty of disaster if we do not.

Elihu, we must act. More than anyone here, you in Washington can see that inaction leaves the canker to spread. Major General Halleck is competent to serve; but the army needs someone to rule. The country has a President to give it heart; it needs a commander to show it strength. Without such, our hopes are orphaned, and the battle lost.

Think carefully upon what I write; but do not let reflection become a disguise for irresolution, for nothing is more certain of ensuring defeat than that. I hope soon to follow this letter with one announcing victory at Chattanooga; you know that in such a case, Washington must be the scene of the next great campaign. Talk amongst our allies in Congress for such a bill reviving the rank of Lieutenant General knowing that the people and the papers talk of it already. You and I will never bring to bear such influence for the country's good as by elevating to this position he who can do so much more to enforce the Union of the states than both of us combined. If we do not defeat ourselves, no enemy will.

I will write more fully when I have more time.

Rawlins

From the window where I sat I could see ambulances in the streets of Chattanooga coming back from the battlefield. They moved through the town like stray thoughts you can't control, reminding you of something you wish to forget.

∽∾

After the fighting, Grant and the other commanders came back to headquarters. Horace was both sombre and excited:

'The rebels supposed we held a grand review. They came

out of their pits to watch. There was not a straggler or a laggard as Wood went forward. The men went to it beautifully.'

I know Ulysses S. Grant, right? Well, we were in the officers' mess – Horace was right next to me, and as his excited voice summarised the battle, I was watching Grant eat. Grant could not eat red meat. If forced to, he'd insist it was burnt to the point of charcoal, and with this brick of carbon, he'd slice one cucumber, dip it in vinegar, and eat it. So, I know Grant, right? Figure that one, 'cos it's fucked me. Horace kept talking.

'The advance was sounded at half-past one. There were 10,000 polished bayonets, Lieutenant, all flashing. The plain looked like a prairie dog village, full of dug earth in little mounds. The company officers could be heard from the parapet where we stood. Not one man lagged! Has this ever before been seen on a battle field?'

Cucumber! Fuck.

'We heard the faint cheer as the breastworks at Orchard Knob were taken. What boys they are!' Horace lowered his voice. 'Old Pap does not show much, yet I can detect in his countenance tonight a glad pride. He has ordered Hooker to demonstrate against Lookout Mountain tomorrow morning. Old Pap's boys will not let the job go half-done.'

The mess was directly below the room where I had sat most of the day. From there, you couldn't see the Tennessee, but I continued to sense the movement of troops still marching in the night-time drizzle. The bottom half of the windows were roughly boarded up, though even these boards had holes knocked through them. The tops of the tents could be seen outside in the light of the campfires.

Horace turned to Grant. 'I am grateful, General, that I could stay this last day in Chattanooga to see the drummers of the

Army of the Cumberland beat the charge, and so gloriously, too.'

'The advantage is greatly on our side now,' said Grant.

'I will go to Washington assured that news of success follows close. The hold of the implacable hand that has for nine weeks threatened to strangle this army is weakened, and will soon be thrown off.'

Grant didn't look up from his plate. 'We do all we can for Burnside and the cause. If I could be assured he could hold out ten days more, I would be more easy.'

Horace was delighted. 'The bloody work of death saddens us all,' he kept on, encouraged somehow by Grant's reply, 'yet who could have thought that it could look so glorious as it did today? The ringing note of the bugle seemed to call out to the boys to expunge the memory of Chickamauga. I have never doubted the Army of the Cumberland. Once those boys are given the chance, they will always show their officers and their country they are worthy sons of the Revolution.'

Grant ate his cucumber.

Then Horace, with all the pride of a good son, safe and approved, ventured, 'General, the vicissitudes of battle mirror that of life. You must think to a time after this war. You must hope to return to Galena again.'

It has just now become clear to me. General Grant ate the aforementioned cylindrically-shaped soft vegetable so that when someone suggested to him he might wish to return to Galena, he wouldn't choke to fucking death. But, no, that was me (as always) doing the coughing. Instead of convulsing, Grant's face mellowed the permanent disappointment it seemed to convey.

'My wish, Captain, would be to return to the Pacific Coast. I have spent time there, and though I find the expense of living greater than in Illinois, yet I feel my family could find a pleasurable situation for ourselves.'

I was manoeuvring to get him promoted to Lieutenant

General of All Union Armies and he wanted to go to San Francisco and set up shop.

'The city of San Francisco was a picturesque place before 1853. Many of the real scenes of life there would, I am sure, have exceeded in strangeness the mere products of the brain of a novelist. Such a place I would not take Mrs Grant; but now the city has become staid and orderly, and the Pacific Division of the army will not be an important one after this war. Perhaps command of such a Division may be granted me.'

I was not with him at Fort Humboldt, and I was never in the officers' mess at Fort Vancouver as he foolishly schemed away his wages, yet I cannot but believe these places were scenes of failure and humiliation for Grant. Did I wish to return to my father's side at the smelter, sweating and choking on dust? Could I not see clearly what that place meant to me? But Grant wanted to go back. Couldn't he see his own past as clearly as I do? Sometimes, the contempt I felt for him! When he wasn't leader of all Union armies, he was lost.

In 1852, after he fought in the Mexican war, Grant had been posted to Fort Vancouver, north of San Francisco on the Columbia River. Outside the officers' mess the ice-green Columbia moved primitively under huge elegiac valleys of spruce and fir, while inside Sam Grant would frantically expedite his own failure. Slicing ice from the river and towing it down to San Francisco, buying into a billiard club, shipping pigs and cattle to the city market, growing vegetables on the river bank – Sam tried and failed at them all. You shouldn't try to be your fucking father; I could've told him that.

His letters to his wife Julia are at first childishly eager:

> *I have in the ground a field of barley every grain of which I sewed with my own hands. The ground is already broken for twenty acres of potatoes, and a five acres for onions and other vegetables. I shall do all the ploughing*

> *myself all summer. You know besides my farming operation I have a large quantity of Steamboat wood cut for which I get $2.50 per cord more than it cost me to get it cut. It has to be hauled but a short distance and that is done with my own private horse and wagon. We're starting two drays which we think will bring in from $10 to 15 dollars per day each. If I am at all fortunate next fall will bring me in a good return which will make me easy for the future, for then I will never permit myself to get the least in debt.*

And then they begin to read like a schoolboy's excuse:

> *I have been quite unfortunate lately. The Columbia is now far over its banks, and has destroyed all the grain, onions, corn and about half the potatoes upon which I have expended so much money and labor. The wood I had on the bank of the river had all to be removed, at an expense, and will all have to be put back again at an expense ... We finally had to pay some of the farmers to haul the potatoes away ...*

I think Grant had some cartoonish conception of himself as a businessman, respectable and competent, admired for his savvy and guile. He was stuck out West for well over two years without seeing his wife; by the time he first saw his son Ulysses Jnr, the child was more than two. Julia wrote to him less and less often. Grant wrote to her on October 26, 1852, from Fort Vancouver, of his increasingly desperate hopes:

> *My dearest wife:*
>
> *Another mail has arrived and not one word do I get from you either directly or indirectly. It makes me restless,*

Dearest, and much more so because I now know that I must wait over two weeks before I can possibly hear. I can write you nothing until I hear from you and learn that you and our dear little ones are well. Just think, our youngest is at this moment probably over three months of age, and yet I have never heard a word from it, or you, in that time. I have my health perfectly and could enjoy myself here as well as at any place that I have ever been stationed if only you were here. It is true that all my pay would not much more than pay the expenses of the table, yet I think, judging from what has taken place, that this expense could be borne better here that the ordinary expenses in the Atlantic States. I have made something dearest for us, and being carried out, by which I hope to make much more. I have been up to the Dalles of the Columbia, where the Immigrants generally first stop upon their arrival in Oregon, coming by the overland route. I there made arrangements for the purchase of quite a number of oxen and cows, and for having them taken care of for the winter. If I should lose one fourth of my cattle I would then clear at least one hundred per cent, if I should lose all I would have the consolation of knowing that I was still better off than when I first came to this country. I have, in addition to cattle, some hogs from which I expect a large increase, soon, and have also bought a horse upon which . . .'

Well, it goes on. That scheme failed too. The past can be so depressing and pathetic, though that's mainly when you're living it. I still wince when I think of some things. Surely Grant must get a lot of that.

In 1854, two years after the failures at Fort Vancouver and still long before I met him at Galena, Grant had been posted to Fort Humboldt. He resigned from the army within four months of getting there. Fort Humboldt was an isolated post north of San Francisco. You can go there now – visit the ruins, read the plaque about President Grant. You catch the plane to San Francisco, and drive up the rest of the way to Humboldt Bay. It gets cold there. I could take you: a CWD tour group. We'd all get out of the bus – the door would suction open, letting out warm air smelling slightly of the toilet up back – the whole fucking geriatric bunch of us, and we'd huddle in the wind and say, 'Oh, I seem to feel the cold more and more now I'm 156.'

At Fort Humboldt, rain and mist cover the road until a yawning drop of grey sky and water presents itself on the last turn in the highway. The perspective it forms seems too huge – one has to look again and again to see it all – but, somehow, it never reveals itself as fully as in that first beautiful glance.

It seems to me Grant's ghost is in the air at the Fort; that many ghosts are there. I did not think I would be so affected. The log cabins and earthworks are as lonely as he was; they stand consecrated by memory in the forest clearing, looking over the freezing harbour. The lawns around the site are impeccably tended (by some tourism board or local historical club or something) and their neatness is like that of a well kept grave, full of devotion and pain. I seem to see Emily, as if real, walking across those lawns to the officers' huts, caught disappearing in the mist and drizzle.

Emily told me once she nearly came to the west: 'I was to travel with my father. We didn't come because he was afraid of the cholera. Instead, we went up north to the St. Lawrence. I was so cold. I had my maroon gloves that I told you about, but they weren't enough, so my father gave me his big ones and I wore them around the whole time. Everyone said it looked fetching, my small hands in his big mittens.'

There were originally 126 men at the post, but a few deserted. Grant hated the commander, whom the men nicknamed 'Old Butch'. Grant wrote to Julia, 'You do not know how forsaken I feel here ...' He used to drink whisky by placing his little finger on the outside of his glass along the bottom, and then aligning his three other fingers on top of that one. He'd fill the glass with whisky to the top of his index finger, and drink it straight.

Standing on that lonely neat lawn, looking out over the huge bay, it is easy to see him, pissed at night at Fort Humboldt in 1854. Grant would climb up the lawns, less neat then, up that drunk's parabola of joy; as he climbed, his feet would increasingly misjudge the track from the mess to the officers' huts. To the left the howling bay is punched by ocean, and the road sways in front of his vision. Grant senses his body as a still image, held like a figure in a video game, and then the road rises up to meet his face. The other officers giggle.

'Grant's at it again,' says one. 'Captain, you are fallen in the mud.'

All the officers laugh, amazed at this wit. One of the other officers points. 'The captain has fallen in the mud,' he announces, like a child showing a picture. They are all pissed. Light can still be seen in the mess, but the officers are outside in the drizzling night, delighted to be wet, climbing up the bluff to the barracks above. Up that rocking parabola; and to the right beyond the low earthwork that bounds the Fort the continent is still empty and pressing in on them.

'Old Butch has got his eye on you,' says the first in warning.

'A mail came today,' Grant wrote to Julia while he was at Fort Humboldt, 'but brought me no news from you ... I cannot conceive what is the cause of the delay. The state of suspense that I am in is scarcely bearable.' And down Grant goes, down that inevitable parabola to despair: 'Write me a great deal about our little boys. Tell me about their pranks. I suppose Ulys. speaks a great many words distinctly. Kiss both of them for me.'

Later, in the mess, Grant puts down his pen. He quietly turns back the fold of his army jacket. Suddenly, he can hear the ocean outside, as if his guilt has made him more alert. He reaches for the hidden bottle.

'Captain,' says Old Butch, 'you will be found out.'

All the officers in the mess are immediately still.

Grant holds up his bottle, as proud as a drunk teenager. 'My wife,' he toasts. 'Sir, my wife.'

Grant looks at the bottle, then up at Old Butch.

'My wife,' he says, and drinks.

The mess is so quiet all can hear the ocean now.

'My wife.' Drinks. 'My wife.' Drinks.

Old Butch stands, outraged. One or two officers also stand up, knowing what the next order will be.

'My wife,' says Grant, about to drink again . . .

I find myself staring at the historical marker in front of me. I'm the sort of guy who reads all the plaques. CWD, for sure. I only go to these places for the historical markers.

The plaque said:

> *President Ulysses S. Grant was assigned to Fort Humboldt on August 9, 1853, when he was promoted to captain, and ordered to take command of Company F. He arrived here in early 1854. He tendered his resignation from the army on April 11 of the same year. Ironically, this resignation was finally accepted by the then Secretary of War, Jefferson Davis.*

'Bit disappointed they haven't got more historical markers,' I say to Old Butch, who's standing next to me in a ghostly drizzle. 'Job's easier if you could pull down those huts' – I point my gloved hand up the frozen green hill towards the pale shacks up the top – 'and put up a huge slab with lots of writing on. Knock 'em down, change it all. Explain the whole fucking thing. Damned historical buildings. Get in the way of the markers.' Old Butch leans on his rake. He'd been looking after this place for years and years now. His face is like a sailor's from the wind and rain.

◦◦◦

The next day was the second of the three days during which he fought and won the Battle of Chattanooga. Some men just can't forgive their fathers, can they? There is much dispute between Civil War Deadshits as to whether Grant's battle plans were followed. They argue amongst themselves that because the battle progressed so differently from his intentions, how far does this mean his orders had anything to do with the victory? As if. As if orders matter. Of course, back then Grant's orders seemed important; but now, I can't think why. As if orders and dispositions and plans matter. God almighty.

Horace's job as a staff officer was to run like a good boy around the battlefield communicating those orders between the commanding general and commanders close to the action. He did this very well. I think the orders weren't as important as the fact that someone was risking their life carrying them. On this second day, we thought the main action would occur on the left, with Sherman's troops. We were wrong (as CWDs down the centuries will note with glee), but Grant needed someone very senior on his staff to be with Sherman and organise communication back to headquarters. It needed someone familiar with the whole plan of battle. Horace had left for Washington, so I got the job. OK, so I volunteered for the job. But it was time, it was time, it really was time. It was time for the real bullets bit.

Sherman's forces began crossing the river upstream from Chattanooga at two in the morning, and by daylight the advance parties were dug in facing the small hills and spurs that were the beginning of Missionary Ridge.

When I think about it and am honest, there are whole continents I don't give a toss about, but there are some square yards of earth that seem to mean more to me than my limbs. There's the coal pits; home; the park outside Emily's house; Grant's tent in the Wilderness; and the few hundred yards of some poor fucking Quaker's farm near South Chickamauga Creek, Tennessee. The first time I saw those few hundred yards was as I came across the new pontoon bridge crossing the Tennessee. When I stepped off the pontoon bridge there was a chaotic sense of the earth being completely dug up. As I walked up the bank of the river I could see mounds of earth from fresh rifle pits stretching out of sight to the right and left. Wounded and bleeding men gathered on either side of where the pontoon bridge met the shore. All the men and equipment I had been watching yesterday spilled unceasingly across the bridge. It took Sherman twelve hours to cross.

Already, this space around the landing was not at the battle proper: the real battle was hidden over beyond the low hills surrounding the landing. Stretching way, way back over the river and past Chattanooga and Vicksburg and Shiloh and Fort Donelson and Cairo, up past St. Louis to Jo Daviess County and Galena, and a little way out of town into the woods, was the route that took me home: just up over there, that route ended, but it hadn't ended yet. There was only one cavalry man as an escort with me. He was from Sherman's army. As I was staring up at those hills, he said, 'I think it best, Lieutenant Colonel, if I find Head Quarters and then report back to you.'

'Very well.' He disappeared into the pushing crowd of men. My job was to attach myself to Sherman's party, and send messengers back to Grant. I kept staring with fascination at the end of the line, up just over that hill.

It was still drizzling and cold. To my left, a group of men, without stopping their shovelling, inexplicably cheered and shouted. I found the distant rifle fire more disturbing than the occasional shell that would land in the area. A burst of earth, and it was over. But the rifle fire was hidden behind the hill: it sounded all that was to come, all that I had yet to confront.

A captain strode up to me.

'Lieutenant Colonel Rawlins?'

'Yes.'

'Sir, I come from Brigadier General Osterhaus. He invites you to join him at Divisional Headquarters.' He gestured down river.

'I have been ordered to attach myself to Major General Sherman.'

'General Sherman has not yet crossed the river. He is not expected for some time, sir. He gave General Osterhaus orders to contact you, and he will communicate with you there when possible.'

'I have just sent my own messenger to General Sherman; that messenger expects me here.'

'Your messenger will take hours to cross and re-cross the bridge, sir. General Sherman is not yet over.'

'General Grant must know where to find me, and must be kept informed of the situation here.' The men digging cheered again. 'Does General Osterhaus's division move to attack soon?'

'Our commands are to wait in reserve, sir.'

'I cannot wait. General Grant must know of our advance. Which division leads this attack?'

'General Ewing's Fourth.' He dropped the 'sir', despite my rank.

'Where are they?'

He looked up and down the confusion of the river bank, and shrugged. Cheeky bastard. At the time, I thought I was curtly dismissing him when I said, 'Inform General Osterhaus I will be with General Ewing.'

Everything around me seemed to be in motion. Except for the isolated men lining the banks of the river, all were animated with purpose. I needed to find Ewing. The men on the river banks seemed as lost as me. I approached one. He was staring out over the river. 'What is your company, soldier?'

He looked up. There was a black powder over his face, smudged either by sweat or the drizzle. He turned back, gazing with longing over the Tennessee.

'What is your company, soldier?' I repeated. He was shivering. I realised he'd been over that hill already, and had decided to come back. 'Where is your company?'

'I helped my Captain back,' he lied. 'He was shot in the chest.'

'Soldier, your duty is to find your company. There are men detailed to help the wounded. Comrades of yours are fighting without you. You may not hear their cries for your help now, but you will never be deaf to them when all this is over, and we must account to ourselves and God for our actions.'

But what do orders matter, when everyone's lost interest? He slumped back on to the river bank, put his arm over his face, and observed with a genuinely disinterested admiration, 'Don't *you* talk fine?'

Now, *that* was a dismissal. I looked again up the banks of the river, and now knew that the growing number of men collecting there were stragglers; they only stopped here because the river made it impossible to go any further back up the line to their former lives.

Across the Tennessee, a small steamboat was ferrying men. The gentle sound of its engine and the slowness of its movements made it incongruously civilian. I remember thinking it looked as if it were running picnickers for a day trip. I could feel a subterranean panic in my stomach, as if sensing in this incongruity the first unusual twitch of the seismograph, and soon I'd realise every thing on this river bank was just chaos about to be engulfed by collapse. The river bank was becoming more and more dense with stragglers and the injured. The men digging and cheering seemed both organised and in good spirit. They could be seen up from the river bank. Behind them, at a slight rise above where they were digging in, the line of the horizon formed by the hill remained as fascinating as the curtain of a tabernacle. I strode to them.

The men cheered because, as they were digging in, the owner of the farm we had landed on, a Quaker, was telling their Captain that they should stop destroying his land and get off. General William Tecumseh Sherman was coming across that pontoon bridge with four divisions, but this guy in the broad-brimmed hat was going to argue us all out of it.

'The laws of God do not permit your presence. This field is my pasture.' The Quaker was angry, but controlled. 'Your digging ruins my land.'

The men cheered: 'He's right, Captain. Let's be off.' They kept digging.

'You are a Captain? Do you think this rank means anything to God? It is his orders we all must obey.'

'True.'; 'Amen.'; 'Form company; shovels down; retreat,' yelled the men.

I looked at the Quaker's face. I could see that my first impression about his self-control was wrong. His face was tearful and distorted. He had turned red with exertion and panic. I thought of my father, and all the land I had cleared so he could wreck it later.

'Captain, is this company part of General Ewing's Fourth Division?' With my entrance, the men became respectful and silent, the Captain looked shocked, and even the Quaker shut up. I was a Lieutenant-Colonel by then.

'Yes, sir. We are part of Colonel Cockerill's 3rd brigade.'

'I wish you to send one of these men to find General Ewing's headquarters, and inform them that Lieutenant-Colonel Rawlins of General Grant's staff is with this company. Send another with the same message to Colonel Cockerill. I will provide written messages for them. Do you know the location of either of these headquarters?'

He told me Cockerill was only half a mile away, but Ewing could be anywhere. I sat down with some paper from his order book, and began to write. The Quaker found voice: 'You command these men to do actions against God. More than them, you will be held to account. You will leave soon, but my farm and my living are being destroyed for years to come. So it is your actions will live after you, to your shame and condemnation.'

I was thinking: Grant thinks I'm with Sherman; Sherman thinks I'm with Osterhaus; Osterhaus thinks I'm with Ewing; Ewing doesn't even know I'm here; and I've been this side of the river for ten minutes. Ten minutes.

You can learn a lot in ten minutes. Without looking up from my writing, I said to the Quaker, 'Don't you talk fine?' Dunno where he went after that.

I finished writing, and handed the Captain my orders. 'No matter where you move, I will stay with this company, Captain, until these men return. It is vital my position is made aware to those in command at the highest levels. If these men have not returned in half an hour, I will order two more men to go with the same message. I do not care if I order your whole company away from you, if that is what it takes.'

And so I waited with this small company just below that magic horizon for the order to advance. The effect of my presence on the men changed. Initially, they were awed and made shy by having such a senior staff member with them. I noticed the Captain was especially awkward; he didn't even have the protection of being just part of the ranks to hide behind. If it was anyone's job to talk to me, it was his. But it was not for him to initiate any conversation. He busied himself with the men – he checked their ammunition rounds, collected canteens to be filled, sorted battle dressing kits – normal bullshit that the men would've objected to in rifle pits before a charge. But they welcomed this officiousness: after their first nervousness, I realised their mood changed to wanting to please me. They were being model soldiers. After the first half-hour, the men looked with eager faces to be picked as the next to run the errand to Ewing. Up, up that gentle slope they soon had to go, and their bodies would be silhouetted briefly in the noon drizzle against the part of the sky that lay on this hill. With me here, the burden of this was made easier. They talked eagerly amongst each other about the prank played on the Army of the Cumberland. They'd heard that some men in the Commissary driving the supply train had collected some of the huge piles of horse dung left behind the wagons. The day before, one by one each wagon had turned off into Chattanooga, and deposited in the street an accumulated pile of dung, on top of which they had stuck an old sheet on a pole with 'Battle Flag of the Cumberland, Chickamauga' smeared across it. This was a cause of slightly illicit pride: they wanted me to hear the story, but didn't want to tell me directly. I could sense they were no longer alone, trying to ignore all that was within them that told them not to go over the horizon. They knew that their battle will be seen, appreciated, not lost in the hugeness of general sacrifice.

But after more time we spent in the pit together, even this was lost. Soon enough, I sensed them turn back in towards themselves. The rain kept drizzling; regular shell fire came over the hill. Looking toward the river, all seemed more and more crowded and confused as Sherman's troops continued to come across. After an hour in the pit, another messenger was to be sent to Ewing; but when the Captain came to order a man, none of them were looking towards us. Some were staring back across the safety of the river, and one or two stood towards the hill, solemnly, wonderingly, gazing up, as if that line of land was the edge of the earth; but most were concerned only with the half-square foot of world around them. Some dozed in that world, others fiddled with any accoutrements they could find in it – knife, gun, boot; one or two were writing to someone they knew in that other world beyond those half-twelve inches, a world they had left, but which they could still remember existed.

You've been waiting all your life for the next five minutes of it to come, but you're not always as aware of that fact as when you wait for them in a rifle pit. In one way, it was orders that were going to send me and these men up that hill. But our thinking on the subject back then seems muddled. I looked up the slope. One of the men began to boil a pan of water for coffee. 'We're between a shit and a sweat,' he said. What good are orders, if everyone's lost interest? It was duty sending me up, but not only duty; Grant, but not only Grant; the Union, but not only the Union. That all told me why I *should*, but in the rifle pit none of that mattered. At the time, the fucking fucking fucking drizzle was beginning to give me the shits. My problem was: who was telling me if I *could*?

'Lieutenant Colonel, we have word General Ewing has been shot.' The Captain's whispering voice startled me. 'I have a message passed down the line. Do you wish to be escorted to Colonel Cockerill?' The report turned out to be wrong, but we believed it at the time.

'Is the attack cancelled?'

'I have no orders to cancel our advance.'

'Then I will stay with this company. Have any men returned from Ewing's headquarters?'

'No.' The whole day, not one man came back. By this time, Sherman was surely sending his own adjutants to Grant.

None of this exchange was heard by the men. I looked at

them. The ones not lying down or fiddling with equipment gazed ahead; none looked in the same direction.

The Captain ventured gently, 'The rain aggravates your cough, sir.'

I knew that Grant would've sent out more of his own staff to contact Sherman once he hadn't heard from me. I'd just get further lost if I tried to find Sherman myself; Ewing was probably dead; and if I went to Cockerill my various messengers wouldn't know where to find me, whereas at least now they knew to look for their own company. I never saw again the escort from Sherman who crossed the pontoon bridge with me. I would have to stay with these men, even if they were ordered to advance. It was almost as if I was planning it.

Little over an hour later, at about one o'clock, we were ordered over the hill. During this hour, our artillery planted on the north of the Tennessee had increased its fire, until a continuous bombardment was kept up. A tired, sweating staff officer from Cockerill ran up to the Captain. 'You are to advance,' he said, 'conforming with the company on your right, on the signal of five repeated shots from cannon. I will stay with you to show you your objective once over this rise.' He saw me, and started in shock at my rank. They didn't even fucking know I was here, or had forgotten or something. He saluted.

'Is General Ewing's wound fatal?' I asked him.

'I did not know the General had been shot, sir.' He looked panicked at the news.

'We heard this report more than an hour ago.'

'Colonel Cockerill came back from the General less than ten minutes ago. He had been summoned to receive the order to advance.'

It's a balls-up, it's a balls-up, this whole fucking idea, and we all better go home and work out our personal relationships in a more holistic fashion – that was the look on his face, and mine, and the Captain's. The build up of the artillery and the arrival of the adjutant had confirmed to the men that an advance was imminent. They had already begun to come out of their surly isolation. The Captain addressed them.

He pointed up. 'On command, we go up this hill, and from there, I will show you our route. Be alert for that direction. Do not waste your fire by using your rifle early. You are clear as to your immediate task. I and all other officers in the Army of the Tennessee will make sure that if you ignore your duty now you will come to greater and more certain harm than if you follow it. Be prepared immediately for my signal and watch for my command as we reach the top.' And then he said, 'Fix bayonets.'

We were waiting for five clear shots, which meant the barrage had to stop. To the right and left I could see long lines of troops, dug in as we were. Most were standing up, but way down the river I could see one man still sitting. An officer was leaning over him. I thought the officer was shouting, but I couldn't see properly. The sight of one man sitting down was scandalous and fascinating. Back near the river, the movement of troops across the bridge went on.

There were two strange things about the order to charge. One was that none of us heard the five shots. There was a slackening in the rate of artillery fire, but down the line, before any clear signal that we could hear, companies started up the hill. As I watched, some of the troops began moving, leaving gaps of other confused companies in the pits. The Captain looked at the adjutant but before they could discuss anything, it become obvious we should go. Whole bodies of troops had begun to move.

'Forward,' shouted the Captain. Then the second thing: it was far clumsier to actually get out of the trench and up the hill that I thought it would be. Although the pits were not too deep, I found I couldn't just step over. I had to put both hands down and raise myself up, put a knee on the crumbled ledge of earth, and then push myself onto the heaped diggings deposited in front. Balancing, I had a moment of foolish, fearful panic that I'd slide back, humiliatingly, into the trench. To my left and right I could sense a similar awkward fumbling; one or two men did slide back. But my momentum was enough to carry me forward. With that unexpected, minor fear uppermost, I left the line back to Galena behind.

I was out of breath by the top of the hill. At the horizon, right at the top, I stopped coughing long enough to hear Cockerill's adjutant say to the Captain, 'Follow that road. Stick with the company on your right. The South Chickamauga is on your left. The Western and Atlantic [for non CWDs, he's talking about the railroad] joins from the right. Halt there.' I looked. The men were already running. There was a road to follow! It confused me. I looked again. From this hill, it all partially made sense. Along my left, the South Chickamauga river, its clear pale-blue course forming a feminine rippled curve, ran to marry with the Tennessee. Beside it lived a family of fields (the Quaker's, I presume) whose happy cultivation was only here and there being twisted by the mad mud holes left by the shelling. The road ran sensible and straight until it curved out of sight behind the green wood, and the wood was to my sight the last solid line before all was overwhelmed by the huge steel haze of Missionary Ridge itself. Across all that ran Colonel Joseph R. Cockerill's Third Brigade, comprising of the 48th Illinois, the 97th and 99th Indiana, the 53rd Ohio, the 70th Ohio, and me.

Truth be told, I didn't do much running. The railroad looked about a mile away. Run or walk, if you're gonna go to Heaven, you'll get there anyhow. I was coughing my guts out. I began with a foolish half-jog, spasmodically stalled to a walk and, depending on my ability to breathe, spluttered back to a crippled running motion. Jee-sus, jesus, jesus: here's the

Lieutenant-Colonel, bringing up the rear. The whole plain below the hill was quiet. Deep thudding shells, more vibration than sound, and the treble of rifle fire could be heard over the rises from the direction of Chattanooga. But right there, right at that moment, as I came down the hill, a hand was cupped around the ear of the land, creating a still hum. The men were far ahead. I could see them forming behind the wood. I could not see one wounded or dead man. I forced myself to jog, until I had to stop, lean and spit. I coughed blood.

'You are wounded!' I looked up. The Captain knelt on one knee, so his face could be level with mine.

'Yes!' he added, as if convinced now of something. 'You must be tended.'

I had, instantaneously, both a sudden absurd panic that I'd been hit without knowing it, and the understanding that the Captain was wrong because he couldn't know that spitting blood was something I'd gotten used to doing. 'I am not wounded, Captain.' I was hoarse. 'I cannot undergo physical exertion without ill-effect.'

He looked at me, and for fuck sake, in all my heaving panic, I can still remember thinking: 'That's like Washburne!' He was looking at me like Washburne did sometimes.

'I have no wound,' I said. 'Where are your men?' I began my old man's jogging.

'The company has joined the Brigade.' He walked beside me.

'I am not wounded,' I insisted.

'Lieutenant Colonel, you must not . . .'

I turned to him. 'I am not injured. Where are your men?'

'I returned to you, sir, to take you to the company. No man has returned yet from General Ewing.' He was speaking very quickly, trying to get out enough information to re-assure me, to hit on the right combination of words to make me understand. 'We will return to the company. I will lead you. No message has returned yet.'

I'd stopped coughing. I could tell he was convinced now I wasn't wounded. I kept running to the line of the woods.

'Lieutenant Colonel' – he started again, with the same tone – 'Colonel Cockerill will not order the advance so soon. Be assured you can be located.'

But I still didn't get it. He tried again. 'I will order another messenger to be sent on our arrival.' He wanted me to stop. 'I have already sent a man to report to General Ewing our new location. Another can be sent. We will not charge again for a little time.'

The charge was over – that's what I finally realised. Of the whole fucking regiment, John A., you're the only one still gallantly rushing the breastworks, givin' 'em the cold steel, doing the hot and heavy work. I'd *made* it – that's what the Captain was telling me.

We were now near to the line of the woods. I could see the troops there, and the railway line. I'd made it. Quick as that. Most of the men were sitting down; some were lying down, dozing. Officers were counting heads, or shouting company and regiment names – but not with panic, just with a standard organisational impatience. Looking backwards, I could see a line of wagons advancing up the road we'd just come. It was the same feeling as when I'd first crossed the Tennessee: the battle was close, but wasn't here yet.

That's what I got, for my first charge upon the enemy: a winded shuffle for a mile-and-a-half across a Quaker's farm. I could see why the Quaker was pissed off. The South Chickamauga lay gentle as a woman's finger on one side and Missionary Ridge rose as stern as justice on another – his farm was a golden space, no doubt. So I was led to jog across his farm. Could've been worse. Looking back, I feel more tender and proud of my failures than my successes. I was there that April day in 1865 when Grant got the note that went:

> *General: – I received your note of this morning on the picket-line whither I have come to meet you and ascertain definitely what terms were embraced in your proposal of yesterday with reference to the surrender of this army. I now request an interview in accordance with the offer contained in your letter of yesterday for that purpose.*
>
> *R. E. Lee,*
> *General*

But that pathetic winded jog means more to me. All that victory, and it's the fucking up that matters. When I lay in Washington dying, the doctor asked, 'What is your full name?'

'John A. Rawlins,' I said.

'Do you know why you are here?'

'I am sick and have consumption.'

'That is right. Let me check you now ...' And he began to undo my shirt. Jesus. Right through that examination, all I thought about were the fuck-ups.

Once their officers had got them back into ordered groups those men about me in the woods sat around with a sort of resigned, sullen grumbling. Ordering them to possible death seemed to piss them off, but no more. Shells occasionally landed back behind us, where we'd just charged, and sometimes a shot would fall among the trees. 'Least we're out of the rain,' I heard one man say, pointing up to the branches overhead.

No-one had come back from either Sherman or Ewing. I thought about going back myself, all the way to Grant. I could get back to Chattanooga, report and return at least to the crossing at the Tennessee before nightfall. It was about three o'clock. 'Fall in,' shouted an officer, and here and there, more officers took up that call. The men shuffled around. I could at least tell Grant Sherman was over the river and making some progress. 'Fall in,' shouted the officers. I half heard, 'Fall in – forward march.'

It wasn't until the troops were leaving the wood that I realised we were charging again. *I will write more fully when I have more time.* I followed. Once beyond the trees, I could see no obvious reason for the charge. The men were walking this time, trying to keep in line with each other. I couldn't see the enemy. Beyond the clumps of trees we'd left was a rising slope crossed by a wooden fence, then boulders and more trees. I had the awful feeling that all our men could turn around and do exactly the same thing in the opposite direction, and it would make no difference. Shells exploded all around us, but none of the men fell to the ground to get cover. The troops were trained not to drop to the ground unless ordered. Sound seemed to orginate from within. Explosions were heard as if some tiny, vital bones deep inside the ear were cracking apart. Trying to block out noise was as futile as trying to stop seeing the blotched darkness full of black blood you see when your eyes are closed.

The line officers were yelling at the men. I could see one whose face was red and exhausted. 'Steady! Steady! Steady!' he kept shouting. I didn't get a sense he was hysterical. He had to shout using all his breath to be even faintly heard. He screamed those words, over and over, so his men could hear him. In all this bedlam, I was astounded at his strength. It was precious and welcome when both inner and outer worlds seemed close to being overwhelmed.

Things ceased being a narrative. I can recall images and sequences, but whatever continuity it is that links separate events in our consciousness seemed missing. My recall is strobed, seems to jerk from one action, or small set of actions, to the next; and though obviously connected, the moment of movement is gone. How my panic escalated so rapidly to this level I do not know.

I could see other officers, but I could not hear what they were shouting. Many men were yelling purposelessly. It was impossible to distinguish the source of the firing. All the officers suddenly looked exhausted with physical effort. Their hair, if it was long enough to be seen under their wider brimmed hats, was matted and damp. One officer had his hat off – from the wild tussle of his hair, it looked like it had been wrenched off his head. Somehow, in one of those strobed flashes of memory, I retain this image as being very disturbing – as if the disorder of his hair was like some form of nakedness, that an officer's dress should never be so personal, so vulnerable. In all that mess, I even had it in me to point senselessly at him – he would've been at least fifty yards away – and then point stupidly at my own head, trying to tell him, I don't know what, to at least slick back the untidy lashes of hair with his palm. Of course, he neither saw nor heard me. There was a profound, immense distance between us. Anything I could not reach out and touch seemed far away from me. Yelling at him and then touching my own head in warning was exhausting.

I could see men kneeling, and firing their rifles. I couldn't fully comprehend everything around me. I can now remember my first actual image of the Confederates – it was the crew of an artillery battery riding to position on a small piece of open and raised ground so as to set up their gun. But it seems that, at the time, that fact could not immediately make sense to me. Instead, I had to first slowly comprehend the splintered wooden farm fence we were approaching, and then the trees in the distance, in which their breastworks stood. Roughly hacked, sheared off logs pointed through the tress.

I remember seeing one soldier who I thought had been with

me in the rifle pit. He was kneeling and ramming, but not firing. He took cartridge after cartridge between his teeth, ripped them open, and rammed them down his gun, one on top of the other. The black powder spilt all around him, and was stuck by sweat to his hands and face. He was furious in all his actions, driven, it seemed, not by fear, but by some terrific, indivertible purpose.

I saw an officer shouting and pointing. He seemed to be looking right at me, but I had that sense he wasn't seeing me. I stared at him, trying to comprehend what he was saying, but he kept on doing exactly the same thing, so I couldn't work out what his meaning was, if there was any.

Earth pushed itself into one side of my body, getting in my mouth. A great slash was across my vision. I realised I had fallen over. I got to my feet, but the ground came up to meet me again. I have no memory of my own movement: it was the grass and dirt that rose up to me. I think I just tripped over, though I could have been knocked over by the force of an explosion. I was not wounded.

I heard, 'Bear to the right!' I could see only a few soldiers left around me. There were no more than ten or fifteen. But they all seemed to be, at last, thankfully, concentrating on one thing. The men in the ranks were all firing at a target. Two men weren't, but then I realised they were officers. All stood. These men seemed to have control of themselves, and had found a purpose in all this. I saw they were firing at the exposed Confederate artillery battery. This made sense. I hoped they had not seen me on the ground. I couldn't be sure how long I'd been lying down.

The officers were drinking. They were not drunk, but one of them had a small hip flask. He pointed the silver tip of it at me, and shouted, 'Whisky.' I shook my head, and I heard him say 'Very good', as if he was primly commending me. He then took another drink, and passed it to the other.

I began to regain a sense of things outside of my own immediate experience. The small group of men I was now with had a comprehensible purpose: to fire at the enemy cannon that had detached itself. The enemy lines beyond the log fence were still very unclear. I could see some breastworks in the trees, and now also in front of them some rifle pits dug into the ground. For the first time, I could see the rifles of enemy troops, and, here and there, I could even make out movements behind them that seemed real and human. But these enemy works didn't seem to form a continuous line. Most strange, neither the men working the cannon we were firing at, nor anyone else, took any notice of us. The cannoneers were working their gun, which was aimed beyond us and to our left. Similarly, not one of the rifles I could now see were pointed at us. All pointed to our left.

We had no cover, but the ground was not flat. It rose up in irregular rises. Beyond the rifle pits and breastworks, it rose in a very steep ascent.

'The men should lie down and continue firing.' I shouted to one of the officers. I wanted to explain that we might get the benefit of some cover from the undulation of the ground. Immediately, as if he'd been impatiently waiting for me to say this, he shouted an order: 'Lie flat, men. Continue firing.' Only those men close to him could hear; and one or two dropped immediately to the ground – others waited, kneeling to finish a shot, and then dropped. Some either ignored him, or did not hear. I ranked this officer. They both walked amongst the men, shouting, until all of the soldiers were on the ground. I saw one or two look around with panic, thinking we all had been shot, but then they comprehended the order, and dropped too. The two officers remained standing. I realised they were waiting for an order from me to take cover. I ordered them down and lay down myself.

I looked around. To our left, towards where all the attention of the Confederates lay, I could see clumps on the ground. They were bodies. It was hard to see any flesh: they looked like bundles of clothing. But, looking again, a hand or head or other limb would appear to be in there too. Some were in remarkable postures: one, on his back, had his head and upper body raised, as if he was pinned by a weight on his stomach. His arms and legs were similarly pinned beside him, straight and regular. He held that position, its pain made bearable by his death. A horse lay on the ground, but not on its side. Its hind legs lay neatly curled beneath it, and its head pointed straight out in front, resting on its forelimbs.

'Catterson has been whipped,' said the officer who had offered me the drink as he nodded towards our left.

I looked at him. His face was shiny with moisture; the ends of his moustache had stuck to his lower cheeks.

'The 97th retreats,' he said. 'There is no chance of taking the Western and General.'

I looked back at the Confederate gunners working their gun. Near us, a soldier rolled suddenly over onto his back.

The second officer panted, 'Thomas has been repulsed at the foot of Missionary Ridge. Bragg has left the top of the mountain and advanced.' He thought he was calmly and professionally facing a crisis, but his repressed panic gave urgent conviction to what he was saying. 'We should hold a line closer to the river.'

I thought the soldier on his back had been hit but, instead, he held his gun between his knees, and, with the barrel pointing up over his chest, rammed a charge down.

I did not want to leave here. The strange sensation of being ignored continued: the battery we were firing at never stopped gunning to our left. If I had been capable of clear thought, I would have realised it was impossible for anyone to know what was happening over three miles away at Missionary Ridge, but that did not occur to me back then.

'I'll go to the fence line,' I said. I pointed at the splintered fence, still twenty yards ahead, and towards which I had seemed to be charging for twelve hours. All the men with me had bloodshot eyes. I don't know if this was from sweat, or from the discharge of fumes. It was the charcoal pits.

I was too tired to use full sentences: 'Look,' I added.

'You must not,' said the whisky officer. He was not being insubordinate; rather, he was protecting me because of my rank, as any officer would do in that situation. 'I will send a man.' But there was more. It was a strange, emotional objection. The words as read are formal, but it was as if he had implored me. 'Don't leave us,' he might have said. 'Don't leave us.' Always, there's a Washburne thing. It reminds me of that. What did he want? I had the suspicion there was a whole world of feeling I didn't understand, that others could hear a frequency I could not. 'Don't leave me' is what he as good as said. Jesus fuck.

'I am here for Grant,' I replied, and, at the time, meant it. I was alluding to my duty to get reconnaissance and an accurate report of battle. 'Staff officer.' Duty. He knew what I meant, too. His face, flushed and dripping, turned an awful toad-grey. Involuntarily, as if he had just begun to feel how exhausted he was, he began drawing long panting breaths. I thought he was going to faint. On my hands and knees, I started crawling towards the fence.

It was worse at the charcoal pits: so I felt, as I crawled the twenty yards. *'You sit in the dray,' I told Alton, who was coughing a lot because of the closeness of the fumes. 'The smoke stings inside,' he said, 'at the top of my nose.' He pointed to the middle of my face, to show me.* Although I could see the fence, my face was too close to the earth to see much else. Turning to the left, way down, I saw where the fence had been destroyed here and there. But directly ahead, it was only splintered. Fresh wood was cleanly bared where fragments had been shot off. Although I saw and understood all this, my feelings were of Alton, as he sat on the dray and faced the fire to get its heat. I shovelled, damp and filthy with dust. Oh, his face! If only I could see him again! Not in memory, but real! I remember thinking, it was worse, harder, at the charcoal pits; I was more exhausted then. As I crawled on, my pity and sadness for my dead brother rose unbidden and strange, from part of that place your mind visits so little, but knows to be home. To me, as I crawled, the charcoal pits were worse – they'd prepared me for those twenty yards.

Maybe it is worse for a twelve-year-old, at the charcoal pits, than a thirty-two-year old, at the extreme right of Sherman's bungled advance on the second day of the Battle of Chattanooga. Could be.

Over the last couple of yards, splinters of wood stuck to my wet uniform. I touched the fence, and looked beyond.

The ground was rising up into the tree line. On my side of the fence, down to my left, the ground was trampled and dug up. Spades, cups, guns, canteens, papers, all the detritus of battle, was strewn up to the fence line; but over it the ground lay untouched and clean. I could see Confederate rifles sticking out from their breastworks, but there seemed less of them than during the charge itself, and they were firing less often. I was exhausted. In my mouth was the taste of a foul sweating stench, and I had a sudden fear of some vague repellent discharge, some deep internal fault. I spat and coughed, but had brought no drink with me. My arms and shoulders started a rapid, involuntary, giggling shake, caused, now I was not moving, by my physical effort, rather than fear. Instead of propping myself up, I lay flat to the earth until the tremors stopped.

I lay there absurdly, as if relaxed.

Then I heard, 'Damn devil. Damn devil.' An unmistakably Southern voice was nonsensically repeating this over and over, somewhere very close to the front of me. It sounded angry, but, like a mantra, the intonation stayed constant, neither building nor diminishing, controlled by unfluctuating fury.

I did not know whether to look up or not. Amidst the slackening gun shots, I could seem to pick out one very close gun. 'Damn devil, damn devil,' went the voice, and every fourth or fifth round of the chant, the gun was fired.

I felt a peculiar, tingling premonition run from the gun's target at the top of my head back down my neck. My cheek was flat and pathetic against the earth. I did not want to look and risk drawing their attention; I did not want to lie there and get shot like a child in bed, frozen in nightmare. I looked.

Two Confederate soldiers knelt in small undulation in front of me. They seemed not five gun barrel lengths away. Both faced away, to the left. One held his gun vertical, and was swearing, and ramming a charge. The other stared, trying to see the field to my left. Two. So close. Before thought, I had gasped a yelled grunt of shock.

I froze, as if in mid-air, falling terrified to the earth. They did not hear. I put my head flat to the ground, and with my eyes closed in concentration I tried to draw my revolver. The holster was caught awkwardly under my hip and I had to lift my body up a few immense inches. My wrist bent in contortion as it pulled the pistol up under my chest, dragging the gun's dead weight behind it like a wolf hauling prey. Everything was heavier; my body was pressed to earth with unnatural weight. I could smell the oiled mechanism of the barrel as it passed my face. I looked. The earth's finger was under my chin, pushing up like a bully who knows he need not fear. With one hand, I held the gun straight out, my arm along the ground. I raised its angle up, so I would not shoot into the ground in front. The smallest movement seemed to have huge significance. I ground the handle of the gun down into the dirt, and fired.

One fell, as if pretending to be shot. For a fumbled second, the other's eyes searched; it seemed his eyes would never find me. I felt amazed they could not immediately see me when, looking at them, they filled my whole landscape. But before that feeling could be complete, the other soldier did see me: he looked straight at me, his sweating red face distorted. He dropped his ramming rod, but didn't drop his gun.

He fell to the ground. I could only guess at his movements. I had the impossible conviction he had instantaneously got back of me, though I knew, rationally, this could not be so.

I half stood, and, bent double, ran back to the group of men I'd left. During the slow crawl to the fence, I was calm enough: thinking of Alton was strange, but it had some order, some form. Running back, I was gasping, almost sobbing. I have thought deeply since about this crazed distress, and I now put it down to the fact I felt I was going to get the bejesus shot out of me.

I think the Confederate must have gone back to his own lines to report, because as I returned, more rifle fire began to be directed towards us. I lay gasping for breath. The whisky officer asked, 'Are we to advance, sir?'

'Drink,' I spat.

He offered the whisky flask. I drank. That one was for you, Dad, you cunt.

'No,' I told him. Spit. 'We will return to the wood.'

1863 - NOW

VICTORY AT CHATTANOOGA – A HIGHER GRADE
CREATED FOR GRANT – IN COMMAND OF ALL
THE ARMIES

At the back of Sherman's army, it looked like retreat, even though it wasn't. Right along the South Chickamauga there were ambulances, artillery batteries, confused groups of jeering soldiers, riderless horses, Confederate prisoners without escort – all were heading back towards the Tennessee. The whisky drinking officers and their men retreated with me. I lost them at the pontoon bridge. We all seemed deceived into thinking it was a disaster.

I'd turned back, and returned to the woods. I would have still sworn to my own honour. But beyond that, when we move from the world of others, with its own scales of knowledge, into ourselves, and so to truths that are experienced in our sinews, that are automatic as the workings of lung tissue, then we all feel, don't we, revelations of what is deceit and what is true come upon us without our will? I looked at the rain falling on the defeated men around me. Every face stared three feet ahead, concentrating only on making it past there.

I arrived back in Chattanooga after nightfall. The rain had finally stopped, and wind had blown the mists out of the valley. 'Night came on clear,' one of the noble staff officers of the army corps wrote later, 'with the stars lighting up the heavens.'

Before I re-entered the busted house that was headquarters, I leant up against its dirty grey wood, coughing and spitting in the dark. The town was full. Tens of thousands of soldiers, some wounded from this day's fight, were preparing to fight tomorrow. 'But there followed a sight to cheer their hearts and thrill their souls,' writes the same, safe officer. 'Away off to their right, and reaching skyward, Lookout Mountain was ablaze with the fires of Hooker's men, while off to their left, and far down the valley, the north end of Missionary Ridge was aflame with the lights of Sherman's army.' I've got to admit I never saw any of it. I wiped my mouth, and walked into headquarters.

The room was close with smoke and perspiration; if I hadn't just coughed it all up, my bile would have risen to choke me again. At headquarters, they thought they knew more about the battle than I did. Sherman had reported that he had taken the railroad tunnel at the end of Missionary Ridge. Grant remained seated.

'We have had news of Sherman's success, Brigadier,' he said to me. 'What information can you provide for us?'

I was confused. I didn't realise yet that I was wrong about the whole thing.

'I find it hard to clearly perceive our position,' I said. 'I have been with a unit of General Ewing's fourth division. They advanced to a point near the Western and Atlantic railroad, but were forced to retreat. I am unsure as to the general situation of Sherman's advance, though my impressions are that it only has a tenuous hold south of the Tennessee.'

Grant didn't believe me. 'Your view of the battle is wrong,' he said flatly. 'Sherman informs me he has taken the tunnel at the end of Missionary Ridge.' His face was matter of fact. I'd come back from a defeat, but he didn't seem to agree. 'We need to telegraph Washington,' he said, handing me a dispatch. I sat beside him, and read:

> *The fight to-day progressed favorably. Sherman carried the end of Missionary Ridge, and his right is now at the tunnel, and his left at Chickamauga Creek. Troops from Lookout Valley carried the point of the mountain, and now hold the eastern slope and a point high up. Hooker reports two thousand prisoners taken, besides which a small number have fallen into our hands from Missionary Ridge.*

Grant didn't think this was a failure at all. He was planning tomorrow's fight. Around the room, there was a sense of calm achievement.

As CWDs love to point out, most of the dispatch was wrong. Sherman hadn't taken the tunnel – he'd misunderstood the ground, and he only found out the next day, when he lost a few thousand men, that he wasn't where he thought he was. Hooker hadn't yet got to the point of Lookout Mountain. But with Grant, battle was less complex than CWDs would like. None of those mistakes mattered, in the end, because we won the following day.

I missed Horace, God help me! If only I could've seen all this with his eyes, and co-authored his book: *Campaigning With Grant* by J.A. Rawlins and Horace Porter (I think it's fairly clear my name would've gone first), 'a remarkable narrative that gives the reader a vivid picture of life with General

Ulysses S. Grant, hero of the American Civil War. Includes recipes for all occasions, and a visit to Tuscany for the leso wankers.' Above us, an animal was scratching around in the top storey rooms I had sat in yesterday. Its claws hacked away hungrily at the wood.

I thought of Horace's grandly-charged dialogue after he'd come back from yesterday's fight. Horace quotes, in full, the order I'd written for Grant requesting to have him on our staff:

CHATTANOOGA, TENN.,
Nov 5, 1863.

MAJ.-GEN. H. W. HALLECK,
General-in-Chief of the Army.

Capt. Horace Porter, who is now being relieved as chief ordnance officer in the Department of the Cumberland, is represented by all officers who know him as one of the most meritorious and valuable young officers in the service. So far as I have heard from general officers there is a universal desire to see him promoted to the rank of brigadier-general and retained here. I feel no hesitation in joining in that recommendation, and ask he may be assigned for duty with me. I feel the necessity for just such an officer as Captain Porter as described to be, at headquarters, and, if permitted, will retain him with me if assigned here for duty. I am, &c.,

U.S. GRANT, Major-general.

I've taken that from *Campaigning with Grant*.

Ooo, *deep*, Mr Disturbing Authorial Voice – you're quoting from a book, in your book, and it's actually from the book in your book you're pretending is your book! Whoa! That's some of the good self-referential shit, man! Disturbing change of narrative position! Fractured Kafkaesque time shit! Like, how William 'I'll-just-get-up-and-have-a-piss-and-when-I-get-back-I'll-use-a-new-narrative-voice' Faulkner! *Je n*'stick-your-French-post-modernist-pipe-up-your-blurter-*pas*. The only good thing I can see about post-modernism is that if you're not a rug-muncher, or an indigenous person, or a lonely fifty-year-old woman with postcards of Tuscany around your flat masturbating about going to writers group after volunteering at the disabled poetry workshop, it's the only way you'll score a government grant. So, given Horace isn't into post-modernist dickpull, why would he quote that whole order asking for him to join our staff? After all, look at our staff: some staff officers had stolen the best lounge chairs they could find in the town. They sat on them now, sinking down into the white and pink floral patterns like great aunts visiting. The bottom of the chairs had been soiled with mud when they had been dragged to headquarters, as if the chairs had been sitting in a flood. One staff officer had hacked a hole in the arm of one chair so he could keep his sword safe by forcing it down into the fabric. Blankets had been placed over the broken windows, and now smelt like wet dogs from the rain they had collected all day. Why, three decades later, would Horace still be so proud of all this?

CWDs weren't the only ones disappointed with the Battle of Chattanooga. Grant reached in his pocket to fish out another cigar, exactly as if he didn't care for their judgement. I kept looking at the dispatch, even though I had finished reading it. So that was it. That was my fight. It was the closest thing I ever got to a Confederate in action. I'd been to the charcoal pits, and that was all. I know courage is the commonest thing you can find in a man; but I had to tell you. Chattanooga wasn't something I could leave out. It felt hollow then, though, as if, reading that dispatch, I was reading about some other battle from a war long ago – from the Mexican

War, maybe – and it wasn't me who had been part of all that. Whatever it meant, whatever its huge purport, that meaning's significance had gone.

Even back then, I knew I'd never write *Campaigning with Grant*. All my life I'd suspected I'd been made unfit to pass the test of manhood – how could I be expected to accept that my father had prepared me perfectly? I'd been right to the battle and back, and found out that shovelling charcoal into a pit is all it took.

I looked at Grant with the dispatch still in my hand. 'Even my father,' I thought, 'could have done it.'

'Washington will be pleased,' I said, handing it back without amendment. 'There is nothing I can change.'

The dispatch would appear in the *War of the Rebellion: a Compilation of the Official Records of the Union and Confederate Armies* (128 volumes). That seemed important, then.

༺༻

If, during those months between the last victorious day of the Battle of Chattanooga and the famous reception at the White House in March '64 when Lincoln met Grant to promote him to Lieutenant General – if, then, we had at our disposal all the accoutrements of modern lobbying, maybe we could have done the thing properly. After the Battle of Chattanooga, Grant moved to Nashville for winter, and Washburne and I worked to get Grant made commander of all Union armies. Oh, the frequent flyer points that would have been earned flying between Nashville and Washington to lobby for Grant's promotion! Surely this is one of the great unknowns of the American Civil War. Mobile phones! Faxes! *Email!* Imagine if the meeting I would have with Washburne and Chetlain in Washington happened today. Ulysses S. Literature Grant. The Post-modernists would lap it up. They'd have me calling

Washburne on the way to the airport: 'Elihu? Rawlins – yes, fine. No, it was a good result in Chattanooga, wasn't it? Yeah, we're pleased, too. Horace arrive OK? Told him to contact you. He's good middle management: you know, get 'em to pull at the oars so they won't rock the boat. Look, I'm in a taxi ten minutes away from Nashville airport. Arrive in Washington 'bout four. I'll come to your office. So how's the Congress going? Read what Bennett's saying in the *Herald*? I've got it here, hold on: 'It is proposed in Congress to revive the office of Lieutenant General. It is stated that the rank is to be revived that it may be conferred on General Grant, in the hope no doubt such a high military position will switch him off the Presidential track.' Yeah. Yeah. Fuck him. Yeah, I'll fax a copy from the airport if you wa – OK, I suppose it can wait. Yeah, I've read all that crap before, too. No, it's OK. Nah, really, it's a little bit worse, but the doctor says nothing major – Yeah, no, I will look after it. Thanks, Elihu. Bye. Yeah. No, I will. OK. Bye.'

I didn't get to the Capitol until half-past nine because of the traffic. I sat in the warmth of the taxi, looking at the monuments standing lonely and abandoned in the cold. I had seen the lines of the traffic from the air, disentangling and rejoining as we descended to the tarmac – who would've thought that, leaving home, leaving Galena, I had been leaving something behind, abandoning something precious? The possibility had never entered my head. I could see the drivers in the other cars, mostly sitting alone in individual darkness.

Washburne had invited good old Chetlain to dinner. I didn't know why Washburne had asked him, but Chetlain, who was now a Lieutenant Colonel, was known in the army for his support of Grant. Apparently, back in Galena, Chetlain had been the first to recognise the commanding general's great abilities, or so he said. We went to Willard's, of course.

'You never drink, that I know of,' said Washburne after I ordered a Budweiser.

'Started at Chattanooga,' I told him.

'Good move. Though it fucks me up when I'm on the piss,' said Chetlain. He took out his mobile and placed it on the table. He ordered the wines. 'That was a good, good result, John,' he said. I raised my hand and shrugged in pleased but self-deprecating acknowledgment. Chetlain's false admiration continued. 'Halleck's more hated here by the radical Republicans than Jeff Davis is. Henry's gone.' Henry Halleck was the current Union commander.

'Grant has no wish for him to go,' I said.

'Yes, mate, and I'm boning Mary Todd.' Mary Todd was ah ... Forget it.

'It's true. Grant knows he can do the job, and wants to do the job, but he couldn't give a shit whether Halleck stays or goes, just as long as it's him and not Halleck who gets the final call.'

'Bullshit.'

'Grant wants command, not headlines.' All this was said in the greatest friendliness, like the two most popular school boys pretending to fight each other in class so as to annoy the teacher. Everyone in the room knows what is bullshit, and why.

'Halleck accepts that Grant is the man of the moment,' said Chetlain. 'He says it's a matter of law: Grant will pull rank over him, *fini*. But all that's just his bullshit. He's pissed off that Grant's the hero. If he had his way, he'd tell Grant to geeeet fuucke –' Chetlain's voice rose, high-pitched in mock indignation, but Washburne stopped him. He turned to me.

'General Grant wants, above all, to stay in the field?' Every time he spoke, it seemed I was a bit ashamed, like he'd caught me out. Yet the tone of his voice was quiet, considered and genuine.

'Yes,' I replied. 'Yes. That's exactly what he wants. He

doesn't even plan to move to Washington. He'll come to meet Lincoln. He'll fly in when he's needed. Otherwise, he'll stay with the Army of the Potomac. He'd leave Meade in command there, but Grant would tell Meade what to do.'

This amazed Chetlain. All around the dining room sat tables of men who looked like us: smart, powerful, conscious of the tone of the room and its sense of exclusivity. The light fittings were designed by the latest nihilist interior designer from Milan; a steel wire and neon post-modernist bar flickered, annoying as a computer's screen saver; and, best of all, only two doors down was the far more formal French restaurant where yesterday's men dined. There were 134 boutique beers to choose from, and Grant was going to command from a *tent*?

I knew where all this would lead. All the way from Grant and Perkins Leather and Hides Merchants to Willard's. All that way; and so I knew, after Washburne had left, Chetlain was going to slyly offer anyone who was still kicking on some cocaine. He and his Republican mates would meet up, and when he begins to sing 'Lorena' they'd all join in with:

> *The years creep slowly by, VAGINA,*
> *The snow is on the grass again;*
> *The sun's low down the sky, VAGINA,*
> *The frost gleams ... blar-dy ... blar-dy – blah*

We wouldn't have done that back in '62 in Galena, but only because we weren't as sophisticated as big city folk.

Chetlain wanted a cognac – he was on the piss a lot. He arched his back to stretch and pushed his arms out in front, as if that part of the conversation was over, and he could take a break and summarise: 'Robert E, that's who he's coming up against. Robert E.' He let out a small grunt. He was telling us what he supposed we had all been forgetting. 'Fuck Halleck,

Grant could get *Lincoln*'s job if he wanted it. Lee's who we need to get rid of.'

'The General knows how to win,' I said. 'He understands what brings victory and defeat.'

Chetlain ordered another brandy.

'*The Union forever, Hurrah!, boys, Hurrah!*' he sang quietly. Idolising the enemy and dumping on the incompetent good old boys of the Union was the current fashion in Washington. Chetlain thought it showed how cynically aware he was of the realities of the war.

He looked at me. I was sick of bullshitting around. Since Chattanooga, I'd been tired. Chetlain and his crap made me sleepy. Something had changed, somewhere; inside of me, some fault had flowered open like diseased tissue but I didn't want to know where. I looked up at Chetlain. I had been coughing, of course; around my lips mucus formed in a bloody web. 'Chetlain, the day you find out you're a cunt, you'll realise that you'd known all the time.'

When I'd finished coughing, even Chetlain had stopped drinking. They were both looking at the blood on my handkerchief.

Only Washburne could break that silence. 'I wish to ask a favour of you.' He looked at Chetlain. Chetlain! Washburne was asking Chetlain's favour. Chetlain, stupid with surprise, took his eyes away from the blood to look at Washburne. 'President Lincoln asked me yesterday to tell him about Grant. He wishes to know this General. I replied that I, too, find it very hard to really know Grant. So I told the President I would ask if you would speak to him, as you know Grant from his days in Galena. I know you helped him with his finances, and in his father's shop. You know him from before his current fame. Who better to speak for the General than a man who speaks about him as he really is, and not as his fame makes him out to be?'

Chetlain may as well have silently mouthed 'Me? The President? *Me*?' The poor fuck's glass was halfway to his lips. He put it down. He was scared.

It was a good question. Why would Washburne pick him? Why not someone like Horace, who was in town, had seen Grant in battle, and was certain to eulogise him? Then, of course, there was me. Why wouldn't Washburne pick me to see the President?

Suddenly, Chetlain's mobile rang. Before he could move, Washburne reached forward and switched it off.

'You have seen in John the sort of men that surround Grant.' Washburne spoke calmly. 'Can you doubt that the General wishes to fight? Major General Halleck is competent to serve, but the army needs someone to rule. The President needs to know if General Grant is this man. We here know he is; you only need to tell the President your honest knowledge of Grant.'

Chetlain picked up his cognac and gulped some. 'War is cruelty. You cannot refine it,' he was thinking. It was too much for him, and even I thought it was miserable, to see him sitting there so overwhelmed. Chetlain was slumped, staring at his glass. Only Washburne looked comfortable. Out of pity, I think, Washburne called for the bill. He paid.

∽∾

We got a taxi together.

'You speak too well, John,' Washburne said to me. The motion of the taxi caused the street lights to pass in succession up over his darkened face. I felt he could see me clearly. 'Your commitment to Grant and the Republic is too well known, too strong, too much admired. Your passion is pure, and will not be argued with. The President's mind cannot be made up for him – he will not allow that. He wishes to form his own judgement, not be swept up in yours. Horace is noble and simple, and idolises the General; his platitudes will tell the President little. Chetlain is out of his depth, and torn. He has been forced to admire Grant, despite his own false judgements. Lincoln will see him for who he is: someone who doubts Grant, but cannot disagree with the General's achievements. Chetlain would see Grant ill, if he could, but he is too small and dishonest a man to do Grant harm, so instead he boasts of him. Chetlain is another enemy Grant has defeated. Praise from friends is one thing; praise from enemies is even more convincing. I hope you do not think me too subtle?'

From anyone else, that last question would have been boasting, but Washburne was really asking me my response to all he had said. It took me a while to work it out. 'Your passion is pure . . .' – that's what I was thinking about, despite myself. I felt a strange, indefinable emotion as I looked at him. I can see, now, how it was gratitude that I felt; gratitude that I could breathe in his cleaner air. He thought something in me was 'pure'. If only for this taxi ride, I could relax under his generous gaze. Back then, I said nothing as the street lights slowed and finally halted, leaving him paused in darkness.

The taxi had stopped for me to get out. I stepped from the cab, coughing because of the sudden cold. 'Together, Elihu, we both do what we think best for the General. I will go back to Nashville, to help Grant prepare for the coming battle against Lee.' I felt ill, but I knew that the greatest part of the campaign with Grant was still ahead. Except that I'm pretending that all this happened now instead of back then, I could add here that this first battle between Grant and Lee would later be remembered as the Battle of the Wilderness. If we'd've had them in 1864, I would have bent down to the cab window and said to Washburne, 'Call me on my mobile. We will talk more fully when I have more time.'

1864 - 1861 - 1864

ENTERING THE WILDERNESS – CROSSING THE RAPIDAN – EMILY DIES – THE FIRST DAY IN THE LACY MEADOW

What wrongs do we think we have done the dead, that we must deceive ourselves they can come to visit us? That we disguise as unbidden the punishments with which we haunt ourselves makes them more surely self-chosen. We know we make our own ghosts; we know it is absurd to pretend the dead can speak ...

That's the sort of shit you seem to think about, crossing over Germanna Ford into the Wilderness. Gloom is laired in the scrub that begins to surround you. It's not like the solid, vaulting wall of forest I used to ride through up in Galena, where disappearing into the trees would make me suddenly feel as if I was entering a new world. The trees in the Wilderness are too scrawny and wrecked for that; instead, they lace around you in a knotty, knobbly lattice, brown rather than green, and at their feet lies an amputated scrub made of broken limbs that look like they have dropped not from the trees, but from high in the sky above the wood, smashing through the foliage, bringing down more wreckage from what might once have been living plants. Leading through this was the mud-scrapped track of the army. Thousands of men, horses and carts had trampled all growth, so any dirt that was not hardened washed filthy into the Rapidan. I felt I'd been there before.

'If it is true that the spirits of the dead walk beside us, we unknowing of their presence, then it is surely so that they walk here.' Horace was as keen as ever. He notes that on this ride 'General Grant was dressed in a uniform coat and waist-coat, the coat being unbuttoned. On his hands were a pair of yellowish-brown thread gloves. He wore a pair of plain top boots . . .'

I looked at Grant, too. His back slouched slightly, and the tilt of his head, even from behind, seemed to communicate some strange blankness, as if he was gazing at nothing.

'. . . plain top boots,' continues Horace, 'reaching to his knees, and he was equipped with a regulation sword, spurs and sash . . .'

Grant's ear and neck were a fleshy red-brown, and his cheek was stubbled. He seemed to be always resisting something, always burdened by some recent disappointment he had heard about, and must struggle through. Entering the Wilderness, Grant alone seemed unspooked.

'On his head was a slouch hat of black felt with a plain gold cord around it,' writes Horace. I realised who his whole mien reminded me of – who could've guessed? Who could've *not* guessed? Though the scrub of the Wilderness had not seemed like the forests around Galena, when I looked again to my right I felt a ghostly sense that I was riding to the drudgery of the coal pits with my father. Fuck, those mornings. My father would ride in front, and to me the skin on his face always seemed to be impervious to the cold. A lifetime's drinking had corrupted his flesh with an insensate leathery rouge. He'd dismount, and walk into the forest some distance, striding with a sense of purpose I always felt was faked so as to disguise the randomness of the task he was to set us, then he'd drive his axe into a tree, and leave it stuck. It was up to this mark that we were expected to clear the bush. He'd ride off, leaving us to it. Who expects more? No matter how I tried, here I was, with him still. Grant led us on. 'Rawlins was on his left,' writes Horace.

It's the decisions you make when you don't know you're making them that are important. There is a plan, revealed later, you didn't know you were following. An incomplete flush of revelation tingled through me as I rode onto that battle field. I looked up to the sky, but we were too enclosed to get any sense of where we really were. 'It's back to Galena,' I thought. '*It's back home.*' That was why I shat myself in the Wilderness.

The night before we had made camp near a deserted farm house, and had the fence rails made into a fire because of the gloom all around. Grant and Meade talked about tomorrow's battle, but neither Horace nor I were really interested. Horace was more concerned to soak up the small, human detail; and I looked into the melodramatic blackness outside the enclosed firelight and thought again about my dead wife. I could no longer sleep for a full night. I would wake up coughing and gasping, sweating, caught in the middle of some unending physical effort.

∽∾

I was not there when Emily died. Even though I delayed joining Grant to be with her, she died without me. Of course,

Emily was irresistible for me because she was a Senator's daughter, and I was a young politician; because she was from New York, and I from the backwoods; because I was full of passionate idealism, and she could laugh and mock me without malice. My politics and ideals were only familiar to her because of her father. She knew her presence and beauty could delightfully force senators visiting her father's house to stop talking together and ask, 'Does Miss Smith grant us permission to say how pleasant is this home and its associations, both of which do honour to the mother and wife your father has lost?'

'Congressman, the duties of my father's daughter are as lightly carried as my dear mother carried the duties of his wife.'

'The grief of your father can only be consoled by the beauty of his daughter.'

'That my beauty were so great as to provide consolation for such a deep grief is beyond any woman's wish, and too much for a daughter's desire.'

But there was more than this that drew me to Emily. There was her physical nature, her slender form and delicate wrists, her face and lips: so beautiful to me that a guilt that never really troubled me would augment my desire for her, a harmless possibility that it was just her physical beauty I loved. It was as if, for me, her body was animated by a lighter, better spirit. She had an elusiveness always beyond me, to which I could never really join.

It's easy to mock – I know you're smirking – but her and me . . . Maybe it all wouldn't mean so much if she hadn't died. On the mantlepiece in the bedroom where she died there was a small painting of her with her father and mother. This was painted when she was very young, before her mother died. She brought this with her from her father's house, along with a purple tablecloth that she put on a small round wooden table near the window. When we moved in, her father gave us all the paintings she wanted from his New York home, and these were too much for our smaller place. The bulk was stored away, and she would choose which to hang. Paintings were hung everywhere. This was delightful to me, who grew up in a house scratched in the dirt. Emily kept changing these paintings around, so there was always something new and beautiful for her to look at. Her bedroom was too small, really. It was all emptied after she died. The day I left for Cairo to be with Grant I remember looking around that room before I closed the door. I knew it was the last time I'd be there. It was dark; I was tired, and felt so full of grief that I was numbed to more pain. It was a while before I stopped dreaming of that empty room.

The many symptoms of tuberculosis include coughing blood, tiredness, night sweats, loss of appetite, and fever – yet all fitted into that one small room. Emily's world when she was dying was, to me, so huge! One bedroom! The distance to the lounge chair became exhausting for her, then impossible to attempt; drinking a glass of water or taking soup represented tasks that the nurse and I would discuss in earnest conference outside Emily's door. Emily never lay down. She always sat propped up, her hair spreading over her pillows. Often this would form a damp mat; she would move her face, but behind her was an arc of hair fixed by sweat.

'John, I am so tired,' she would say. 'I must sleep, and everything will be all right.'

I would sit there, amazed and helpless.

'I will sleep, and everything will be all right.'

The room seemed to have its own odour. There was an astringent cold scent, strange and incongruous. I think the nurse was the cause of this. She was constantly arranging dried flowers and placing bowls of coloured water in the room. However, underneath there was always a fleshy, humid smell this deodorant could not disguise. It seemed like some distant mountainous fire, some consuming, exhausting heat, was burning far away.

If I was at a meeting in Jesse's store, or discussing the position in Cairo with Chetlain, or even writing letters to Washburne, I sensed I was surrounded by people who were seeing not only me, but also my dying wife in her consumptive, nineteenth century melodrama, like a ghost already by my side. 'Grant is now entitled a captain, who would be also acting adjutant general,' I would say to Chetlain. 'The move to Cairo needs to be carried out so that there is more than a piecemeal approach to the control of the rivers.'

'This is true. Grant needs to move soon,' he would reply. The tone in his voice was ludicrously gentle. He always wanted my job, the fucker, but he let me play the tragically bereaved husband without competition. Our house in Galena was the only one with cable, the only place you could see the sequel to *Meet the Rawlins – The Place Where Emily Rawlins Was Dying*. Her father had paid for the nurse to come from New York, and she went around the town buying food, basins, medicines and linen. Everything she purchased was noted and discussed later by the women of the town, dividing those impressed by the newness of her Yankee ideas from others outraged by her misguided abandonment of traditional care. There was a new war and a romantic death: everyone was happy. I would come from the newly-constructed Galena drill hall, where the talk was of the strategic points on the Mississippi and Ohio, back to that miniature, huge world of Emily and her room.

'She has not taken broth,' the nurse would tell me, 'and she feels more pain in her chest when I replace her pillows. She is no more feverish, but still keeps talking of how she wishes to sleep.' It was like receiving the latest dispatches. She would continue as I took off my overcoat, 'I have changed the flowers. There is more blood-stained sputum being produced, so I will purchase linen and some undergarments. Your wife requested the paintings in the room be moved around. I have suggested to her you may wish to do this for her.'

Emily would ask for one of the paintings from her father's home to be brought from the storeroom; I would hang it, and she would turn to look, that halo of hair, as if it were dead already, unmoving behind her face. The sicker she got, the more restless was her search for the picture that could comfort her. If she was strong enough, she would direct me with her hand to make sure I was hanging the frame straight on the wall. At other times, she would just look. I would return to her bed, and she would ask for another move. Sometimes I'd note later with shock how askew I'd hung a painting. It was like seeing a tiny fissure in the face of a rock wall about to collapse. The ugly crookedness of the painting, scribbled there by a panicked child, seemed to make me aware of all that was amiss. Emily could be lying beautiful in bed, the nurse could be efficient and capable, I was home again – it all could be fine, except there the ill-hung painting tilted, proving how much was wrong, giving away how hard I'd been pretending.

Her father wrote a small, rushed note to me – as if it were he that was dying – sent via the nurse:

> *John, you must keep me informed of all that occurs. I can only stay here in Washington at this time, for you know how McClellan now needs all men to guard the Potomac and the nation. The race of Philip Sydneys lives on! My daughter is my heart, and if this is to be sacrificed for the Union, so be it! Well, this is a beautiful way to die! Beg her keep a brave heart, for brave hearts are all that deserve to live in these times. Write to me. I will try, but I can see no way I can be spared to come.*

And he signed it with his full title, 'Senator Alexander Smith.'

I think, now, how like him I was, for her. In our melodramatic arrogance, we thought her death mattered only as a test of our resolve; as if her illness was a trial for me which I must complete before joining Grant. Sometimes I was numbed sitting by her, but numbed not by grief or pain; instead, I had the secret, awful awareness that I was feeling nothing. What if my wife was dying and this was uncovering only the shallowness of my love for her?

Yet at other times, I'd have the sense that everything around me was the same: this chair, that bed, this room, Galena – but the Earth had shifted, leaving what was close unchanged to my sight, but placing me in a different orbit. Nothing was to be the same now.

Chetlain knew that with Emily taking so long to die, he could work the delay to his own advantage. Grant needed a chief of staff. He was in Cairo, drinking with the ABDs. People were impatient for battle – at that early stage of the war we all thought time was short. I would leave Emily and go to the Drill Hall, where Chetlain, Orvil and I talked about Grant.

'Your brother has achieved much,' Chetlain said to Orvil, 'though no more than we all expected of him.'

'Our father is immensely proud.' Orvil was wearing what he thought a gentleman in New York wore. Now he was never seen in the shop apron. He was in waistcoat and jacket, and around his butterfly collar was a striped cravat, worn as a tie. His brother was gone to be a general, and that made him a business executive. In April 1861, I would've just been talking to Jesse Grant's younger son. Now, in August 1861, I was conferencing with the CEO of Grant and Perkins, multinational.

'I have been communicating with Senator Washburne,' Chetlain told me. 'We are all agreed that the General must now build on his success. The country calls for action.'

'We all do our duty, not letting what pain may befall us distract us from that task,' said Orvil.

'Sam needs around him men whom he can trust, whom he knows from home. He is one of Illinois' sons, and we are all brothers now,' said Chetlain.

'The move from Cairo must be made soon. We are all aware of this. At such a time my father and I would wish around my brother Ulysses only those who love him as we do.'

'I will write to the Senator again, explaining our wishes.'

Both would pause, and look at me. They were waiting for me to agree that we should write to Washburne, telling him Grant should offer Chetlain the job in my place.

One day I returned home to find Emily stretched back in a grim contortion, her head fallen from the pillows. Her mouth was open. I gave a strange weakling's yelp, as if from a lesser fear, and ran to her. I felt no hesitation or repulsion when I touched her, as I thought I might when the time came to feel her dead skin. I lifted her head, and yelled for the nurse. What a time that was! Looking back, how hard it was. I know now that all my life I made everything too hard – even this, I made too hard. Emily's neck seemed strangely stretched, and as I lifted her shoulders her head tilted back in an even more grotesque angle. Her mouth gaped. It seemed as if each new fraction of a second brought so much fresh horror that my perceptions slowed to try and imbibe it all. Her body was warm. I was overwhelmed by the experience, but I must tell you, the only conscious thought I had – that I can remember, anyway – was this: 'Chetlain has no chance now.' Her nightgown was damp in the small of her back, and I could feel her breast on my chest as I held her to me: but in all my distress, like some weird involuntary memory, I thought of Chetlain, and what the news would mean to him. As always, I was mistaken. By the time the nurse had entered the room, Emily was awake.

'I need to sleep, John,' she said to me, frightened by my yelling. She coughed, and holding her I felt how her coughing came from deep in her body, but it was now less harsh because she no longer had the strength to sustain such wretched convulsions. 'I will sleep, and then I think everything will be all right.' The nurse looked at us.

'We should let your wife rest if she can, sir,' she said to me, as if I were an idiot. Looking back now, I can see that I had been so panicked, so moved. But I would see Emily die and display only feigned emotion. My long apprenticeship in self-deception provided that for every event in my life, I had, by reflex, a disingenuous response. My fleeting thought of Chetlain only made me more resolute in my beliefs. I was unfit to feel even grief.

Washburne turned up three days before she died. He had been reading between the lines in Chetlain's letters, and knew not only that Emily was dying slowly – as Chetlain repeatedly stated – but that this was being used as a possible means of influencing my position with Grant. He had been in Chicago, but he had told no-one he was coming further west. He got off the at the dock in Galena totally unannounced.

Emily was very ill. She had asked for the painting of her family to be placed at the foot of her bed, propped on a chair. Through strain, exhaustion, or some more fundamental physical collapse, she could not see very well. The painting was her favourite – of her, her dead mother, and her father. In it, she sat below her father, he with one hand placed carefully on her bare shoulder. After that, she never asked for another painting to be swapped into or out of the room, or any to be moved around – she just looked at that one when she was strong enough, as if she had finally found what she most wanted to see. In these last three days, the slow nature of the deterioration of her body ceased. In its place was a process of change that was amazing and shocking even to my numbed reactions.

Every time I saw Emily some new and drastic disaster had occurred. Her chest – all down from her collarbone, her sternum, to her epigastrium – seemed as if it had caved in, like some weakness in the crust of the earth bevelled out from underneath. Similarly, her face changed: her forehead and brow were stark and bulging, her cheeks sucked inwards, and her gums and teeth seemed to grow in her jaw. Her loss of muscle and weight produced this illusion. Looking at her in those last three days, her body seemed more like a corpse than a living thing. Death for Emily was not one single instant, but had come hours – days – before, leaving her to gradually follow. Seeing her face on the pillows, fixed beyond her will towards the ceiling, some profound point in her illness had been passed, so that to those around her she was no longer a healthy body which had become critically sick, but a destroyed body remaining alive. Washburne arrived to see her like this.

He was red and puffing from the steep walk up from the Galena River. Of all the people who met me during Emily's death, he seemed to be the only one who was unaware of the hierarchy of grief in our house, and the level to which he had been assigned on it. He didn't act as if he were stricken by sadness.

'I have come to see you, John,' he told me. The nurse had called me out of Emily's room after she had received Washburne at the door. 'What a time of hardship this must be for you.'

I was shocked by his presence. I thought maybe he had come at Chetlain and Orvil's request. As my mind worked it out, I felt a rush of anger. I thought he was circling here to inspect the state of the corpse himself, to see how long things would linger.

'My wife is dying, Senator, but she bears her pain with the greatest dignity. I can only hope to follow her example.'

'Oh, yes. John, you care and love your wife. How hard things must be.'

I could hear myself, curt and defensive. 'No matter how hard, I will always try to serve the country I love as I try and serve the people I love. In these times, of all times, it is when we are faced with crisis that we can find how deep our ideals are within us.' I would have left then, if he had asked. I would have run down to the wharf without waiting, like a child who'd been dressed up for play in his father's shirt and trousers, and then, with my hand held to my mouth to stop my gasping, I would have looked up at the windows jewelled by the sun on the side of the high Galena hill and tried to find Emily's in that pile of treasure. I would have searched as it receded from me until I lost hope of seeing where I'd left her, and then spat over the railings of the steamer that was taking me down the river to Grant.

He reached out and took my hand, not shaking it, just holding it in both of his. 'If it's possible, John, may I pay my respects to your wife?'

I felt tears come to my eyes at this: he was speaking of Emily as she once was, the wife of a small town lawyer in 1861 whom one called on in a formal visit to pay 'respects' – not as the ghost left on the bed in the other room.

'It will delight me to present her to you,' I said, proud of her again.

I walked him to her room. That scent, subliminal and noxious, struck me as if I were he, and it was me entering Emily's sickroom for the first time. Washburne walked without hesitation close to the bed, so Emily could see him, and he took off his hat.

'I am very glad to make your acquaintance, Mrs Rawlins,' he said, without pity or condescension.

Emily looked at him.

'This is Senator Elihu Washburne, Emily. He has come from Washington.'

'Oh, no John, not so far,' Washburne assured Emily. 'I was

in Chicago, and so the trip has not been so lengthy. I wished to see how you are, Mrs Rawlins, as Augustus Chetlain had written to me saying you are unwell.'

Emily did not try to speak, but she lifted her hand up. Washburne took it in his, and kissed it in formal greeting. 'Of course, I know your father as well as your husband. I have often debated against him in the Senate.'

'We are all together now,' I said.

Emily's hand was still in Washburne's. I could see her grip tighten. She spoke with her normal voice, but we heard it as if from a long distance away. 'Charmed, Senator,' she said, like this was a dance.

Washburne smiled broadly. I didn't see him look around the room, but he said, 'What a delightful room you have, Mrs Rawlins. May I ask, John, with what material is that tablecloth made? Is that not a rich purple?'

'Emily's father gave it to Emily as a present.'

'It is beautiful.' There was my dying wife, but I found myself looking at the fucking tablecloth, thinking it was beautiful. I looked at Emily. For this fraction of a second, I saw pleasure and pride in her face, instead of disease.

'I wish I had your taste for such things,' said Washburne to her. She smiled. 'Mrs Rawlins, in this grave and painful time for you and your husband, it is a great comfort to me that we should meet. I think your husband has an important role to play in the war we are now in. I will use all the power I can exert in the government to have him with General Grant as soon as he is able to leave your side. I must allow myself the relief of saying that it matters not how long he remains here by you, I will stand fast in my efforts to ensure John his place with the General. This is my clear duty, just as his is here.' Washburne took her hand again, making to leave. 'Mrs Rawlins, my admiration for your husband is only increased for having met his wife.'

'Can you help me . . .' said Emily.

For the first time, I felt maybe Washburne was taken aback. He had just met a ghost; but here was something he didn't expect. However, he showed no hesitation in taking her hand again and bending close to her, saying, 'I will do anything I can.'

'I need to sleep,' said Emily. 'Everything will be all right.'

Washburne repeated, 'I will do everything I can to help you.'

'Senator, don't leave me.'

For a long moment Washburne held on to her. Her eyes closed. She was clearly very tired. When she fell asleep, Washburne looked at me. 'I will come again to visit, John.' He rose from her bed.

I made such a big production of it – of her death, and my own. It's like getting married, or having a child: for you, it's the biggest thing to happen, but for everyone else, it's no big deal. Same as when you die. It's happened before. But I was thirty-four when Emily died. It's hard to understand you're not the first person to die, you know. All the men who fought the Battle of the Wilderness died – most of old age.

It took about the same time to fight the Battle of the Wilderness as it took for that last part of Emily's death. Washburne was there most of that time, like a commander-in-chief. The nurse or I would call the doctor when Emily seemed to be having some especially grave crisis, but there was an element of futile play-acting in this, as the doctor's presence meant nothing to Emily, and he could do nothing for her. She seemed, physically, to undergo a circle of decline. She would move towards a point of extreme panic and distress: unable to feel she could breathe, she became hysterical and frantic, coughing and choking; but just at its zenith, this pain would subside, leaving her weaker and exhausted, and so even more vulnerable to the next cycle of attrition, which at the very point of her least despair began in her again. Washburne would sit by her, and this seemed to give her some comfort. She was not conscious most of the time. I had the impression maybe that she felt Washburne was her father, that somehow he and the painting of her family at the end of her bed were merging in her understanding. Once, she asked for mittens. She was sweating and fevered, and at first we thought that she was cold. I put extra blankets on her bed, and fed the fire.

'I do not think she is feeling cold, John,' said Washburne.

She asked for mittens, but she asked Washburne, as if she expected him to have some, as if he should know what she was referring to. He was puzzled. I worked it out. She meant a large pair of mittens that her father used to wear, and that she kept when she came to Galena. I found them, and handed them to her. She only held them, not attempting to put them on.

Washburne's visit put an end to Chetlain and Orvil's plans. He told Chetlain he'd got him a position as Lieutenant Colonel in the 12th Illinois. Chetlain was delighted: he'd only wanted to be with Grant because of Grant's success, but here was a position that would gratify his desire for status. It also meant he didn't have to hang around with a drunk. The letter of condolence I got from him after Emily died was delivered via the US army postal service, and arrived when I was in Cairo. He'd written from his post in Springfield. I don't think I got to his first full stop: 'This is a melancholy duty in the middle of a sad and terrible time to have to write to you of my deep pain upon hearing of the death of your wife . . .' and so on. He was a happy man.

Emily began dying when Washburne arrived, as if his presence gave her permission to leave. I didn't think she would be capable of any cogent thought at the end – it seemed to me she died of exhaustion as much as anything else. For years and months and weeks her body had been battling with lung tissue reclaimed by bacilli, as if the tuberculosis was the original occupant of her body, and she the aberrant tenant. She was so hard on herself. She fought and fought to stay, like it was her duty. 'Everything will be all right,' she was saying, even in those last three days. Her desire for sleep seemed not a desire for peace, but a wish to regather her strength for more battle. It was so courageous: just one sleep, and things would be better then. All it would take was sleep. Washburne didn't seem to do much; he just sat near her, or close by in the room, or talked to me or the nurse.

I was not there when she died. It was September 3rd, and the air outside was just beginning to feel cold. The nurse, sensing another, possibly final, crisis had come to get me again from the Drill Hall. I was with Washburne. I ran through Galena, leaving him puffing far behind me, feeling the cold holding its chilly palm of air to my face. I entered her bedroom, and in its sudden humid warmth Emily seemed to be concentrating, holding with an act of enormous will onto some impossible weight. She was full of pain.

I was alone with her. I'm not sure if she knew someone was in the room, or, if she did, whether she could tell who it was – but there was so much anguish in that moment I do not trust my perceptions of it. This seemed the single culmination of some life-long battle. I never saw her more ugly with the disease. After she died, especially after her body had been tended to, she looked more like herself than she did then, with me there. I was conscious of all the room, of her on the bed and me with her. Everything in the room seemed poised with me beside her. Bottles of medicine left on the table near the window had their labels turned so I could read them. For a meaningless instant, I was taken back to the porch of the recruiting office in St. Louis – *Marvellous Cordials, Refreshing to Enervated Limbs*. My memory, as if not my own, returned to me again, entire, that old entrapment. I leant down and put my cheek as close as I could to her mouth. Emily seemed to hardly breathe. There was a fraction of space between my face and hers; I held my breath, trying to hear. She did not move. I abandoned her, and ran to get the doctor.

That was the last I saw of her. It's a strange memory, the memory of the last time you saw your wife alive. In the Cairo barracks after she died I dreamed of her often. I wished and longed to touch her again. How much it seemed, in my dreams, to be able to sense her wrists and face, and how she carried her self, her walk and her poise! I was not alone! How powerful to me that was; how amazed I would be when I'd wake and look at the muddy barracks in confusion, as if she had just spoken.

When the doctor and I arrived, Washburne was in the bedroom holding Emily's hand. Washburne looked at us, and then let her hand go and stepped back from the body. The doctor examined her, but he was very brief. He took longer with me than her, telling me clearly that my wife was dead, and that soon – within the week – he would call in again to give me some paperwork I'd have to complete for the registries. The nurse came in as he left, and we three stood so still, as if we were waiting for something delicate and frightened to arrive in the room, and we wished not to scare it away. We stood and stood there; Washburne moved to the chair after a while, but he did not leave. Finally, the nurse left the room, and I was surprised to hear her in the other part of the house continuing her chores. What job had she left to do? It seemed absurd to me she could be busy. I wasn't thinking clearly.

'Did she say anything?' I asked Washburne.

'No,' he said. 'She held my hand.'

I touched her face. Her hair was damp. I saw now that in his examination the doctor had discreetly fixed her features: her mouth was shut, her eyes closed, her hands folded in front like a corpse's.

'She is asleep at last,' I said. I'd thought about it first, making it sound false and melodramatic.

Washburne said, 'I am glad her pain has stopped.'

I touched Emily's face again. 'She bore it bravely. She wished to sleep, so as to fight on. She thought nothing of herself.' I do not wish to report to you what I said. I was never more false, never more unable to understand. John A. Rawlins, by his dead wife's side, wanted to give a speech. 'From such an example henceforth will I draw my own courage.' I looked at Washburne: 'How could I not do my duty, seeing how Emily died? Who could fear the pain of death, armed with such foreknowledge of how it can be borne?' I stood up.

'Let's stay here with Emily,' he said. 'The nurse may come in soon . . .' He meant, to tend to her, to dress her.

I know now I should have started crying out to him. I should have asked him, 'Will I be lost? Will I be lost, in battle?' I should have grabbed his hand and said, 'Don't leave me.' Instead I said, 'I will get the nurse now,' and I left the room. But I don't suppose it matters, in the long run, precisely when things happen.

The moment she died, I moved to join Grant. I was campaigning with him still the night before we entered the Wilderness in 1864. Grant sat on a log next to the fire, his face turned away from Meade. The fire was finally getting warm enough, and there was a lot of activity: telegrams arriving and being sent off, adjutants reporting from various commanders, servants setting up tents. Meade had already begun affecting his general's mien; he relaxed in a folding deck chair, as if on cruise. Grant offered him a cigar, and I could sense Meade's surprise and appreciation, pleased that his commander would also be part of this act. Horace was impressed. I don't think

Meade or Horace understood yet that when Grant casually lit up around a brooding camp fire, commanding 118,000 men all more or less fearful that the sharks of gloom and darkness were soon going to take them, there was no pretence. All he wanted was a smoke. So, would they be more or less scared? Horace captured the moment:

> *The general-in-chief offered Meade a cigar. The wind was blowing, and he had some difficulty lighting it, when General Grant offered him his flint and steel, which overcame the difficulty. The general always carried in the field a small silver tinder-box, in which there was a flint and steel with which to strike a spark ... The French would call it a* briquet.

Horace had an eye for that sort of stuff. We subliminally masked ourselves with subtly calibrated body language. Here, at the commanding officers' headquarters, the servants and men in the ranks were stiffly formal if they were in the presence of commanding officers; if not, they slouched as if just released from a physical burden. Meade, as General of the Army of the Potomac, was duty bound to affect his nonchalant unconcern, just as the other members of the General Staff were duty bound to follow his example in front of the lower ranks, and adopt the stiff deference of those lower ranks in front of him. It seemed to me only Grant was outside this set of formal, unacknowledged rules. He had no skill for these subtleties, as much as he would have liked to. When he tried to adopt the pose of a General, he became absurd; Grant just wanted a smoke, and that's what Horace couldn't understand, and why his book gets that moment all wrong.

Like all the veterans preparing for the Battle of the Wilderness, that night I thought of the other great battle I had witnessed. Let me admit it now. Here's the most painful thing

I have to tell you. As Horace went off to his tent and the guards stood posted around the encampment, this is the knowledge that visited me: Emily's infection was mine also. A reedy breath of shock rattled my throat as I thought of it. This knowledge stood dumb behind me for years, and now, with gentle and dark touch, it reached out and held its cold finger on my back. I had seen the disease's progress, horrible and unalterable, and knew that it was to take its course through me. *The infection was mine.*

I looked beyond the fire, but my eyes would not adjust to the darkness. I seemed to see a skeleton, left from years ago, unwanted amongst the trees. Thousands of men camped in the woods, waiting for tomorrow's battle. We were watched beyond the firelight by unreal visitors. An army had come to haunt the ghosts in this wood. I can see myself now, struggling heavily by that fire. All despair that night was self-inflicted. But is pain any the less painful for that? Is hurt any the less bruising for being self-created? Was she not still beautiful, and now gone? I wanted to reach out and touch her forehead, lightly enough so as not to wake her, yet fondly hoping she sensed I was still here. I could not. How long it can be before what you have done is undone.

All I refused to know about Emily's death seemed to come unbidden. When you watch another's death, you watch your own death also. It was my disease I could not face. It was my undoing that I would not stay to see. At the time, I had not the moral courage to halt and consider what to do. I kept right on. Understanding comes as lightly as if from the air above.

> *Without hail or tempest,*
> *Blue sword or flame,*
> *Love came so lightly*
> *I knew not that he came.*

Bang that up your ginger.

I was prevented from sleeping by the normal chills and sweats. The fire was let burn down, though occasionally a guard would softly place more fence rails on it, as if, in the middle of the night and unseen, he could for just this one task let himself be gentle and weak. From my tent, I watched it burn away. I tried to sleep.

On the morning of May 5th, 1864, about daylight, the General Staff had breakfast while Meade went further down the Germanna Plank Road. Horace tells us that at 8.24 a.m. Grant sent a message to Meade, stating that 'If an opportunity presents itself for pitching into part of Lee's army, do so . . .' At 8.41 Burnside was told to hurry up and meet with Sedgwick. Grant ordered us to move camp, and a mile down the road we met a messenger from Sedgwick – Colonel Hyde – saying that the enemy had advanced further down the turnpike to meet us. We kept riding, more quickly now, and soon met Meade four miles deeper into the scrub. 'It had become evident,' says Horie, 'that the enemy intended to give battle in the heart of the Wilderness.'

For CWDs, the story of these two days we spent in the Wilderness is like a child telling the tale of the first Christmas, or a happy couple recounting how they met. Each element of the story is familiar and loved; it forms a grand and safe ballad, a myth from which deeper poetic truths about horror and distress can be distilled. How we found and stayed in Lacy's meadow; the Orange Plank Road; the attacks by Hancock and Longstreet and Gordon; and all this leading up to the command 'Forward by the left flank', the command Sherman called the 'supreme moment' of Grant's life. Everything, every loss and defeat, is turned to victory in the retelling.

You like war stories? Not this war story, bud. This ain't *Saving Private Ryan*. It's more *Saving Ryan's Privates*. Look, it mightn't turn out to be the story you wanted, but it's not the story *I* wanted, either. If only it was as easy as Horace made it look – if only we could all sit down and write the expurgated version and believe it. Why, my fucking father could have written *that* story: *Death Wears a Poncho*, the haunting tale of one man's adventures in the Mexican War of 1846. James Rawlins is a man torn between the wife he loves and the country he serves. Leaving his adoring family, he and General Scott fight in the ancient blood-drenched Halls of Montezuma, knowing that the savage heart of the enemy knows no mercy, and that in this land Death itself wears a poncho.

I mean, so my father couldn't read or write – but why should that stop him writing a novel? It never stopped Horace Porter. For too long, literature has been restricted to an elite circle of self-appointed guardians, people whose only qualifications are that they are literate. Time to break down the walls. Open literature up to everybody, I say. Why, the other arts did it long ago. Dance? By God, just jerk around on the stage in disrhythmic fit while your lover plays an out of tune cello. Call it 'Resonances of Grief – an exploration of the Self, the Unself and the Total Self'. Drama? One spotlight, one chair, one actor who walks to the centre of the stage. Long silence. Silence continues. More silence. Cello starts to play in background. Actor cries in pain. Silence. *Finis*. 'Resonances of Grief – an exploration of the Self, the Unself and the Total Self' is the hit of the festival. Art? Well, Christ, the last thing you want in art is to be able to draw. That's not gonna get you anywhere. Worse than Hitler, that. What you do is dig up your mother's corpse, put a cello up her arse with a swastika on it, and display the body in ultraviolet light. It's an *installation*, arsepick. I call it 'Resonances of Grief – an exploration of the Self, the Unself and the Total Self'. I don't know much about art, but I know what I fund. And if you can't do anything else, just become a photographer.

So, why should writing be restricted to the writers? We should be able to choose the story we want, create the history we wish to have lived. Let me quote from *Death Wears a Poncho*:

> *The Mexican sun was taking its revenge on the earth below. James Rawlins, despite his leg wound, staggered towards the citadel.*
>
> *'General,' he gasped to his leader, 'the Greasers are crafty. Maybe we should split up.'*
>
> *'James,' said General Scott, 'I need you here.'*
>
> *Rawlins looked up. The ziggurat seemed to be moving further away, shimmering evilly in the heat. Around them, the brown, flat impassive faces of the peasants stared, some not even bothering to look up from the fields they were tending. He thought of his son and how the young child's face cried as he was leaving the Galena wharf. He knew no-one could be trusted. Death wore a poncho, in this land . . .*

That's the story he wanted. So shut up. Shut up. He didn't get it. We didn't get it. You're not gonna get the war story you want, either.

That's not exactly what I was thinking about as the orderlies set up camp in Lacy's meadow, but I was spooked all right. It was the battle when I shat myself. It did not take long for much of Lacy's meadow to be turned to mud. Telegraph wires were carried in reels on the back of donkeys, and the animals could be heard braying beyond the trees as the wires were strung. Everyone was waiting for the sound of gunfire, but the strange accoustic tricks of the scrub meant we heard only the bellowing of oxen, or the New York accent of a reporter's voice, or men chopping wood, or any one of the millions of noises that are not gunfire. A dog barked near the edge of the meadow. Old mining diggings ridged the land, and deposits of junked soil and wasted bearings lay everywhere. Any track that the soldiers had marched along was littered with discarded blankets, canteens and overcoats; all sorts of unidentifiable clothing lay trampled into the mud, and some overcoats hung absurdly from the branches into which they had been tossed, as if placed there with mocking care. Standing in Lacy's meadow that morning, I could smell the baking bread of the quartermaster's corps, and see the baskets of wines and cheeses that Meade's little dickslip staffer Adams made sure were part of Meade's table. No matter how much I spat, I could not clear the blood from my throat.

At about midday, Warren's corps began the battle. It seemed to me as I stood in front of the map table that I could smell the fumes of gunshot. Grant was sitting on a cut log whittling, and I looked to him to see if he could sense the odour. He kept whittling. The sound of gunfire blew unmistakably across the encampment. Meade was talking to Adams, and as they heard it I saw Adams' slight involuntary flinch, as if he'd been lightly pinched. At least he was spooked too. He and Meade kept talking for just long enough to make the point that the gunfire was not what was making them stop, and then Meade walked towards Grant. I was distracted by a sudden drop of moisture hitting the map in front of me. I looked up to the sky, but it was sweat, I realised, falling from me.

It must have seemed I was looking at the sun, because I heard, 'Brigadier-General, it is for us the glorious sun of Austerlitz.'

If someone had said to me just then, 'Be bop a loo bop a bop bam boom', I would've known it was Little Richard. If someone had sung, 'I wanna rock and roll all night – party *everree* day,' I would've known a member of Kiss was in the ranks of the Union boys. And it was with equal certainty that I knew Horace Porter was at present my interlocutor.

I will admit to you frankly that Horace had become more and more a favourite of Grant's. Horace's idolisation of the General flattered him. Grant was able to be flattered, though he was never really convinced.

The tops of the trees began filling with smoke. At first it seemed like a delicate trick in the back of the eye, a mist floating over the retina, but as the gun-smoke increased, a pollution-blue haze crept definitively around the skyline. Adams made a point of chatting quietly with the New York journalist, even picking up a newspaper and reading to him a short extract as evidence in some piffling debate. This attack of Warren's involved thousands of men. The gunfire at times sounded pleasantly puny.

'General Grant has ordered all commanders to attack if he finds the enemy unentrenched. No commander need wait for disposition.' Horace looked admiringly at Grant whittling. 'We'll pitch into 'em,' he said.

A short time after the first gunshots, Warren rode into the camp. His horse was sweating, but Warren's uniform was clean and his face composed. Grant and Warren rode out to inspect the lines. Grant chose Porter as the aide who would ride with them.

Horace writes: 'The party moved to the front along a narrow country road bordered by a heavy undergrowth of timber and bristling thickets. The infantry were struggling with difficulty through the dense woods, the wounded were lying along the roadside, firing still continued in front, and dense clouds of smoke hung above the tops of the trees.' And he couldn't help himself from adding, 'It was the opening scene of the horrors of the Wilderness.'

The hallucinogenic quality that pervades every headquarters

during battle was never more strong than during the Wilderness. The circle of understanding in which effective action operates is reduced and reduced, narrowing what can be seen and known, as in the disorientations of fever. In the Wilderness, the bush around seemed to be a physical manifestation of this blindness. In Lacy's meadow, no matter how hard I tried or in what direction I looked, all I could see was forty or so yards of cleared scrub, unless I looked to the miles of sky directly above.

Horace was still riding with Grant and Warren when Adams wandered over to me, smirking.

'Brigadier-General, I have been talking to a newspaper man.' His voice was like a lawyer so assured of his case that he disdains courtroom theatrics. He spoke just a little too softly, forcing you to listen to him.

'He was still shaking. I had to offer the fellow some of the General Meade's best whisky.' He acted as if he were trying to contain his amusement, and had come to share the yarn with me. 'This news man rushed back here from the pike Warren is on. He says he couldn't be sure, but he thought he was very near Warren's lines when he heard the sound of guns and rifles. He says his horse refused to go any further up the road, and as he was urging it on he was nearly collected by a wagon hurtling down towards him without a driver! He says he'd just jumped out of the way, and then the roar of guns was accompanied by some sort of strange rumble and the sounds of men yelling. He was still shaking by the side of the track from his miss with the wagon, when suddenly, he says, down the road came men running, ambulances, wagons, horses without riders, officers – the whole of Birney's division, he says! He told me he would've joined 'em in the direction they were going, but they were too impolite to let him back on the road.' He looked for my reaction, then kept going. '"That's not like our troops," I told the reporter. "Our boys have more practice retreating than others, and they wouldn't be so uncivil about it."' Adams was an out-and-out-wanker. He shook his head. 'I don't know where these stories you read in the papers start,' Adams jeered. 'He says Hays is dead.'

Horace and Grant returned. Grant took up his whittling again. It was about two o'clock in the afternoon. Gunfire could be heard from many directions. At the very edge of the scrub, I could see two of the camp guards sleeping. Others played cards at a table nearby. Adjutants rode in, nervous and exhausted, continually bringing reports. Dogs followed camp everywhere, living off scraps, alternately feted and cursed by the soldiers. Mostly they disappeared when gunfire started, but every time an adjutant rode into the meadow, one dog would begin an absurd growling, barking as if this was the time for an ostentatious display of bravery. I could see it running at every adjutant's mount, full of bravado, but keeping enough distance to prevent itself from entering any real conflict. The adjutants would dismount and report, their faces flushed and sweating; one or two had horses with bullet wounds.

For the hour from two to three, all of them were reporting an attack on our left. Hill was moving up the Orange Plank Road. Another one would leap off his horse, the dog would prance around barking, and the adjutant would run to the command tent and gasp: 'Hill. Coming up the Orange Plank Road.' Horace was sent to bring back a report about Hancock's troops, who were bearing the brunt of Hill's attack. A. P. Hill was a very famous general: one of theirs, not one of ours.

Horace rode to Hancock, bending athletically low in the saddle to avoid the overhanging branches at the edge of the meadow. Watching as Horace galloped off with the dog chasing behind, I felt the strange sensation of suddenly wanting to sleep. I thought I might faint, but, instead, my eyelids closed to the narrowest slit. Horace's image was lost. I let my chin fall, rolled my neck, and then shook myself.

'Perhaps you may like to take a chair?' said Adams. He held the camp chair in front of him. I couldn't see him properly, but I knew he was sneering.

My sight cleared. 'I will return to the maps,' I told him. 'I will take a drink.' Cunt.

I could not guess at, nor control, the cause of my convulsive exhaustion. It passed as I walked away from that prick. I wanted to sleep. Things were too much.

Two of the camp guards stood by the edge of the wood. One held up a piece of meat for the dog. He waved it and coaxed the dog over. As the dog moved towards them, the guards in turn moved closer and closer to the edge of the cleared grass, teasing it to come further. The dog was used to begging, and moved swiftly to them. When they allowed the dog to reach them, the guard with the food placed it carefully on the ground, and took three large steps back. The other levelled his gun and shot the dog in the belly, and then, as it fell, again in the head. Together they picked up the dog, one guard by the front two legs, one by the hind legs, and on the count of three swung the carcass deep into the bush. They returned to their cards.

Horace returned from Hancock. As he dismounted, I could tell something was wrong. He looked as if something deeply personal was happening, like he'd blundered in on an argument between married friends, and he was pretending to ignore it. Instead of going to Grant, he came over to me.

Horace was sweating. I could see his young face beaded with healthy exertion. 'General Hays has been killed,' he told me, solemn despite his panting. 'Did not General Grant know him as a cadet and during the war?' Horace meant the Mexican War.

'They fought together in the Battle of Monterey,' I said. 'What do we know of General Hays' death? How can we be sure of this report?'

'I am certain. I was with Hancock's troops when they moved on Hill. I was near the attack. Hays has been killed, and Getty and Carroll wounded.'

'Is Birney's division routed?'

'I do not know. I have not heard of this.'

'I have heard a report Birney was pushed back down the pike.'

'He may have been. I know only of Wadsworth's division of Warren's corps. They have began to move towards Hancock.'

It felt suddenly as if we were both acting. Like the onset of a sudden twitch of the eyelid, the same spasms of revelation, mutual but unacknowledged, began in both of us: Warren is breaking up, most of Hancock's corps is gone, A.P. Hill ('A savage fighter' – CWD) was coming up the Plank Road, and the Plank Road, via a winding yet irresistible route through the malevolent wilds, led directly up our cornholes. We were wrong, but we didn't know it at the time. Horace reached up to rub his eye, at the same time trying to disguise the fact it was a tense and unnecessary movement. Grant had moved from the log he had been sitting on. He was sitting on the ground, whittling, his back up against a tree. I couldn't see his face. His head was bowed, watching the stick he was stripping. His knife cut into it near the bottom, and Grant pulled through the bark, until, with a sudden controlled release, the blade and wood parted, his knife jerking away as the off-cut fell onto his lap.

I walked towards him. 'General Grant.'

He looked up at me.

'Colonel Porter has returned from Hancock. He reports that Hill continues his advance. Getty and Carroll are both severely wounded. General Hancock has not yet linked up with any of Wadsworth's corps.'

He kept looking, his face turned up to me. From where I

stood over him, the angle made his face like that of a bearded and bothered nine-year-old boy. His mouth was opened slightly in anticipation as he listened, but he was unsurprised, as if some familiar drudgery was being demanded of him by an adult.

Horace came up behind me and spoke. 'General Hays has been killed, General. I learned of his death when I was close to General Hancock's lines. He was leading his men into battle to encourage his troops, and was instantly killed.'

Grant looked down at his lap, and swept the shards of wood away. 'I knew Hays at West Point and in Mexico,' he said. He wiped his fingers hard against his trousers twice, banging the smallest splinters out of the material. He looked up at us. 'He was a gallant officer.'

Horace was behind me; but I am sure I heard him draw in a long breath so he could began a speech of condolence. It seemed to me that Grant meant to cut him off when he said, 'With Hays it was always "Come, boys", not "Go".' He held his knife at the torn bottom of the stick he was holding. 'Go find Wadsworth and tell him to hurry up,' he said to Porter. 'We may run out of daylight in which to attack Hill further.' As Horace strode off, Grant's knife pushed into the skin of wood, but he got the angle wrong, so the incision was such that it was impossible for him to draw the blade up the torso of the wood easily. He pulled the blade out, and carefully restarted his cut with a shallower grade.

I turned to leave. Adams and Meade stood near the entrance of Meade's tent, looking at us. Adams wore his sword. The leather of his boots rose tightly over his calves, opened over his knees, and then fell stylishly away. Their polished blackness emphasised the assurance of his stance; his hand rested naturally on the hilt of his sword. The swaggering tilt of his hips was defined by the shining braid of his belt, and his officer's jacket swung open carelessly, showing the effortless superiority of his white dress shirt. Meade stood beside him like a proud father, unconsciously aware not only of his son's success, but of his own challenged but undiminished power. His thin older face had a greying, pointed beard and moustache, professorial and precise, which hid his lips, leaving his eyes to place you in the hierarchy of his esteem. His hands were folded behind his back. He looked at Grant and me as if all of his breeding were needed to hide his concern. They stood, the two of them, and were caught in my memory as in a Mathew Brady photograph, except some more modern flash of perception meant that instead of holding themselves with stiff self-consciousness their bodies were framed by an easy awareness of their own worth.

I'll tell you what I know. I know the only reason why any one of them – Adams, Meade, Chetlain, Horace, CWDs, fucking Lincoln himself – abided Grant for even the smallest moment was his success. Yet all of Grant's life had been bound with defeat. He had been raised on, suckled by, joined to, born from defeat. Horace looked at the 'sad havoc' Grant's whittling had played with his gloves, and fondly notes 'before nightfall several holes had been worn in them, from which his finger nails protruded'. But I know there would've been no fondness for the shabby dilapidations of a drunken thirty-eight-year-old Galena clerk bumbling at the back of Jesse's shoddy shop. I, however, was raised in familiarity with such circumstances.

> *No terms except unconditional and immediate surrender can be accepted. I propose to move immediately upon your works. I am, sir, very respectfully,*
>
> *Your ob't se'v't,*
> *U.S. GRANT,*
> *Brig. Gen.*

He learnt this at breakfast, not at West Point.

I have come to understand, at least a little, about my feeling for him; now, others were coming to find him out, too. Meade and Adams were looking over at Grant and me as if they'd just heard some rumour about us that was cowardly but true. I was finding out, now, what I'd always known: in battle, here in the East, up against Lee, the fight was coming to an end. Adams looked at me, then turned away.

'You have a very serious cough, I fear,' Meade called out. He walked closer. 'I will get Captain Adams to call my doctor.'

'No need, sir,' I gasped, between huge breaths that were always too shallow to fill my lungs. 'I need only to sit . . .'

'Captain,' he called to Adams, 'bring a chair for General Rawlins.'

'I will return to the maps,' I said.

Meade was too embarrassed by my gasping to object. 'Do not allow yourself to be weakened,' he told me. He was trying to be kind. 'The country and General Grant need true men now.'

'I could not leave the General, sir, any more than I could abandon the cause.'

'Come,' he said to Adams. 'We will give our condolences to General Grant for the loss of Hays.'

180,000 men fought the Battle of the Wilderness, but sitting sweating at the map table with a shaft of panic lancing through me, there was no-one else with me. Fighting my body, I was all alone. I could see Grant, still sitting on the ground, talking to Meade and Adams. It was about four o'clock, but seemed later because of the darkness of the scrub.

Like some corny re-enactment, a cheer was heard from the south. It sounded fake to me, as if rehearsed. Hancock's troops were too far away to be heard. The small of my back, and lower, was covered with sweat. I wanted to sleep. Three adjutants, in quick succession, almost together, rode into the meadow. Their horses were exhausted. From my map table I could see them dismount. All three strode towards the commanders with an exaggerated urgency and panic. My half-delirium seemed to make them move in the distance like actors, framed on stage by the edge of the table and the curtain of trees behind. One of them, in his panic, rushed straight into his report without saluting. He must have been rebuked for this, or remembered himself, for suddenly his head jerked slightly up, and he broke off his speech to perform a contrite and formal salute. Yet Meade, Adams and Grant all listened with rapt attention, ignoring his gesture. Without even waiting for the adjutants to leave, Meade and Adams began talking to each other. I could see the three messengers' confused body language; they wished to appear attentive, yet sensed this conversation may be outside their station. They had brought news of this crisis, but it was not seemly for them to witness its effects on their commanders. They shuffled unconsciously together as Adams punched his fist into his open palm, turning to Grant in his alarm, and then back to Meade when his demonstration was made ridiculous by Grant's lack of response. The adjutants, with one move, turned to leave; they must have been dismissed. Another cheer, formal and on cue, came from the same direction as the first.

This exhausted, despairing sense of being removed from the scene left me when I saw Adams, amazingly, begin to jog towards my table. Adams, even half-running! He was heading for me, shouting directions I couldn't quite hear, either at me or at the departing adjutants.

'Where is Baxter's brigade?' he panted out to me.

'Brewster?' I said, confused.

'Baxter. *Baxter*. Robinson's Division.'

I looked at the maps around me, and before I could move to them he leaned over and began scattering them, looking for the one he wanted.

'Baxter must go with Wadsworth to help Hancock,' he said. He seemed to have nearly lost his composure. No more smarmy whispering courtroom theatrics. For nearly the only time I ever saw, he was for real. Oh, fuck.

'General Grant orders Baxter's brigade to support Hancock. I must tell the adjutant where to find Baxter,' he said.

'Robinson is on Warren's right, near the turnpike. You may best –'

He cut me off. 'It's enough,' he said, and turned to run to the adjutants.

I said, 'Wait. Hancock may need more men to stop Hill's attack. We should send Denison as well. Warren is under less pressure; Hancock's crisis is greatest.'

He turned round to fully face me. 'Stop?' he said, in surprise; and then, as if angered by the news and blaming me for it, he told me, '*Stop* Hill's attack? General Rawlins, Hancock is *driving* 'em. He's *drivin*' 'em.'

He ran full-pelt to the adjutants, and they galloped off. Things were stranger than even I had imagined. We were winning.

1864

THE FIRST DAY IN THE LACY MEADOW (CONT.) –
THE FIRST NIGHT IN THE LACY MEADOW –
THE MORNING OF THE SECOND DAY IN THE LACY
MEADOW – HANCOCK FLUSHED WITH VICTORY –
THE SECOND DAY IN THE LACY MEADOW –
THE CRISIS ON THE SECOND DAY

We weren't winning. It was very late afternoon. Over the top of the bush, the smoke from different areas of burning trees rose in separate columns, each bent by the wind in exactly the same angle across the sky. The discharge from rifles and artillery was more diffuse, creating a haze scented with sulfur. I leaned back in my chair. I could feel the dampness of my shirt pressed onto my back. My sense of exhaustion grew.

'Wadsworth will not meet Hancock before dark!' Horace said. He was standing in front of me. I hadn't seen him ride in. 'He encounters great difficulty working his way through the woods. I have informed General Hancock of the probability of having no support today from that quarter.'

'Hancock is also to be supported by Baxter,' I said to him. He had a crumpled map tucked into his belt, and his cheek and brow were smeared with what looked like ink or gunpowder. His gloves were rank with sweat and grime.

'I have been with Wadsworth. He will not meet Hancock,' Horace repeated. 'He is too encumbered by the woods. I do not like how this place restricts the movement of our troops. Our superior numbers are not used as they might.' He seemed ill at ease, as if suffering from toothache or stomach cramp, or some such minor pain. 'Hancock fights close to the enemy.'

'Hancock will get more troops to complete his victory.'

'I have talked to officers in his command. They tell me they cannot see the whole length of their regiments. Advance or retreat must be judged by the sound of the firing. The enemy comes on with only the flash of muskets and the noise of their passage through thickets as warning.'

'Wadsworth may not arrive, but Baxter is sent also to help Hancock drive Hill.'

He looked at me. 'Does Hancock advance?'

'Reports are that —'

'He does not advance,' Horace told me. 'I have come from there. It is impossible. There is gloom in these thickets, and it prevents understanding of the battle. Who reported this advance?'

'Three adjutants from Hancock's corps, nearly one hour ago, all reported an advance.'

'This is not so. I have just returned, and reported to General Grant and General Meade. This information you have is mistaken.' He took off his gloves, shoving them into his belt on the opposite side to the map. 'General Grant did not mention this information during my report to him.' Behind Porter, I could see some guards sitting on the muddy grass, one lying with his feet out comfortably and raising himself casually on one elbow. His leg was bandaged from his thigh to his foot. 'Your information is wrong, or out of date,' Horace told me again. 'We will spend a night in the Wilderness, I think.'

It was four more hours – well after dark – before the main fighting stopped, and Horace was shown to be correct. Lee had succeeded in halting our march south. We could go no further. As the light faded, our sense of entrapment grew.

So me, and 180,000 other men, some dying faster than others, spent the night in the Wilderness.

The things that were too trivial to notice at the time – the old style typeface of the lettering on the top of the endless Army forms I filled in, the square labels pasted to the boxes of telegrams and maps, the dirty tent flap forming a triangle of darkness in the firelight diffusing through my tent wall – all these are very powerful now, when I think back. I never got closer to fighting than that fence line in Chattanooga. Back then, I always thought that being close to battle would be the sort of thing that would burn itself into my memory. But the recollections of my folding writing table or the smell of stacked horse feed now seems to me to loom as large, as if every small memory, discarded because trivial, is retained: and the more disregarded they were, the deeper and more potent they become. My tent that night in the Wilderness had no flooring, so I could spit on the grass and dirt. I could hear the weird sound of my breathing. Each breath sounded like I was frantically shaking something that was almost empty, and I could hear only deep clicks of mucus and phlegm. The battle that was to resume before morning had such a looming presence it was like trying to sleep under the huge retaining wall of a dam. In the night occasional gunfire was heard, but there were also all the unaffected rustling sounds of the scrub. How could an animal call out, or even the branches of the trees sough in the wind, as if there were not so many thousands of men here? How could this all go on as it must have even one night ago, when the Wilderness was not full of the Army of North Virginia and the Grand Army of the Potomac? Yet it was impossible not to be always aware of the huge volumes of men that would very soon flood back up against each other, flattening the wood.

'Before eleven o'clock,' Horace tells us of that evening after the fighting on the first day, 'the general-in-chief remarked to the staff: "We shall have a busy day to-morrow, and I think we had all better get all the sleep we can to-night. I am a confirmed believer in the restorative powers of sleep, and always like to get at least seven hours of it, though I have often been compelled to put up with much less."' And – this is what Horace wanted us all to remember – then Grant commented on stories that Napoleon could do with four hours sleep: '"Well, I for one never believed those stories . . . If the truth were known, I have no doubt it would be found that he made up for his short sleep at night by taking naps during the day." The chief then retired to his tent . . .' Bet you're glad you know that. I myself didn't care, either. I was on my bunk, shaking.

If ideas alone can cause disease, what I thought that night were of the sort that make you sick. I had seen Alton die, and Emily. I thought I would die very soon. I knew I had been asleep on my army bunk when my own cry of distress woke me. The camp guard had tended the fire, and it still burnt. My tent was stuffy with perspiration. Meade had ordered an attack for six a.m.; Grant had changed this to five.

We spent the whole of the second day, like the first, in Lacy's meadow. It remained closed around us like a neurosis. The General Staff gathered before daybreak. Although it was still dark, the bottoms of the clouds were lit by the orange glow of burning trees. It made even the darkness before dawn seem theatrical and artificial. The only freshness came from the cold; on first getting out of my tent I could smell the smoke, but very soon this scent was sublimated into the events of the day, making it even harder for me to find clean air.

'The dawn breaks, its cheek pale as a dead man's, and this

morning will soon reveal the horrible face of the coming day,' said Horace. 'The resin in the saplings makes the trees burn like torches.'

I looked at him. The meadow was lit only by the central camp fire and the small lamps placed near each tent. He was wearing his gloves, and they were stained by yesterday's sweat and dirt. He was twenty-seven, his hair parted like a good boy's neatly on the right, and his face remained healthy and unlined. The shadows under his dark eyebrows contrasted with this boyishness. He looked peculiarly intense in the faint eerie yellow. 'But by dint of extraordinary exertions,' he said, reassuring himself, 'great numbers of the seriously wounded are being brought to where they can be cared for.' It reads like Horace, written down; but I looked at him again. His face was strange. Whatever change was in it, whatever caused the change – the campfire, the morning air – I couldn't quite pick.

'Everything that can be done, will be done,' I said to him.

'General Rawlins, I have –' He stopped. 'All things seem like an omen in this wild,' he said. 'Presentiments hang in the air.'

I spat and coughed. This was so common that neither of us let it interrupt the conversation.

'The army cannot move in this bush,' he said. 'We must try to be out of it, and fight in the open.' We were walking to the mess table. He stopped.

'General Rawlins,' he said, again. 'Sir, let me take your hand. I wish you to know that I will never regret serving General Grant, and will never forget it was you who gave me this chance.' He said this resolutely, as if he'd been thinking about it all night, and was committed to this moment. He was solemn, moved by his own words, as if he were reading his own epitaph. It made sense: he thought he was going to die. Looks like every fucking one of us had a bad night. But I was shocked. Not *Horace*. Horace's job was comic relief, not introspection. It was 4.30 a.m., May 6 1864, in Virginia, and maybe or maybe not the United States. I suppose that's not a bad time to do some thinking. I don't think that he'd lost his belief in Grant. I think, rather, he'd had some sort of young man's revelation about his own death. He had glimpsed mortality during the night, its cheek as pale as a dead man's, and the morning had revealed its horrible face to be his own.

But young people – aren't they amazing? You know what it took to get Horace back on the job? The brief staff breakfast was nearly over. We discussed the situation. Hancock was to attack on our left. Adams and Meade sat together, both in new uniforms. Horace remained uncharacteristically quiet, until Grant spoke to his personal servant:

'I need more cigars,' Grant said.

'Yes, sir. How many will you want today?'

'It will be a long day,' Grant said, as if in excuse. 'Bring me two dozen.'

Horace's delighted face showed he was writing that down in his memory so that in 1896 it would be ready to be inserted whole into his description of 'Grant's preparations for the second day in the Wilderness'. That's what it took to make Horace forget his own death. Grant's inspired leadership had worked again.

I quote from Horace's work:

> *Stretch your arms out, like you're on a crucifix. Up above your head to the north is Washington, the Union capital down near your toes to the south is Richmond, the Confederate capital. Grant has begun a march down the long plank where they've nailed your torso, going from head to toes. At the cross beam, where your arms are stretched out, there is a scrub called the Wilderness, miles wide across your chest. Just as Grant gets there, suddenly from his right comes Lee, who has been hiding somewhere up your right arm.*

Grant swings around to face this attack. Instead of facing your toes he is now looking straight up your right arm. Your throat is on Grant's right, and on Grant's left is your stomach, the road to Richmond.

Grant could go backwards, up your other arm, but behind him is the Potomac River, somewhere near your left elbow, so that way is no good. Grant could force Lee back up your right arm, but he'd have to win the battle on your chest first. If Grant continues to lose that battle, he could do what all other Union commanders have done, and march to his right, running squealing back up over your head, home to Washington. Or Grant could go to his left, marching south, further down your chest, towards your stomach – further away from home, deeper into enemy territory, knowing Lee will come after him and meet him again somewhere down there. Imagine – the American Civil War was decided when Lee defeated Grant, way down south in the Battle of the Testicles.

This is not really Horace's. His was more homo-erotic.

Grant stood on the edge of Lacy's meadow, lighting a cigar as the weak light of day took over from the weaker light of the fire. We were all waiting for the crash of Hancock's guns. Grant's uniform was patched with white dust, especially where his hands touched it most, round the collar, fly, and near the button-holes. All his clothes seemed crumpled, as if every night his servant in some mad ritual rolled up his uniform and jumped on it, instead of hanging and ironing it, like other generals' servants did. He took another cigar, and lit it. Horace was rapt; and I, too. A CWD quotes a private from the 5th Wisconsin who saw Grant and said, 'He looked like he meant it.' And that was right.

The gunfire rose slowly with the sun. Grant stood, waiting and smoking. Anyone bored enough could have picked emerging patterns in the random shots. The individual shots coalesced into a swell.

Almost immediately after the crash of Lee's artillery we got a succession of adjutants reporting success. These reports were too consistent and came from too many different sources to be doubted. Most convincing was the fact that on the roads outside of the meadow, instead of ambulances and empty supply wagons and small groups of our troops receding back from the battle, there were columns of Confederate troops under guard. Hancock's adjutants were greeted with a genuine surprise that would have been masked if the news was of defeat. Meade and Adams could not prevent showing shocked delight as they came away from interviews with adjutants. The sun was not yet up enough to shine directly into the meadow; it was still cold, and the canvas of the camp chairs and the top of the map table were annoyingly damp. It was a great two hours. If only the tops of the trees could have held the sunlight still. I saw Adams not even allow an adjutant to get down from his horse. Instead, like an eager girl, Adams stood looking up as the adjutant in the saddle talked down to him. The young officer's face was hot with physical effort, and behind him the darkness entwined in the top of the scrub was being disentangled by the morning light. I noticed my own breath frosted in the air, and felt as if its diseased heat were being cleansed in the cold.

It was easy to get the impression there was something missing in Grant. Long ago, he had been shown the dangers of hoping for too much. He seemed to feel no excitement during these two hours; he reacted to Hancock's success as he did to Hays' death yesterday.

'Go to Hancock,' he told Horace. 'Tell him to expect Burnside to assist him soon.'

Horace wouldn't agree, but I think Hancock was who he really should have written a book about, not Grant. Horace only dedicated his life to Grant and Grant's memory because Grant won. But Horace wanted a hero so much that he didn't want to see who Grant was and who he wasn't. When Horace found Hancock that morning in the Wilderness,

> *... all thought of the battle which raged around us was to me for a moment lost in a contemplation of the dramatic scene of the knightly corps commander. He had just driven the enemy a mile-and-a-half. His face was flushed with the excitement of victory, his eyes were lighted by the fire of battle, his flaxen hair was thrust back from his temples, his right arm was extended to its full length in pointing out certain positions as he gave his orders, and his commanding form towered still higher as he rose in his stirrups to peer through the openings in the woods . . . It was itself enough to inspire the troops he led to deeds of unmatched heroism. He was well dubbed 'Hancock the Superb'.*

It was so easy, when you were winning. At least Hancock didn't wear a poncho.

∽∾

Victory or defeat: they both mean peace. But who could blame us all for not thinking that way back then, on our second day in the Wilderness? At 8.30 in the morning Hancock the Superb sent us back one complete column of 3,000 prisoners, all from Hill's corps. No-one wants another perspective then, except maybe the prisoners. But from then, for the rest of the day until the battle ended after nightfall, we were beaten. That was the last of our false victories.

It was still cold in the enclosed clearing, but my shirt clung to my chest, already damp with a mixture of old and new sweat. The news of Hancock's advance spread, and everyone moved with a happy promptness. Adjutants received and delivered messages with cheerful eagerness. Lacy's meadow seemed to be suddenly full of purposeful staff officers riding off or striding from one tent to another, each grimly trying to hide their new enthusiasm. I noted Adams was wearing a bow tie and a dagger with his fresh uniform. Instead of the virginal blouse of the day before, he had on a checked gingham shirt; buttoned up, his immaculate Captain's jacket revealed the check only in the V exposed between the jacket lapels. The bow tie was part of dress uniform, but the shirt was his touch, you see, to show that he could with impunity augment the uniformed conformity of an army with his own dashing style. The dagger, I assume, was for slicing Meade's camembert. Grant sat stooped on a tree stump, as if defeated.

Prisoners were brought to be interrogated. Meade and Adams stood together questioning them, slightly to the side and front of Grant, who would very rarely ask anything. He would continue to whittle, abstractly listening. I doubt whether most of the prisoners knew who he was. They only looked at Meade and Adams. There was no cockiness or arrogance in the manner of Meade or Adams – they affected a businesslike assurance. A very distressed prisoner was offered a chair; another was dressed in the jacket of a Union private, possibly because some lower officer had decided the prisoner's sopping, filthy uniform was unpresentable to the commanding generals. Not one of the Confederates was in any way defiant. Most stood to attention, as if these Union generals were now their commanders – which was true. They were scared mainly by the change, by the novelty of their defeat. They were used to winning. Their dirtier skin and matted hair gave them a curious incongruity, like they were people from another, far away country, and they had just arrived. It would have been interesting to ask what they thought of us.

Horace was back from Hancock. His uniform was wet through. I saw him report, his face solemn and willing, as he always seemed to be with Grant. Grant was sitting on the ground, his legs straight out. This was awkward for Horace: should he sit on his haunches, to make it easier for Grant, or was this too familiar with the Commanding General of all Union Armies? Grant's neck cricked up to Horace, but either the uncomfortableness of the angle or disinterest meant Grant soon looked only at the whittled shards on his lap. Horace managed to be half-bent and half at rigid attention as he spoke, getting no cue from Grant to put him at ease.

Then, very quickly, while Horace was still reporting to Grant about Hancock's advance, we seemed to be in the middle of the battle. Men without guns were running past the command post; those too wounded to run, but whose fear overcame their pain and weakness, moved with a distorted, perplexed shuffle. Shells fell in the trees and into the clearing itself. Because we were enclosed, it was hard to hear the shells coming. There was a diffuse, unstopping and distant bass vibration of cannon; then the shells would smash into the trees, tearing at them like a screaming animal. Everything that lived in, on or under those trees began bolting around the undergrowth in terror – except, of course, for the Staff Officers of the Grand Army. Smoke and a smell like burning chemicals filled the clearing. When a shot fell directly into the meadow, it smacked into the earth, with a spout of dirt exactly as one might expect; but, unlike those which fell into the trees, a shell in the clearing also caused a *whump* of concussed air, blasted by unguessed-at pressures. Officers and men were careful to move upright. No-one wanted to be seen cringing before the fire. The horses' panic could be heard hissing around the circle of the trees like steam from a bursting engine.

Grant was standing up now, next to Horace. He was smoking, and looked up, checking the sky. I took a map to them, with a self-conscious inability to judge if I was walking too slowly or too fast.

'These shots,' I said, 'must be stray artillery from in front of Warren.'

Grant didn't look at the map. 'A portion of Warren's line is being driven.' It was logical – unless it was total disaster, Warren's troops were closest. Surely Hancock's charge could not have been reversed so dramatically.

A small group, no more than five, from the mass of retreating troops had been herded at gunpoint into the clearing by our guards. Almost at the same time, adjutants came bursting in, reporting to Meade. Soon, Adams walked to us, his hands held behind his back like a school teacher doing yard duty.

'The retreating troops are from Warren's front, sir,' he said. 'Wadsworth's division,' he added with a sneering pause, like he'd said '*Fuck*-ing *Wads*worth'. A little way behind Adams I could see a servant, as if on cue, lead Grant's horse closer. 'General Meade has ordered General Warren to move Crawford to cover the line while Wadsworth's men are reformed.' Another insolent pause, then: 'General, wouldn't it be prudent to move headquarters to the other side of the Germanna Plank Road till the result of the present attack is known?' I looked at Adams. His face was all composure, held blank so no trace of insult could possibly be read into the question. He was a right little cunt. The little prick was suggesting a retreat. I don't know if Grant was aware of the insult, or, if he was aware of it, it didn't bother him. Grant dealt with the question straight, taking his cigar out.

'It strikes me,' he said, 'that it would be better to order up some artillery and defend the present location.' His tone neutered all of Adams' cockhead play-acting. I think maybe Adams thought Grant was just too dumb to be provoked. The servant expectantly holding Grant's horse looked discreetly to us for a sign to come closer. Adams strode past him back to

Meade, waving him away. In the midst of it all, this wave seemed to affect the horse more than anything else. It began to convulsively rear.

Some troops collapsed a tent, cutting the lines with an axe.

'Go order those men to stop,' Grant told Horace.

There was a continual sound of crashing trees, as if one by one each tree lost its courage and attempted a panicked escape. Grant walked forwards, me following, and he kept looking at the sky, like the captain of a ship trying to intuitively sense all conditions.

'Pack only the most secret materials,' Grant said to me, still walking slowly, his face turned to the sky. 'But do not send them away yet. Leave the money and gold where it is.' We carried with us both Confederate and Union bills, and some gold bullion, used to pay off Confederate spies and equip our own. Grant reached and took the end of the bridle of his horse from the servant. In one automatic, assured movement, he sharply pulled the horse's head down, grabbed the bridle to shorten it and so bring the horse closer to him, and, holding the rein with one hand, put his hand on the other side of the horse's head and pulled it even nearer. I couldn't hear him say anything to the animal. He stood, looking again at the sky and around the meadow, stroking the calmed horse absent-mindedly.

The papers I needed to pack were in Grant's tent. Inside the enclosed tent, it seemed somehow more likely a shell would crash in on me. Grant's desk had lockable drawers, and the most important documents – codes, secret orders, secret unsent dispatches – were held in different places, each needing a separate key. I felt I'd been through all this before in some nightmare, fumbling the simplest of movements. I had all the keys. I could hear a man panting, almost crying, on the other side of the tent wall. In front of me was a childish problem: which key, which drawer? I had every key; had used them for all the years I'd been with Grant. But the simplest knowledge seemed inaccessible. I took a guess, and fumbled a key into the lock, but it would not turn. I had, for all my panic, enough self-possession to be immensely glad no-one could see me.

'One by one,' I said aloud to myself. I wanted a plan – it didn't matter how long it took, I'd just try them one by one, each key for the first lock, until I got to the right one. I'd given up trying to remember what I should've known immediately. The soldier panting behind the tent wall seemed to suppress a wail when I'd got through all the keys, and not one of them worked.

I stood up – I'd been crouched over the desk – and looked back to the flap of the tent, just to check no-one was standing there, watching my humiliation. This onset of panic was like the sudden collapse of a shaft that had been weak for years.

'You try one by one,' I kept repeating, absurdly whispering it to myself, just in case, in the middle of an artillery attack, I might be overheard. At last a key turned. Later, thinking about it, I couldn't've been in Grant's tent for more than a minute. I placed the papers in a pile, and worked through the next drawer in the same way: try every key. As each successive drawer opened, the task lost its urgent difficulty. The sobbing man stopped. For the final drawers I could abandon my plan of trying each key: I could remember, of course, which to use. Finished, and with the small bundle of documents and folders in front of me, I realised who I'd heard sobbing. I hoped no-one else had.

Walking out of the tent, I could smell the sulfur in the air. I felt a calm exhaustion after my panic. Men were running to build a line of entrenchments. Straining horses pulled artillery into position, and I could hear the occasional screech of a shell in the brush beyond. Grant was sitting on his usual tree stump, but not slumped over. He still gave me the impression of an animal using all senses. His face was tilted up, like a snout to the wind. He got off the stump, and seemed to pace around it, not going far in any direction. In one hand, he held a broken stick. Instead of looking up, his eyes prowled the ground in front of him. For a second, it seemed to me that in battle, a deeper instinct had taken hold of him, and he was possessed by some more elemental, more bestial will. But that idea was just me bullshitting, because then I saw what the beast was hunting: Grant leant down, and picked up his lost whittling knife. He returned to his stump as if he knew he'd be less bored now he had something to do.

Horace was magnificent under fire, I've got to say. I could see him striding around Lacy's meadow unflinchingly. He helped place the artillery caisson that was brought up, and oversaw the entrenchment. We weren't under fire that long, after all: but he acted as resolutely as his book recommends to young readers who may wish to know how to look brave. He saw me standing at Grant's tent, and walked over.

'"Stand fast, Craig Ellachie",' he quoted. He was, I think now, in many ways a gem. Only Horace . . . I looked at him blankly.

'That is the motto of the General's Scottish ancestors,' he told me. 'And is he not always true to it?' Bugger me, Horace, you defy your own insipid self-chosen role as Side Kick To The Great Man. You're a cigar-counting suck, but at times I misunderstood you as deeply as I did Washburne.

'There has been no general collapse of our line?' I asked him.

'Wadsworth was out of alignment because of the rapidity of Hancock's advance. Wadsworth could not conform to his wing because of the bush. Hancock has sent reinforcements.'

'Even if they have been stopped, we cannot stay here if we are within range,' I said.

'There have been no shells for some time. General Grant feels they have been pushed back.'

'We definitely stay?'

'Without doubt. The attack could not have been made with more than one division.' Horace snickered. 'I myself have always doubted Lee's brilliance, but even his hardiest supporters would not suggest he could move us with that.' Fucking Horace is cracking funny ones now. I take it back, Horace. You are a dick. 'We stand fast, General,' he said, moving towards Grant.

I hadn't noticed, but the shelling had stopped. It couldn't have lasted more than ten minutes. CWDs know that it wasn't much after ten o'clock, and they always quote the regimental commander who said, 'There was a lull all along the line. It was the ominous silence that precedes the tornado.' He got a job after the war writing preview copy for video-only movies.

I turned back into Grant's tent to return the documents I was carrying. I was shocked. The drawers were hanging open – a couple had been pulled right out, and lay on the floor of the tent – and around and on Grant's desk papers were scattered everywhere. Fuck, I must have been shitting myself. Then, from behind the back of the tent, I heard again that same distressed panting I had heard before, though weaker now, as if exhausted by grief. That despair, I realised, was not mine this time. On the other side of the canvas there was someone else who shat himself in the Wilderness. It was nearly as startling as that first artillery shell had been. All this time, and I'd thought panicked humiliation was my own unique curse. I left the desk, and went outside and around to the secluded back of the tent, without even the presence of mind to sneak.

Adams was standing, but he was bent over like an exhausted athlete after a race, his head hanging, supporting himself with his hands on his knees. I saw him draw himself up, taking in a long shuddering breath. His face should have been red with exertion, but instead it was a gruesome white. As he drew himself up, his hands went to his waist, but this seemed too much effort, and he let them fall pathetically down in front of himself. There was a quality of childish tantrum about his posture now, as if some adult had demanded of him a level of self-control he found brutal and unfair. I was too amazed to feel even triumph. Instead, almost without choosing to, I left him. He hadn't seen me. I knew straight away this was something I did not want to disclose. Of all people, I can keep a secret coffinned till it rots. Even before he proved it later that very day, I knew that little turd wouldn't have done the same for me. I was puzzled: his teary face was another enemy I had triumphed over, but I felt none of that. Instead, I held my hands behind my back as I walked steadily away from Grant's tent, clutching them together too hard for comfort. I didn't need to see his face. I didn't want to know how things really were.

One hour later, at 11.00 a.m., we all found out how things really were. CWDs know that with hindsight we can say

> *Tactically, Grant was in far worse shape than he or anyone else in the Lacy meadow seemed to know. In addition to the unmanned gap across his center, he had both flanks in the air. No blue army had ever remained long in any such attitude, here in Virginia, without suffering grievously at the hands of Lee . . .*

There is a description by a Union soldier, somewhere, of a corpse he saw that had just been struck by a cannon ball. He swears that out from under the collar and cuffs of the clothing on the body he saw smoke seeping slowly from some buried core of fire. We never shared a deeper, more buried fear than that which ignited in Lacy's meadow for the next eight hours. We could hear all the accumulating suppressions of the last day, of the last months, groaning in the weight of the gunfire that collapsed onto us at eleven o'clock that morning. Grant had never fought Lee; and he was losing, we realised, just as all the others had. We thought panic had been burned out of us. But we found even that was wrong. Today, with this attack, Lee called from us reserves of fear the existence of which we were unaware. In the end Grant was made President; Horace was his aide; Washburne became Ambassador to France and I, Secretary of War: but no country demanded more of us than Lee's did during that half day.

When the attack began on Hancock's front at 11.00 a.m., Adams was with us in the meadow. He seemed unchanged. For the next eight hours the circle of trees closed around us. No-one would admit to what they imagined was happening outside in the shrub. The adjutants seemed to always bring with them a new defeat, making even those visionary fears seem childish in comparison.

Within one hour of his morning victory, Hancock the Superb was defeated on our left. If you reach in and feel your chest now, it's warm, and all seems well; but the hard bones and heavy flesh feel like a cow's cold carcass when you're dead. It's a peculiar mixture of emotions, being undeceived. Horace rode back into our circle of trees, coming from Hancock.

'General Wadsworth is dead,' he told us. His uniform was slightly askew everywhere, as if he'd been putting off and pulling on his uniform over and over in manic repetition. 'Hancock has been attacked in both the front and flank. The enemy come suddenly out of the dense wood, not firing until over our lines.' He was a child, and just learning how to dress.

Meade said, 'Who are the commanders in Wadsworth's division? We must find out who is most senior, and affirm him in command. We need a list of his Brigadiers.'

For the first time in two days, Grant came over to me to look at the maps.

Behind us, I could hear Adams' voice, calm, reciting for Meade: 'First Brigade: Brigadier-General Lysander Cutler, commanding the 7th Indiana, the 19th Indiana, the 24th Michigan, the 1st New York Battalion Sharp Shooters, the 2nd Wisconsin, 6th Wisconsin, 7th Wisconsin.' His voice moved smartly on: 'Second Brigade: Brigadier General James C. Rice, commanding . . .'

Grant shuffled with mild discomfort at having to ignore some small irritation. Still holding his whittling knife, he traced along the line of the Rapidan, the river to the north on our right.

'. . . 84th New York, 95th New York,' continued Adams, '147th New York, 56th Pennsylvania. Third Brigade: Colonel Roy Stone, commanding 121st Pennsylvania, 142nd Pennsylvania . . .'

There was no fire directly at us. Hancock's line was over a mile away to the west. But all around us we could hear guns. A huge glass oven dish seemed to be placed over us, trapping the sound and the smoke. I could smell the hysteria in Adams' calm control.

Meade walked to Grant. 'I will send to Cutler, to inform him he has charge of the fourth Division. I will also inform Major General Warren, and his other divisional leaders.' Meade's beard hid his mouth as he spoke. He looked extremely tired. Most of the Union army in 1864 were under twenty-seven years old; less than half had turned twenty-five (CWD figures). But Meade looked like an old man.

Grant said to Horace, 'Go to Burnside. Tell him to connect with Hancock's right at all hazards, and then prepare an attack.' And then he said to Meade, 'Order every man not now engaged on the lines to report to Hancock. I wish to attack soon there. Order the wagon train guards and bullock drivers to report to Hancock. Ensure there is enough ammunition.' Then after that, without any change of tone, he ordered all the pontoon bridges on our right taken up, so we couldn't go north back over the Rapidan River to Washington.

The smothering circle of trees seemed to trap the smoke. In many places, the trees were on fire; this mingled with the fumes of the guns. I had to force myself to ignore my panic at finding it harder to breathe.

When Horace came back, he was expressionless and exhausted.

'Burnside cannot connect with Hancock,' he said to Grant. 'The bush is too thick. The men fall into unseen swamps.' To me, out of Grant's hearing, he said, 'Every bush seems hung with shreds of bloodstained clothing. Wounded men burn. One of General Burnside's aides told me he was retreating from the flames, and the incapacitated men along the bush track begged him to shoot them. First one yelled, and this seemed to give courage to the others. Soon all were screaming at him, asking him to shoot them.'

There was clean air, I knew, up, beyond the circle of trees, up there. I thought of the Dubuque hills, and how I'd look down on the Galena river from high. There had been no battle, it seemed, until now. Adjutants no longer bothered binding their horses' wounds. They would ride them away after reporting, the horses still bleeding. One horse crashed down, and the carcass needed to be hauled from out of the meadow.

Meade sat on his camp chair, staring straight ahead. He received the reports from his adjutants with increasing politeness. One panting officer reported Hancock was retreating and a Confederate body of troops had moved up near the Brock Road, on Hancock's rear flank. 'Very good, sir,' Meade told him. Soon after, Meade and Adams mounted their horses, and went out to talk with some commanders in the field. They rode out together, conspiratorial and alone.

When Meade and Adams rode back into the meadow, they did not come over to us. Wounded soldiers were being placed by stretcher bearers on the fringes of the meadow, but all were ordered away. Hancock's troops had been fighting since five – over seven hours. I thought I could hear the sound of screaming carried by the wind, but surely that could not be so.

I could see no camp guards, no servants, no oxen drivers or telegraph stringers. Except for sweating adjutants crowded around the water barrel, movement seemed to have stopped in here. No-one remained who didn't absolutely have to be here.

Longstreet was fighting us now, we heard. Lee had taken personal command of the centre. We heard that the unit behind Hancock's flank was a column of our wounded marching away; or that it was a division from Longstreet sweeping up our rear along the line of the Germanna Plank Road; Burnside was seen dead; we heard that a whole section of Potter's division had simply put down their arms and marched through the bush until they found someone they could surrender to. Much of all this was false, but it was all reported to us. The worse the news, the more stoical the adjutant forced himself to be. Adams had taken to waving them away over to us, while he and Meade talked together.

I think Meade and Adams were working out a good quote for the New York papers, something tabloid and pithy – something like over the forty-eight hours, or 172,800 seconds of the two days we were in the Wilderness, we lost a man, killed, wounded or captured, every ten seconds, give or take a second here and there. Every ten seconds for two days and nights a chime went off – *ping*. Open the microwave, another one's done.

I was never hysterical. My moment of most paralysing panic had come and gone in the tent earlier. But as the day went on, I could sense in me a growing recognition of what was to come. I knew Grant's history too well. Defeat, here, against Lee: was this not what would happen if a shopkeeper from

Galena got his failed drunk son and told him to fight General Robert E. Lee? Grant had no friends, only allies. How had he come to mean so much to me? I felt as if I did not care for this war anymore. There was another battle, somewhere else, that Grant was losing. This was my battle. I could see the reporters' faces as Adams dictated. Defeat or victory, allies leave. We would be left here alone.

In the middle of the Wilderness, I felt the terror of this abandonment. The wind moved thousands of yards of scrub as if leeches and maggots were creeping under the skin of the forest. Great hunks of the brush coalesced, broken branches and shorn trees merged in fearful premonition, until I could only stare in horror at the vision revealed: Grant's face. I heard myself moan in disbelief.

Lee's attack escalated at 4:15 in the afternoon. His attack, according to the maps in front of me, should have come from directly ahead of us. But Lee seemed to come from everywhere – he came at us from the north, to our right, where we'd have to go to escape back to Washington; he came from the South, our left, where we'd be dragged as prisoners to Richmond; and he came at us right here, in the centre of the Wilderness, where we'd be buried.

The accumulated smoke of the last two days meant the sun shone red, stuck at sunset. Things seemed reversed. Gunfire, wounded men, panic and fear – these seemed to be normal now, and seeing sunlight, trees, or the sky caused me to look up in eerie surprise. Even though it was only mid-afternoon, someone had lit some lamps around the meadow, and halos of fumes circled in the air. The emptied meadow was filled again by a procession of adjutants galloping in, reporting the new action. Whoever started this fight, whatever its causes, no matter the rights and wrongs, it was now out of our control. We had picked on the wrong drunk, in the wrong bar.

Horace's face was full of small, nicked cuts, caused by

branches whipping him as he rode. Most of the adjutants were damp and filthy: they had passed through small creeks, and grime stuck to them. Many were sullen and exhausted, some going to the water barrel even before reporting. In the extraordinary red air, things seemed more beautiful. The maps seemed to glow, diffuse transparent light coming as if from behind them. I only heard the loudest explosions. Horace told me the fire moved quickly enough to sometimes overtake whole trains of ammunition wagons.

Word came that Meade was going to send an order for commanders to count their numbers. It is an order only sent before a retreat. No winning commander needs to know exactly how many men he's got, at least not in the very moments victory is unfolding. Grant countermanded it; yet, for the next hour, we still had adjutants coming back from the front with figures. When Grant wandered near I seemed to smell his cigar smoke, a fond memory unpolluted by the subconscious envelopment of the burning wilderness. I was panting with every breath.

It was five o'clock on that supernatural afternoon when Grant finally came over to me. I knew that this had to come. He got up from the ground, stiff from prolonged sitting, and turned for a second to drive his whittling knife into the stump he had been leaning on. His face was neutral – he could have been bored in the shop. I felt suddenly as if I had been impossibly linked to my own history, like a narrator displaced by degrees of latitude and hundreds of years from the events in which he is placed. That story was ending now.

'General Grant.' I spoke to him first. My voice sounded strange, as if I'd been unknowingly shouting for hours, and this was my failed attempt at a whisper.

'General Rawlins,' he said, 'I wish you to help me draft an order for the whole army.'

Who knows what he was thinking? I have done some study

on his life. A string of defeats had led up to this, the final scene of failure. Was he thinking of Fort Humboldt? Of Galena? Of the dirty wagon he drove into St. Louis in '54, dressed in his old Mexican army overcoat, so he could stand on street corners selling firewood, until he made enough to go to a bar? His face looked as if he were about to greet me as an old army buddy, and ask to shout him a shot for old time's sake, like when we retreated north after getting our arses kicked in the Wilderness in '67 . . . or '63 . . . whenever that was. That's the biography of U.S. Grant that would never have gotten written.

I stood, frightened. My fingers gripped the order book, like I'd gripped the frame of the door outside that office in St. Louis. I waited for Grant to speak. His small eyes seemed narrowed in resignation.

'There is a great conflagration in the woods,' he said. 'Our breastworks are burning. Men suffocate in this air.' I looked at him. I seemed to hear his voice alone; the rest of the world was reduced to a small murmur in the background. 'This attack by Lee exhausts our troops. I will revoke my order for Hancock to assault. He has not enough ammunition. We must draft an order for the army to move.' Even though it was the smallest of movements to get the quill and open the order book, it made me want to gulp for air. I knew I could not, in front of him; I inhaled only as little as I needed to prevent panic.

'We shall move forward, out of these woods. I hope to swiftly bring this campaign to an end. We will advance – south, out of the Wilderness.'

1869

DANBURY – A TRAIN RIDE SOUTH – IN PRESIDENT
GRANT'S CABINET ROOM – WILLARD'S HOTEL – UP

In the end, I had to be led out.

In late August 1869 I vomited more blood than I wanted to look at behind some stables in Danbury, Connecticut. I was President Grant's Secretary of War. Either because they could hear my retching, or because they could smell the blood, the horses in the stables became agitated, so I only had time to shuffle some dirt onto my mess before I stumbled back home. I told no one. In the days after, I felt, as I expected, weak and exhausted. I was unable to exert myself physically in any way. If I was in the presence of others, I often pretended to stop and look at a shop window, or admire a well groomed horse, or fabricate some other excuse to allow my dizziness and distress to fade. But I had stranger symptoms. I felt a general diffuse warmth in my body. At times, this would seem to concentrate into an identifiable, localised heat in my chest, but, more often, it was as if I had been given new, warmer blood to replace that which I had lost. I was shocked and horrified, and because of this I found it hard to distinguish between what was really happening to my body and what I might be conjuring with my mind. In those days, before the train ride to New York, I sensed a sort of changed awareness. At times I heard small and inconsequential sounds, like a maid sliding open a window or children's voices from another room as if they had occurred very close to me, almost as if the source of the sound was right next to my ear. More than this, I felt, despite my exhaustion, intensely aware of some things. Looking at a garden, or down a streetscape, I could not help having a strong sense of distance and perspective, as one does automatically when looking down from an unusual height. However, I was more worried about how to hide what was happening to me. These disjointed eerie sensations seem far more important to me now than then.

During this time I got notice of a cabinet meeting in Washington, which meant first a train trip to New York. On the train to New York, things seemed to go in a delirious cycle. It was August, and hot. As soon as I was in the train, after the heat and farewells of the platform, it was as if some huge struggle to ignore pain was over, and I allowed myself to feel for the first time the full extent of my extreme exhaustion. It was like finally unstifling a groan. That sense of being released from some effort of containment repeated itself right throughout the trip. I would be overcome by successive waves of pent-up distress. All the rhythmic noises of the train's movement seemed to be jumping and creaking right in the shell of my ear. For so long I had concentrated on my every breath – for years drawing in each one involved repressing the panic of suffocation. Wanting to beat the shit out of my ox that day high in the Dubuque hills was the last time I felt I could exert myself without gasping. Now this long, long effort of enforced calm was coming to an end. The slow curved rate of the destruction in my lungs was exponentially accelerating, curling up in successive cycles of distress. During this hallucinogenic time in the train, I was also thinking of Emily as she lay on her bed and Washburne said, 'Let's stay here.' In the humming, hot carriage the scene revolved and revolved before me. I could see her face, struggling with pain. Washburne would say it again – 'Let's stay here' – and at this climax I would be overwhelmed by my panicked gasping for air. I would return again to a calmer but weaker exhaustion. I knew I wasn't thinking right.

In the train, there was a moment that came again and again at the same point in the repeated cycle of my fever. This was a moment when I doubted my own recollection of what had happened, and tried to be convinced that, in my grief and pain at Emily's bedside, I had stayed in that room. But as my thoughts went on, I became aware that this was a safe lie, and that Washburne had said 'Let's stay here', but I had left those grim eyes fixed upwards.

It is still with horror that I think of how I left her.

I didn't think I was dying. I knew I was very sick, and that I was having to make a great effort to get to New York, and Washington, and to Cabinet – to still be John A. Rawlins, Secretary for War – but I didn't think dying was a train ride south.

In New York another great involuntary upheaval of blood left me almost unconscious. I lay on my hotel bed, cold and numb, attached apathetically to awareness until I couldn't be bothered even with that. I passed out. I retain a fearful dark feeling for this time. After coming to, I could sense I had not been asleep. Rather, there was a strange, dank, gruesome quality to my unconsciousness, as if some deep failure had occurred. There was no part of me that did not feel sick.

Pains reached from my abdomen down my side and through my limbs. My hotel room was hot, and this heat seemed to be putrid and fetid; I have no desire to tell you all. I noticed that there was a filmy, cellular distortion in my left eye. To me, now, thinking back to the hotel room and remembering myself staring in confusion at the bright summer whiteness of the wall, wondering, even in the enormity of my distress, at the glob of hazy greyness floating there in my vision – it's pathetic, like a boy staring at his dead father's boots, unaware of the huge adult disaster about to overwhelm him. The bell boy started with repugnance when I opened my hotel door.

'I have a booking on the train to Washington,' I told him, as if he had asked me, as if it answered for the calamity he could smell in my room. He said, 'Yes, sir.' I did not know how ghastly I seemed to him. I was already too ill to understand how humiliated I would have been feeling if I were well and this had happened. It almost makes me cry out now in pain.

∞

Everything in Grant's White House of 1869 was smaller than you might expect – the impression it made was similar to that which the scenes of childhood give to a returning adult. Incongruously, the cabinet room was furnished more like a domestic drawing room than a place of government. Long, draped ceiling-to-wall curtains fell over the two large windows; a side board with files, odd books, bric-a-brac, and candle holders with half-burned candles stood against one wall; the other had a fireplace, and on the mantle-piece were miniatures of Grant's family. The cabinet table in the middle could have been for family dinners. The two small secretarial desks, with writing lamps, file holders, quills and stationery, seemed to be out of place – it was a strange family that allowed such business-like things here.

Grant sat at the head of the table, with me next to him. Grant would sit back in his chair, bemused and lost. The cabinet ministers around him were not careful about concealing their superiority over him. The Secretary of State had a family history reaching to the roots of Yankee prestige; the Attorney General was a judge, and son of a famous Yankee lawyer; the Secretary of the Navy was a rich merchant – and so it went, each man more successful than Grant in everything but fighting. Grant, I could tell, still wanted to be like those men, and, as always, in this he was defeated.

I don't know what other governments are like, but it was rare for a cabinet meeting of Grant's to have all the members even bothering to sit around the table. This family ate dinner with the TV on. One minister's chair would be turned to the next, and they would talk to each other as if the rest of us weren't there. Right now, two of them were discussing the government sale of gold, and how this would influence the new tycoons like Jay Gould.

'That's not what the tycoons are after,' said the Attorney General. There was always a corruption scandal during Grant's presidency, always another smart deal being done.

'Their interest in the government sale of gold is only natural for bankers in their position,' the Secretary of the Interior confirmed. 'This prevarication by the cabinet is wrong.'

This shithead would sit on an armchair to one side, reading minutes and memorandums from his Interior Department, as if that were the real government business, and it was an annoyance that these sort of meetings had to distract him from that task. 'I don't know,' he'd often say if pressed for an opinion, looking up from his folders with impatience, and meaning 'It's too small an issue for me to worry about'. Grant would raise his hand a little, just like Horace once described him doing, and then let it fall on to his knee, hopeless. He was back in the storeroom in Galena, searching for stirrups.

Looking back, I think I was the only one at the cabinet meeting on September 3rd, 1869 who did not know I was dying. When Shithead for the Interior walked in to the cabinet room, with a servant behind him carrying bundles of documents, I don't think he noticed me at first. But even with the haze that had developed in my left eye, I wondered at what it was that passed over his face when he seated himself, and looked up to see me next to the President.

'John!' he said, shocked; and then remembered himself. 'Sir,' he said, nodding to acknowledge Grant, who was, after all, the President. 'John,' he said to me again, this time his voice composed.

I could not have understood this, back there. I never had time. The last three days, from the Cabinet meeting to the final day in the hotel, all that happened to me happened without my volition – so much so that it seemed I was only incidentally involved. It was as if by accident I was there at my death. I was thirty-eight. By the time I worked out someone was dying, I was barely able to remember who it was. During the cabinet meeting, and the day after, I thought I was doing a fairly good job of deceiving those around me about how sick I felt. Something else strange was happening to my vision. The light coming in through the windows in the Cabinet room was blinding and intense, but only in swirling patches, which would float across the window and force me to squint. Apart from these patches of brilliance, my sight seemed normal. I also remember that after the collapse in New York I lost for a while my sense of exhausted distress. I was no longer overtaken by faintness. I felt not on the edge of a smothering dank slumber, but rather of airy delirium. The facts and opinions of the Cabinet meeting floated past me in a way that made them seem instantly comprehensible.

'The liquidation of debt through the retirement of the bonds issued during the war will return the value of currency towards it being possible to redeem face value in specie.' These words were heard at a hallucinogenic distance that helped rather than hindered my comprehension. The point seemed simple and clear and I could almost hear what was to be said next. The contraction of the amount of money would hurt businessmen like Jay Gould because . . .

'. . . the lowering of the price of gold will lead to stagnation. There will simply be less money to spend, to do business with.' The debate had, for me, a physical clarity; each idea seemed substantial enough for me to touch, if only I could stop coughing and get my hand to move where I wished it to go. I also understood there was a more muted, solemn tone to the meeting. The casual disrespect of Grant was less overt. Even Shithead for the Interior made some effort to pay attention. It was as if some disaster was looming – the collapse of the gold market, or the public announcement of corruption at the highest level – and we were all still and waiting so we could feel the first small tremor of the quake. 'Something terrible is happening,' I thought, sensing things with my new inner clarity, 'and these men are all somewhat cowed by it.' In the silences, even in between fits of coughing, my wheezing was like unused breath echoing around my empty lungs. Not one of the men in the room looked at me. If I turned to face them, they would avert their eyes, coy and embarrassed. 'I have caught them out,' I thought to myself. 'Something is being planned for me.'

The day after the cabinet meeting, Grant was to leave for a trip to Saratoga. Before he left, I saw him at the White House. It was September 4th. It was my final conversation with Grant, but only he could have suspected that at the time. Most of the White House was shabby – the carpet in the room we sat in was worn near the door and in front of the fireplace. It smelt stale.

'You must not allow the interests of the speculators to influence the currency debate,' I said to him. 'The Attorney General is too involved with the bankers. He must not be relied upon in this matter.'

His small, crumpled face looked miserable. He said to me, 'That is what I think, too.' He looked straight ahead, not at me. After a silence, he said, 'I fear you are very sick.'

I was a little surprised. I thought it wasn't that obvious.

'My cough has worsened. The summer heat and dust aggravates me.'

'I see,' he said. He held a quill in his hand, very much as if he wanted to start whittling it down. I seem to remember this scene as if I were not there, and the person talking to Ulysses S. Grant is someone I met long ago, but have since forgotten. 'You have had this for so long.'

'I am convinced,' I said, 'that Jay Gould controls more members of Congress, even members of cabinet, than we may think.'

'John,' he said. 'My brother Simpson and sister Clara died from consumption during the rebellion. The disease was in my family. Two of my father's brothers died from it. When I was young, in the months before my graduation from West Point, I had a cough like yours. I was very much reduced in weight, and for six months my cough never stopped. It was, however, not what was thought. I recovered. It is a disease that disguises itself well.'

I looked at him. I had a ghostly awareness of my own body – I could almost see the bony reduction in my face, feel the skeleton of my chest pushing up for air, sense the delicate brittleness of my posture as I held on against pain. The distance between us seemed palpable, as if it were an object too, like the desk or chair.

'Of the three of us,' Grant said, '– Simpson, Clara, and me – I seemed by far the most promising subject for that disease.'

I was wrong about me and Grant; almost totally wrong. I found that out when he ordered us south, out of the Wilderness. I think he did not need me for much. I get three mentions in Grant's book. Three mentions, all small, in a 600 page book. Two are totally incidental. The other contains Grant's only summing up of our life time together:

> *He was an able man, possessed of great firmness, and could say 'no' so emphatically to a request which he thought should not be granted that the person he was addressing would understand at once that there was no use of pressing the matter. General Rawlins was a very useful officer in other ways than this. I became very much attached to him.*

And that's it. It's better than 'With him it was "Come, boys," not "Go",' I guess. Grant leaned back in his chair, and his arm made a small, futile brushing movement, sweeping some non-existent shavings off his desk. He twisted his quill. Whatever disappointment or pain was in his face, it seemed there despite me. Maybe, later, after, he broke down in some tent somewhere, and wept.

'I am leaving to holiday in Saratoga.' He paused, uncertain as always. 'I hope,' said my commander, 'we can both of us get some peace.'

I left his shabby house then, and went to the Washington hotel room that had been waiting for me to book in all my life. Willard's was comparatively empty. Everyone was getting out of town for summer. As I lay on my bed, the strange, acute distortions of my hearing made each thing I heard seem to exist a foot from my head. The hollow whistle of the gas jet, the jingle and clanking of a team of horses, the Negro voices of the maids calling down the corridor – all seemed to revolve just above my drenched pillow. I could hear more than this, however. There was also the constant, almost rhythmic, straining of the rigging on the ships in the Potomac; I could hear the thin, combined note of the voices in the restaurant on the ground floor, and water running in a trickle from a jug controlled by an unsteady hand, and a muffled cold voice commanding something of somebody next to me, and I knew I was to be ordered next, and that the order was harshly made and unwelcome. There were times when I realised I was lying in bed in my room in Willard's, but I had no sense of the missing spaces connecting these clearer moments. I knew in those spaces I had also been hearing my father's voice, and my brothers' and my mother's, and that this was impossible, as they were all dead; yet I could think it was beautiful and wonderful to hear them again, exactly as they were. How rich an experience, to hear what I thought was lost forever – precious still, even if it were only a hallucination.

'What is your full name?' I was asked.

'John A. Rawlins,' I said.

'Do you know why you are here?'

'I am sick and have consumption.'

'That is right. Let me check you now . . .'

I became more aware of what was happening, either because of something the doctor gave me, or because of the activity of having to sit up and let my shirt be taken off. A little while later he placed cups on the flesh down my back. As the vacuum in the heated cups drew blood up through the yellow swelling of my skin the pain was unlike the exhausted collapse of the rest of my body. It was rather as if an immense, giant hand, with fingers the size of the room, had reached down and, after fumbling for a while because I was so small, pinched my back as a nasty prank. I screamed without inhibition.

'I will not leave you, John.' I looked up. Washburne was close to the bed, seated. Behind him stood two or three women I didn't recognise: probably nurses or servants from the hotel.

I assume they had found me unconscious in my room. I was enough returned to my old self to feel embarrassment at being seen like this. Washburne held my shirt in his hand. Even to my eyes, it was a repugnant yellow. He turned to one of the others, gave it to them, and asked for a few clean ones to be brought to the room straight away. 'You will find some in the room I am occupying, if needed,' he told the maidservant. 'Take those.'

And, oh, I shat myself then. I figured it out, not by some inherent awareness of what was happening to my body, but circumstantially, inferring from what was happening around me. If Washburne was here, and a doctor, and if the doctor looked so calm and solemn and business-like, then it was possible to work back logically from these circumstances to me. They were acting as if I were dying; and so I was.

It was about here, to my mind, that John A. Rawlins, that whole campaign – all that father and son stuff – all of that – all that was going. It was John A. Rawlins, again, brought back briefly by the doctor's treatment or ill-treatment, who was looking puzzled at Washburne and embarrassed by the maids. It was a brief, childish last look. After that, it was all battle. In those last few hours, the very effort of fighting to stay destroyed me as much as anything else. I fought so hard to stay.

After that examination, I was terrified. I kept calling for Grant. I was being consumed by my body. This was a fight in which I felt elementally alone. I find it very hard to describe. The physical pain I felt was, of course, more and more overwhelming, until that was all I felt, and then not even that. But to the extent I was able to think, I felt the greatest terror. I would feel a panic that seemed to rise from the deepest part of me. This was irresistible and overwhelming. There was no hope of conquering or controlling it. I was alone, and I was lost. Whatever belief I had that made me certain a part of all existence could be called mine – whatever worked to separate me from all else, and did so as automatically as the cells and nerves that work to make us breathe – it was now being undeceived. Every second, every thought, like every cell, we only assume needs to be bound to the next: and now that binding was being unwound.

And at the moment of greatest terror, at my most extreme exhaustion, I would call for Grant. He was what made me John A. Rawlins, Chief of Staff. At this moment, at this point of crisis, I would see Washburne sitting with me. There was a blank, white, moving square of light, and a sulfuric smell, and damp heat. I could not connect these isolated sensations to work out what was the window or the doctor's matches or my sheets, and put them back together to make sense of the room. Underneath all was disintegration, and then everything began again to move away, leaving only it.

Washburne sat with me the whole time. 'I will stay,' he would say.

In Saratoga at 4:45 p.m. while walking back from church with Horace, Grant got a telegram saying I was calling for him. He got the 5:50 train to Albany. You can find out these details from books. I tell you, even in that sixty-five minutes, the tombstone on my chest pressed too heavy for my ribs to hold. To breathe, I had to push it up, push it away to clear those half-inches of space that my lungs needed to fill with air; and down it would come, cold as the veteran's tin cup on my chest, and I would lie there with my arms straight down by my side and my head held stiffly up at the neck by the pillows, as if I were trying to peer awkwardly over its mass and read my own name on the slab. Maybe it was the doctor's hand, as he pressed lightly and cruelly on my sternum to gauge my strength.

I was trapped in this cycle, trapped underneath its weight. I remember, when we were young, Alton and I slept for a while in the same bed. I saw him once. I think he thought I was asleep.

He was trying to lie down. He was stuck, propped up on the side of the bed, too frail and frightened to let himself fall back onto it, too weak to pull himself upright, and clinging desperately to the bed rail, holding on as if he were far up above the earth. Full of pity, I looked at him holding on there, knowing he needed someone to ease him down. I waited for seconds before I helped him, because of my amazement and wonder at his helplessness.

'I will stay,' Washburne would say. I saw him take the doctor's hand off my chest, and when the doctor looked questioningly at him, Washburne smiled at the doctor and told him that he would stay with me and that 'I will call you if you are needed. Maybe you would like to dine downstairs? You have been here for some hours now'.

Washburne and I were alone. You can read that Grant, by this time, had reached Albany at 7.00 p.m., but missed a special train arranged to take him to New York. He took the night boat, which sailed slowly up the Hudson with him smoking alone on deck. For the time it took for every one of the million things to happen to Grant on the ten-hour journey on the night boat to New York – every dark headland he stared at, every cigar wrapper he carefully examined before pulling apart and discarding, every idiot looking at the President sitting alone with what I suppose we'll assume was his grief, every gust of wind and spray of water and thud of the hull back into a wave – every one of those things turned to clods of dead weight and fell onto the stone under which my chest was forced to rise. I called for him; and now that call seemed nearly dead.

What I didn't know then, but was soon to know, was that my pain came not from me stopping the stone pushing down, it was from the stone stopping me rising up. I think Washburne knew the whole time. 'I will stay,' I heard him whisper to me in the morning, when Grant was still miles away having breakfast with Jay Gould in Astor House while waiting for a

Jersey City train to arrive. 'I will stay.' He held my hand as I stared at the ceiling, concentrating hard over some small puzzle I'd read on the back of a packet of matches. There was someone in the room in trouble, I knew: but it wasn't me.

It was easy.

Grant got there at 5.15 p.m., but that was an hour too late.

I didn't know what happened until after, and I had gone. And after – sadder than what we cannot be shown is what we do not want to see. When we rise above, so all is revealed: what a heaven that will be.

Back in the battle, I could hardly see anything. I was lost, really, and all I could do was keep on going. I had not the moral courage to halt and consider what to do. Me and Grant: we both made it so hard. Washburne knew things at the time, or at least some things. He knew things are easy, and peaceful. It was me that was at war.

1864

REFLECTIONS ON THE MOVEMENT BY THE LEFT FLANK – THE FINAL CRISIS – OUT OF THE WILDERNESS

Was Grant wrong when he ordered us to advance south, rather than retreat north, and so lead us out of the Wilderness? We didn't know at the time. I suppose it depends from where you're looking at it.

CWDs see it as the beginning of the famous Forty Days. In the next month, Grant would order a move to the left another five times, all trying to get between Lee and his capital Richmond. In the course of those forty days, we lost 50,000 men. Those two days of the Wilderness were just the beginning – not the end, as we all feared – and were to happen again and again. But in those next battles we lost more men, and more quickly. Four weeks later, at the Battle of Cold Harbor, in the space of seven minutes 7,000 men were shot. I'm only counting casualties on our side. So CWD opinion is divided about

Grant's move out of the Wilderness. He never did get between Lee and Richmond. After the Forty Days, he and Lee fought the Siege of Petersburg. This lasted ten months. It wasn't until April 9 in 1865 that Lee surrendered.

General William Tecumseh Sherman called it 'the supreme moment' of Grant's life:

> *Undismayed, with a full comprehension of the importance of the work in which he was engaged, feeling as keen a sympathy for his dead and wounded as any one, and without stopping to count his numbers, he gave his orders calmly, specifically, and absolutely – 'Forward to Spotsylvania'.*

'Surprise and disappointment,' wrote George Cary Eggleston in *The Century Magazine*'s 'Battles and Leaders of the Civil War', 'were the prevailing emotions in the ranks of the Army of Northern Virginia when we discovered, after the contest in the Wilderness, that General Grant was not going to retire behind the river and permit General Lee to carry on a campaign against Washington in the normal way.'

Eggleston was a Confederate Sergeant-Major of artillery:

> *We had been accustomed to a programme which began with a Federal advance, culminated in one great battle, and ended in the retirement of the Union army, the substitution of a new Federal commander for the one beaten, and the institution of a more or less effective campaign on our part. This was the usual order of events, and this was what we confidently expected when Grant crossed into the Wilderness. But here was a new Federal general, fresh from the West, and so ill-informed as to the military customs in our part of the country that when the Battle*

of the Wilderness was over, instead of retiring to the north bank of the river and awaiting the development of Lee's plans, he had the temerity to move by his left flank to a new position, there to try conclusions with us again. We were greatly disappointed with General Grant, and full of curiosity to know how long it was going to take him to perceive the impropriety of his course.

But by the time we reached Cold Harbor we had begun to understand what our new adversary meant, and there, for the first time, I think, the men in the ranks of the Army of Northern Virginia realized that the era of experimental campaigns against us was over; that Grant was not going to retreat; that he was not to be removed from command because he had failed to break Lee's resistance; and that the policy of pounding had begun, and would continue until our strength should be utterly worn away ... We began to understand that Grant had taken hold of the problem of destroying the Confederate strength in the only way that the strength of such an army, so commanded, could be destroyed, and that he intended to continue the plodding work till the task should be accomplished ...

Of course, Eggleston was writing years later – 'Battles and Leaders of the Civil War' wasn't published until 1889 – and it seems to me his version tells as much about what he was feeling twenty years on as what happened at the time. His tone of fond sarcasm, bordering on being patronising – it's so like we all were then, so full of sentiment and grand ideals. Everyone's a self-effuckingfacing hero.

His face lit by artificial red light and leathery with mild

disappointment, Grant looked at me and said we were moving toward more battle.

'We will advance south, out of the Wilderness.'

I inhaled, trying to hide my shallow shuddering.

'Sam,' I said.

I saw him move his fist up across his stomach. I was shocked by what I had called the Commander of all Union armies. He held his arm there, awkwardly. There was no threat in his posture. I was amazed by my thoughts. Grant looked away from me, one side of his profile red with firelight and the other merged black into the forest behind him.

His small head bent down. All of Grant was described in that profile, features reduced by flame to outline the untransformed self. He was like a child with disease. If I can write words that remain unchanged by time, I wish to write them now: how I pitied him his battle.

'General Rawlins,' said Grant. He paused, waiting to make sure I was ready to make notes, and then continued with his plan for a move forward. 'Hancock will stay on our left, and we will move our right wing and centre behind him. Warren will move first. Burnside will move to Piney Branch church along the Plank Road. Sedgwick can move along the pike to Chancellorsville, and then to Spotsylvania.' This moment could never be changed. I scratched the quill over the paper. 'Warn all commanders a heavy attack may be made on Hancock. We must keep this move unknown to the enemy for as long as possible. Move the hospitals to Chancellorsville. I will need a draft order detailing these movements.'

It was the order, I knew, both of us must follow. My pen moved as if by another's hand, controlled by the pity I felt for him, and the pity I felt for myself. No matter how far you march, you are the same man's son.

Then, late on that second day, before I could complete any draft of Grant's order, the crisis I've told you about already –

way back at the start – began. This was the final crisis. It was nearly dark. Colonel Hyde, of Sedgwick's staff, came galloping up to Meade. Hyde was bleeding.

As he reported, I could see Meade, whose exaggerated, deferential nodding was part of the polite ceremony he'd been performing for the last six disastrous hours, suddenly leap up with ugly surprise. Hyde moved automatically to attention, shocked into this instinctive response by a commander's rage. Meade's voice was made ridiculous by its new power.

'... this is nonsense!' Across the dark clearing Grant and I could hear his screaming, his face inches from Hyde's. Adams came running across to us, as if he was scared.

'We have a report of disaster,' he told us.

For Grant and me, this could only be a distraction. No-one else knew, but we had a plan – we were fighting on, going south eventually, and defeat or victory here made no difference to that. Sick soldiers and well – all were to be moved alike. At last, I came to understand: there was to be no changing course. I felt no panic. Grant, too. There was a streak of mud down Adams' checked shirt. Grant stood and looked at Adams, with his hands in his pockets, and white dust patches and crumpled uniform still visible in the dark. Grant's shoes were scuffed; he wore boots like a labourer's. His beard was itchy. He took out a hand and scratched just below his jaw line, tilting his head. That's all he did.

Adams looked from Grant's face to mine.

'Colonel Hyde had reported that Wright's division has broken. Our wagon and train are in danger.' Adams, I felt, seemed to think this problem hugely complex. *No need for change*, I thought to myself. I looked at Adams as he tried to work out what he should hide or reveal. We will march forward, win or lose, to more battle. That was our way out of the Wilderness. 'Even if cowardice is the commonest thing you could find in a man,' I wanted to reasure him, 'it would make no difference to this campaign.'

I looked at Grant as Adams ran back over to Meade. He stood slightly slumped over, small and incomplete. Lee was coming at us, wanting to prove we were all defeated soldiers in a beaten army.

'General Grant,' I said, 'I fear Captain Adams would wish for a retreat.' He didn't say anything, but gave a little laughing grunt, as if I'd stated the obvious.

'Only fighting,' said Grant, 'will finish this war.'

'Nonsense!' screamed Meade again, jabbing at a map he was holding in front of Hyde. Hyde's face was white with exhaustion and strain. Below his ear there was a knot of congealed blood. He was cut and bleeding along the back of his neck, and the blood formed a smudge near his collar that rose and stopped along the thin straight line of the cut. When Meade dismissed him, he walked with a stiff artificiality, carrying his head awkwardly, as if he was balancing something on it.

In the dark, it was impossible to locate the gunfire precisely. It seemed to swell to our right, but other officers in the meadow looked left. After so long under fire, all men were spooked by the distorted accoustics – it seemed the whole circle of bush was full of Lee's army, that he was magically able to attack from all sides. Adjutants ran to us from every direction.

An officer walked out of the darkness into the spotted yellow shadows cast by the lamps hanging from our tents. He stumbled foolishly over a tent line, but did not fall. We realised with surprise he had two General's stars on his jacket. He was wet through, sopping with moisture, and his dark shirt clung to his side. He seemed to walk onto this scene like a ghost. He stood in front of the map table, and raised his bandaged hand in imprecation.

'General Grant,' said the Ghost General, but he didn't look

directly at Grant. I don't think he could guess which of the commanders in front of him was which. 'This is a crisis that cannot be looked upon too seriously. I know Lee's methods well by past experience. He will throw his whole army between us and the Rapidan.' His eyes moved from Grant to Meade to Adams to me; he did not move his head. His hand looked like it was bleeding in the bandage. 'Lee will cut us off completely from our communications.'

I thought Meade was going to shout 'Nonsense!' at him, or Adams demand to know which division he was from; but they were both silent, awed by his strangeness.

He showed us his hand. Dark blood ringed fresh wet blood. Even the bandage had been mangled, as if caught in some huge, brutal piece of machinery. He was trapped still, trapped in all the old defeats Lee had inflicted on him. He looked at his fist with horror, amazed and shocked, as if this was the first time he had seen how bad the wound was. I was about to say to him 'You need not fear. We will not abandon our course,' when Grant spoke up.

'Oh, I am heartily tired,' he said, and stopped. He said this with the cigar in his mouth, but for the next bit, he took it out, as if the effort of speaking with it between his lips was finally too much. 'I am tired of hearing about what Lee is going to do. Some of you always seem to think he is suddenly going to turn a double somersault, and land in our rear and on both of our flanks at the same time.' At this, Horace let out a little simpering, obsequious giggle. I'd forgotten about Horace. 'Go back to your command,' Grant told the Ghost General, exactly as if this ghastly spook was a whining toddler, 'and try and think of what we are going to do ourselves, instead of what Lee is going to do.'

The staring General lowered his hand, and held it strangely behind his back, as if he was hiding a sweet from a child. Grant turned away. Horace said, 'General, I will provide you with a horse, the faster to return you to your command.'

It was very dark now in Lacy's meadow. The only light came from the soiled lamps, with their pungent silky fumes. The ghost let out a deep grunted sigh. He was wounded, I realised, in his side, and blood was saturating the whole left side of his uniform.

'Colonel Porter,' I said to Horace, 'I will direct the General.' I got up from the map table. Even this small movement caused me to feel winded, but it didn't matter, I knew. The ghost was still slightly hunched over. Meade and Adams had stiffened in embarrassment. They were not aware of his wound. The man had been dismissed – more, he had been reprimanded publicly. It was amazing and outrageous for those two that he should stay. I put my hand low on his back. He seemed icy cold. 'Come, General,' I said.

I led him out of the circle of the lamplight. 'We will not abandon you,' I told him. 'We will not turn away from our course against Lee. Have no fear.' Of course, both commanding generals had their own doctors with them. I called over a guard. 'Take this general to General Grant's doctor,' I said. I don't think the Ghost General heard this. He made no change to his stiff awkward stance. The ghost wasn't with me anymore. Pain had led him out. I was going where he was going, but not yet. His head was bent down, his chin frozen onto his chest. I didn't see him again.

As I've told you, they kept coming, though. Out of the Wilderness they came, back to us, pleading for us to find a different way out. Meade thought it was all so complex, so intricate; he was tangled up in this forest, and he could never have extracted himself. But I knew how simple Grant had made it for me. They all kept coming in, and Meade was more and more trapped, trying to find some way of getting out of this battle. His general's mien was nearly gone. I could see him jerk his head in the direction of every loud explosion. Unaware of his actions, he tugged his grey-black beard, the skin under his cheek bulging, then sagging slowly back.

I told you, way back at the start, how Lee's final attack ended. At eight, Hancock came from his front. To me he looked plainly exhausted, and seemed unaware his hair was matted down on his damp forehead. Horace fawned around him. Horace noted that when Grant offered Hancock a cigar he 'found that only one was left in his pocket'. The three of them – Horace, Meade and Adams – grouped around Hancock, as if for warmth. They didn't notice when Grant moved away. Soon, Meade, Adams and Hancock rode back to their own encampments.

At 8 p.m., Grant went to his tent.

Now here's where I got frightened.

I followed him into his tent. Grant collapsed on his cot and began weeping. I could feel myself suddenly without air. My breathing became convulsive. I'd forgotten how to breathe involuntarily. I needed to consciously bellow air in and out of my body.

Grant was face down. He had abandoned all pretence. The tent walls were dimly glowing yellow from the lamp outside. I moved to Grant, amazed.

'General.'

He was crying, and the child's tears looked impossible running down the adult hide of his cheeks. 'I'll just try and sleep,' he said, still weeping. 'I'll just have to try and sleep, and it'll be all right.'

I can detail my physical actions, but my feelings overwhelmed me.

'General,' I was whispering. 'General.'

I cannot remember hearing anything but Grant's sobs. Then I turned to find Adams staring at us. I do not know how long he had been there. Adams didn't look shocked; his face was unnatural, ugly and contorted, unable to assume any one guise.

When Adams turned and left the tent, I knew I would go after him.

I could not abandon Grant. When I walked out of that tent, it was like walking out of a temple, out of a more perfect world, and back to how things always seemed. I did not think about it. All my instincts lean towards deception. I was raised, suckled, joined, born from it. Adams, I knew, needed to be deceived as much as I once had.

I caught Adams. I was coughing and gasping. 'The General is stirred to the very depths of his soul,' I said.

'Sir, the General is unmanned, and unable to command himself.'

'That he has given way to the greatest emotion is true. The last two days have been ones of great crisis.'

Everyone has a story they repeat like a myth! Everyone has a history they longingly bury themselves in!

Adams bounced up on to his horse. I continued, 'But General Grant has not displayed any doubt or discouragement about the progress of our arms, or the course we have followed and must continue to follow.' It didn't matter what I said. I knew what I'd seen earlier that day, behind Grant's tent wall. I knew Adams would leave. He looked down at me.

'That the General is confident about the progress of arms is welcome news indeed, sir, as in that he truly stands alone. Let us hope that confidence is more inspiring for the troops and the nation than it seems to be for himself at present.'

And so I told him about the move by the left flank. We all know, now, about that famous order. Back then, Grant was weeping on his camp bed. There are facts you can't change, no matter how many different histories are written. But what do facts matter? All can be changed; everything. Even deception, I learnt, can be changed to truth, when viewed from above.

'Captain Adams,' I said, 'General Grant has ordered a movement by the left flank. The objective is Spotsylvania Courthouse.' I kept my tone as neutral as possible: no arrogance, no combativeness, as if I were just reciting a sentence I'd read in history books. I could have cried to Adams, 'Don't leave! Don't abandon me!' – but, frankly, *fuck* that.

'General Grant orders a forward movement?' He looked at me. This was an idea that was too sudden for him. He didn't understand me. 'When?'

I said to Adams, 'General Grant has not asked me to draft final orders yet. I presume you will receive these sometime tonight.' I wanted Adams to ride off, before he could find out what was real and what wasn't. I'd seen the truth about him earlier; I'd seen his white face, undisguised. I knew what he was hiding, and how much more that would make him want to expose Grant. Adams, Meade, the whole Union: none of them would forgive him this weakness.

'This is absurd,' said Adams, his pompous face returning now that he had time to understand the idea of a move to the left. 'General Grant would surely expect General Meade to be informed of such a move immediately.' Adams had just seen Grant weeping, had just walked out of the tent of a defeated commander. He got down from his horse. He wanted to see more; he wanted to confirm Grant's failure. Finally, at last, I had run out of words. What did it matter that I could forgive Grant his defeat? All this time attacked by Lee, who would have thought we'd get exposed by Charles F. Adams? I didn't know then, like we all know now, that inside that tent Grant was already sitting composed at his desk, writing in his own resolute hand a rough draft of the order to move left.

Up, like a child tossed in his father's arms – who could have guessed that's where I go at the end of this story? It changes everything. When Horace reported looking in Grant's tent later and saw 'him now sleeping as soundly as an infant', Horace knew that failure had been turned to victory. Up, from that higher distance, things look different.

I find it hard, of course, to explain my experience of flying upward over the Wilderness. I don't think it is literally true that I left the Wilderness, but, at the time, it seemed more real, less strange, than all that had happened for the last two days. It was not dream-like, if dream-like means nebulous and hazy. In contrast, I sensed myself more deeply aware of what was happening. Adams was walking from his horse; and then I felt myself breathing a cleaner air. I felt cold. It took me a moment to work out that the circle of dotted lights below me were the lights in Lacy's meadow. I had to crane my neck to look straight down. Smoke was blowing across between me and the lamps. I was breathing again in a way I had forgotten. I could feel in my limbs, right through my body, relief from suffocation. The lights of Lacy's meadow became indistinguishable in the midst of all the hundreds of campfires that spread below. I wished a similar cathartic benevolence could be granted the men around them. No doubt this escape was my reaction to the stresses and collapse of the Battle of the Wilderness. There's nothing strange about that. Even though I was moving away from the wedge of land between the Rapidan and the Rappahannock Rivers, I could clearly see the campfires. Their brightness seemed unaffected by the distance between me and the land. Up high enough, the Potomac, and even the huge edge of ocean, were dark patches outlined by the joined wash of innumerable campfires. The clouds around me seemed to cease their downwards movement, and then began to rise up. Below, the stream of fire began to separate and move apart, changed from one blanket of light back to individual circles of flame. As they came closer to me, I caught their smoke, and coughed. It was all returning to me. I knew again where I was.

I saw Adams reach out for the flap of Grant's tent. He hesitated, deciding between respect and disbelief, slightly bowed his head and walked in.

It is the vividness of my vision that is most startling still. Back then, back in Lacy's meadow again, it seemed as if I had returned to a world that I was unable to know, that I could only vaguely remember from the past. There was an exhausted pain in my chest, as I tried to adjust to this older, staler air. It might make it less believable, the whole thing, for you, that I should insist on this experience. Washburne would understand. I'd been guided up, if only for a moment. I'd be lost again, but I was unable to deny what I felt as Adams walked to Grant's tent. I insist on this, because now I can look at the rest of my life and things are made a little easier: I was able to glimpse where I was going. Up, that's where. Up, where everything looks different, and where the facts might stay the same, but the story changes.

∽∾

I know plenty of different stories have been written about all this. Grant wrote his book just before he died; and Horace wrote one too; and if I was going to write one now, this is what I reckon I would write.

ACKNOWLEDGMENTS AND SOURCES

On page 53 I quote Shelby Foote from page 271, *The Civil War: An Illustrated History* by Geoffrey C. Ward with Ric Burns and Ken Burns © American Documentaries Inc, 1990; first published 1991 by The Bodley Head, 20 Vauxhall Bridge Rd, London SW1V 2SA.

On page 67 I quote William S McFeely from page 85, *Grant: A Biography* © 1981 by William S. McFeely. Reprinted by permission WW Norton and Company Inc, 500 Fifth Avenue, New York, NY 10110.

On page 69 I quote four lines, and on page 71 I quote 3 lines, from the poem 'The Brothers' from *Collected Poems 1921–1958* by Edwin Muir © 1960 by Willa Muir. Reprinted courtesy of Faber and Faber Ltd, 3 Queen Square, London WC1N 3AU.

On page 89 and 99 I quote two lines each from 'Folsom Prison Blues' by Johnny Cash, reproduced by permission of Warner/Chappell Music Australia Pty Ltd. Unauthorised reproduction is illegal.

On pages 111–13 I quote five lines from the song 'Lust for Life' (Bowie/Osterberg/Pop), published by Tintoretto Music, administered by Universal Music Publishing Group, reproduced by kind permission of Universal Music (42%); and EMI Publishing Australia Pty Ltd/EMI Virgin Music Publishing Australia Pty Ltd (58%).

On page 238, I quote from p 71, *The Civil War, Volume 3, Red River to Appomattox* by Shelby Foote © Shelby Foote 1958, 1986, Pimlico.

Other sources and quotes used are *Personal Memoirs of U.S. Grant*, published by Charles L. Webster & Co, New York, in 1896; and *Campaigning with Grant* by Horace Porter, published by The Century Co., New York, in 1897.

Stormy Weather
Michael Meehan

'an imagination of another order' *Australian*

'You don't want to make up your mind too quickly about swamps,' the rabbiter said, 'until you seen out swamp. Our swamp aren't like other swamps ...'

A troupe of vaudeville artists arrives in a tiny country town in northwest Victoria. It is 1955, the year before the introduction of television. Their impact on each other – and the inhabitants of the town – over a single day of almost continuous rain, reveals exhausted hopes, secret dreams, plots of betrayal and anarchic optimism.

Story Weather demonstrates Michael Meehan's inspired rapport with the Australian landscape and the characters who cling to its remote areas – characters as diverse as the subversive rabbiter, the pale English girl with her saxophone, the weeping soprano, and the enigmatic, endlessly scribbling compere, for whom this town may be the last curtain call. They all have their stories, and their revelations, in the course of this lyrical – and at times blackly comic – work.

Lucia's Measure
Angela Malone

The Story of a Giantess

I'm no liar or madman ... I didn't see any wooden sticks underneath that girl's skirt on Harvest Night. No I didn't. What I saw when she ran were real legs. Real legs with bones inside, real feet with cracked soles like a gyspy's ... And this I promise. 'Inches for secrets,' she said to him. 'Inches for secrets.' And then she was gone.

Something eerie is happening in the little goldmining town of Reedy Creek. When George Clancy Tynan's wife married him he was four feet ten inches tall. Then he became a nine-feet-tall giant. A giant obsessed with a woman named Lucia Peddler.

Now George Clancy's granddaughter, Kitty Charlotte O'Reilly, seeks the truth about her grandfather. And as she does, she gives us a town, a love story, and an enduring mystery, as her own height increases, inch by inch.

Angela Malone captures the life of Reedy Creek, its Irish immigrants and their magic with exquisite language, deep affection and a soaring imagination. A mesmerising new talent.